ROCKY MOUNTAIN GOLD

ROCKY MOUNTAIN ROMANCES
BOOK TEN

VIRGINIA FOX

DRAGONBOOKS
PUBLISHING HOUSE

Names: Fox, Virginia, author.
Title: Rocky Mountain Gold (Rocky Mountain Romances, Book 10) / by Virginia Fox.
Description: First Edition. | Boulder, Colorado: Dragonbooks, 2024.
Subjects: BISAC: FICTION / Romance / General. | FICTION / Romance / Contemporary | FICTION / Women.
ISBN: 978-3-907357-66-8 | LCCN: On file.
Editor: John Palisano
Associate Editor: Eric J. Guignard
Cover Design: Juliane Schneeweiss
Interior Design: Damian Jackson

FREE ROCKY MOUNTAIN PREQUEL

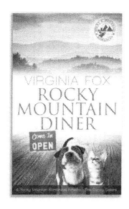

If you are new to my world, you might get a kick out of the FREE Novella *Rocky Mountain Diner*. Sign up for my newsletter to get insider information, more recipes, give aways and receive the FREE ebook of the Rocky Mountain Romances prequel, *Rocky Mountain Diner*.

https://books.virginiafox.com/rmdiner_novella

CHAPTER ONE

Zelda Chastain scurried through the aisles of the convenience store with her head down. Thank goodness it was winter. At least here, in the middle of the Rocky Mountains, the weather stayed cold through March. She pulled the collar of her thick down jacket a little higher until she was bundled up to the tip of her nose. Unfortunately, here in the store, she couldn't pull the hood over her head. She'd be mistaken for a burglarer. Too bad, because that'd hide her distinct dark curls. Even though she had grown up in Independence, the last few years she'd spent in Arizona had made her much more sensitive to the cold. Which meant she was dressed like a polar explorer half the year.

On such days, when she was in danger of stumbling across well-meaning acquaintances at every turn, she was grateful for the camouflage her voluminous winter clothing offered, no matter how much she resembled the Michelin Man.

A relatively warm wind had come in the last few days. The ground was no longer frozen. In a fit of premature enthusiasm for the nicer weather, Zelda had bought flower seedlings for her garden. She presumed they wouldn't survive. But she simply had to try. Maybe they would inspire the weather to hurry and warm up, she reasoned.

"Zelda? Is that really you?" a female voice asked from behind her.

Zelda sighed and eyed the cash register, visible several steps ahead. Should she just pretend she hadn't heard the woman and rush forward? She glanced at her almost-empty shopping cart. She desperately needed something to eat. There was exactly one jar of pickles in her refrigerator. Not enough. Her stomach grumbled. Zelda abandoned her childish thoughts of escape and faced what was pretty much certain to be another cross-examination.

With a put-on smile, she turned. When she realized who stood behind her, it went genuine. The speaker was one of the oldest residents of the city: Eve Lartimer. The woman was already ninety-five years old and a real original. As always, she was impeccably dressed. Pink lipstick adorned her lips, perfectly applied, and a cheeky little hat perched on her silver hair. She radiated elegance from head to toe. She still moved as lightly as she had for decades, the result of being a lifelong dancer. If the rumor mill was true, she'd taken up yoga and was a regular at Jaz Carter's yoga studio. Eve, it seemed, was so good she intimidated the other students. The other rumors? Well, Zelda preferred not to think about Eve's various, much younger lovers. It was rather depressing to realize a ninety-something-year-old had a more active social life than she did.

"Eve," she said, grabbing the older woman's hands. "How nice to see you. Somehow, we always miss each other."

"That's because I'm always healthy," Eve replied.

Zelda had recently begun running the only pharmacy in Independence. It was a request from the Business Women's

2

Association of Independence, or VGI, that had brought her back to the city. The prospect of owning her own pharmacy had assuaged her reservations. After more than ten years of working for her parents, it had seemed like a godsend. Whether her impulsive decision had been wise remained to be seen; especially since she hadn't received all the facts, she thought grimly.

"But what about you, child? You look a little pale around the nose. And that thick jacket. Haven't you noticed spring has sprung?" Eve raised both eyebrows.

Cold was no reason to forgo style in Eve's eyes. Her facial expression made it clear that Zelda's outfit did not meet such criterion.

Zelda grimaced. "Well, I don't know if I'd call this spring. I'm sure it'll snow again next week."

"Nonsense. That's not a reason to hide."

"Oh, you know, hiding sounds pretty good these days." Zelda looked around to make sure no one else was close. "Every time I'm not paying attention, some concerned resident corners me and wants to know how I'm doing and..."

"And? Have you met Cruz yet?" Eve finished the sentence for her. A knowing smile flitted across her face. "Well, have you?"

Zelda groaned. "Not you, too."

"Always so melodramatic. All that's missing is you grabbing your chest and sinking to the floor like Caesar during the last school play. So, what about Cruz?"

"No. I haven't met Cruz yet. And I don't plan to," she replied, feeling stubborn.

"No easy feat in such a small town," Eve said, blunt as ever.

"Tell me about it," Zelda agreed. She bit her lower lip. "This wasn't the plan."

"I can understand," Eve said. "Quite troublesome when the dead don't stay dead. Outrageous, that sort of thing."

That's exactly what it was. Outrageous. Zelda mused angrily recalling Eve's last sentence about the dead not staying dead, taking it out on the hard ground with her little hoe. Anger and frustration over this tiny fact, which the VGI representatives had carelessly forgotten to mention during their many conversations, gave her unimagined strength. Hopefully, her might made up for the fact her tool was completely inadequate to perform the task assigned to it.

Why wasn't Cruz dead? He had to stay dead. Zelda maltreated the brittle earth so that the clods of dirt flew around her ears. It really wasn't fair. First, she had mourned the bastard for years, only to run into him after she was over him.

Her psychologist, to whom she had gone to for many years, would be delighted to learn of this development. Zelda guessed she'd probably point out an urgent need to tack on another five years of therapy. After her parents had been at their wits' end, with a daughter who slid through life completely passive and uninterested, they'd sent her to therapy. With her therapist, Zelda had learned she had exaggerated her childhood love, overshadowed by the tragedy of his sudden and violent death, to immeasurable heights. Which was why, according to her therapist, no other man ever had a chance to get close.

Understandable. After all, it was damn near impossible to compete with a ghost. Supposed tragedy, she corrected herself grimly. Beautiful ghost that didn't even have the decency to stay dead. She continued to attack the innocent ground, imagining it was Cruz. I wonder if it's punishable by law to bring a presumed dead person back to life, just lurking right around the corner, she thought, sullenly. At least the hole in front of her knees was beginning to look like a hole. Such a small ray of hope, even if it was only big enough for a baby hamster.

Cruz Ruis said goodbye to the mayor after a very satisfactory meeting. Mr. Wilkinson had been sympathetic to his proposal to form another committee for start-up businesses. Cruz had expected nothing less. Unlike the program the city had created to attract budding companies to the region, which was funded entirely with tax dollars, his proposal included the cooperation of private investors. In the current low-interest environment, it was a win-win situation for all involved. His company would take care of the selection of suitable candidates in return for a percentage share, thus providing additional relief for the municipality.

Cruz suspected there was a much more personal reason behind it all. Some businesswomen in Independence had gotten together and set up a private association called VGI that offered women entrepreneurs the opportunity to get a foothold in town. The offer was aimed exclusively at women who wanted to take the plunge into self-employment. Unlike the mayor's efforts, VGI emphasized that the new businesses added value to life in Independence. VGI already had success stories to show. A spa had recently opened at the Diner Sisters' bed-and-breakfast. A bookstore had opened its doors, and there was finally a pharmacy in town.

Due to the fact that the residents directly benefited from the efforts of VGI and were able to witness the changes with their own eyes, VGI was the talk of the town. Thus, a real competition had developed between them and the community. Presumably, this had to do with the fact that Miss Minnie, one of the founding members of VGI and co-owner of the diner, was Mr. Wilkinson's longtime on-again, off-again mistress.

Cruz didn't care. As long as it gave him an advantage in his negotiations with the mayor, their situation was just fine with him.

He was about to leave the boardroom when Mr. Wilkinson casually asked, "Have you been to the pharmacy yet?"

Cruz wished he could have rolled his eyes as soon as he heard the question, which apparently intrigued all the residents of the small town, even its mayor. Instead, he forced himself to keep a stiff upper lip. "No reason to do so. I've not been feeling sick at all. I'm in the best health I've been in my entire life."

"Best health ever? Huh," the mayor said, eyeing him. "Well, well. Glad to hear it, I suppose. I just thought you might be happy to see Zelda."

"You and all the other 1,467 residents of the city," he muttered.

"What did you say?"

"Nothing. I'll hear from you in the next few days?" he inquired politely, in an attempt to steer the focus back to business.

"Absolutely," Mr. Wilkinson replied.

Cruz was already focusing on the next item on his to-do list.

Satisfied with the end of the conversation, Cruz left the office and stepped outside. Coat draped over his arm, briefcase in hand, he stopped for a moment to enjoy the warm chinook blowing off the Rocky Mountains.

He glanced at his watch. Should he go to the diner, get something to eat? His eyes fell on the newly erected sign at the intersection pointing toward the pharmacy. A long-forgotten memory rose. A pretty girl with the most enchanting laugh he'd ever heard, holding wildflowers he'd picked for her, sitting in his aunt's old pickup truck. Had he really been that young once?

Zelda.

Of course, he knew she was back. He couldn't think of a good reason to seek her out until that moment. *Do I need one? After all, we were once close friends.* A second snapshot from their past popped into his head. A hot summer evening by the river. Naked skin. Hot kisses. *Okay, so, friends wouldn't quite explain it, especially considering how dramatically both our lives changed since then.* He was sorry when he'd learned about the rumors a few years back. That couldn't have been easy. She'd been one of the good girls. Even so? She showed him a different side of herself, and he smiled at the memory.

There was nothing to stop him from calling her and saying hello. They'd have that behind them, and life could go back to normal. Maybe then the never-ending, miserable questions from his incredibly curious fellow citizens in Independence would stop.

So he went there. Once inside the pharmacy however, he met a young girl substituting over lunch. "Do you know where I can find the pharmacist?" he asked.

She just shrugged and popped her gum bubble.

At least she was probably too young to know his and Zelda's story.

After searching as inconspicuously as possible, but unfortunately unsuccessfully—the diner, the new pizzeria, its accompanying arcade, and Café Sweets—Cruz decided to try Zelda's home. Thanks to the ubiquitous gossip in Independence, he knew Zelda lived in a small, ground-level house not far from the city park. The tract, with its modest individual homes built close together, had been constructed the previous year and been popular with the community.

As he strolled through the park, passing playing children and dogs, he wondered what Zelda looked like now. Would she appreciate a surprise visit from her past? Amazed at the strange mix of emotions inside him, he shook his head, amused.

Quite uncharacteristically for him, he was making something complicated out of a very simple story. If he didn't know any better, he could be forgiven for thinking he was on his way to a date. Maybe even the first date of his life.

In fact, Zelda had been his first date. Cruz remembered that day all too well. *That was then and this is now*, he reminded himself. Several years had passed and they'd both grown up. *All the more reason to finally rectify this ridiculous situation and welcome Zelda back*. He wasn't sure what it was that he felt but he couldn't help but detect some butterflies in his stomach as he continued on his way.

"Whatever it is you're trying to kill, I'm sure it's dead now," an amused voice, unfortunately forever stored in her memory, called over the fence.

Zelda looked up, caught off guard. She couldn't believe it. She felt her blood rush to her face since it was the memory of him and his presumed death that made her so vehemently hack the ground.

"You!" she cried accusingly, brushing an unruly curl from her face before turning back to her gardening. She had absolutely nothing else to say to him. Nothing at all. At least, that's what she tried to tell herself.

Well, that wasn't the reaction I was expecting, Cruz thought. *Maybe this wasn't such a great idea. Doesn't seem like she's been eagerly waiting to see me.*

That didn't stop him from noting, however, that the past few years had done her good. She'd grown in very interesting ways. The waifish girl had developed curves in all the right places. Obviously, she was not one of those who subsisted only on lettuce. Unabashedly, he continued his scrutiny. Her hair was still exactly as he remembered it. Long, wild, and untamed.

Most important? She still had that pointed intelligence in her eyes. Thinking about all their deep conversations from years ago, his heart literally skipped. His stomach tightened.

Forget it, he thought. *Before we have even a hint of a chance to pick up where we left off ten years ago, I have to fight through several layers of hostility.* Zelda's negative vibes were unmistakable.

He met her gaze and involuntarily took a step back.

Zelda's dark eyes sparkled dangerously. He had no idea what he had done to cause such a reaction. After all, he had just arrived…

Disgusted, Zelda tore her attention away from the outrageously handsome ghost from her past who had landed so unexpectedly outside her garden fence. Didn't she have a job to do? In a bad mood, she contemplated her rather pitiful digging progress. Critically, she eyed the small hole to see if she could fit inside. Unfortunately, it didn't look like it'd be able to serve as a hiding place for her anytime soon. Too bad, she thought. *I would have loved to play ostrich. I would have been spared seeing Cruz.*

Where was the justice in this world? At least he could have gone bald and grew a paunch since she'd last seen him. But no, he looked at least as good as before he became "a ghost." If not even better.

She'd only glanced at him briefly, but his looks immediately caught her eye. Cruz had always appealed to her. Like her, he wasn't tall, but possessed a solid, muscular build. He had always reminded her of an athletic bear. His black hair was cut short and contrasted sharply with his green-brown eyes. A scar on his chin gave him a slightly dangerous appearance. Nevertheless, she had always felt safe around him.

He appeared like he had just come out of a business meeting, while she, of course, had thrown on her oldest jeans and a stained wool sweater for the gardening. She knew there were women who elegantly planted their flowers in a white dress with a small shovel and looked sexy without getting a stain; sadly, she did not belong to that category. She had other qualities, she knew. Even if none came to mind.

"Go away," she snapped at him when she couldn't stand the silence anymore.

"Leave?" he asked, surprised. "Why would I do that? I just got here," he added incredulously. "Is there a problem?"

"You should be dead," she snapped. "That's the problem."

Life definitely had a strange sense of humor.

CHAPTER TWO

Cruz thought about the rumors he heard after returning to Independence. According to them, he had been shot and found burned beyond recognition on the day his family moved to California on that foggy night. He still didn't understand. It wasn't clear how something so obviously completely false had taken off and found a life of its own. On the other hand, the inhabitants of Independence were notorious for their vivid imaginations. Knowing full well that he hadn't died that night, he'd never bothered to find the underlying cause of the rumors. He just didn't have time for absurd gossip.

After the first few weeks of his return to the small town had passed, and it became clear to everyone he obviously had no intention of turning into a ghost anytime soon, calm returned. Meanwhile, his business was thriving. He bought a house and met friends once a week at the diner to play billiards. For this reason, it had never even occurred to him that Zelda might not have known. It still didn't explain why she preferred the supposed dead version of him to the living one. Did he even want to know? He wasn't sure.

"Are you talking about that robbery story where I supposedly died?" he asked with a laugh.

Zelda gave him a murderous sideways glance from her position on the floor. "From where else? After all, that robbery story has had no small influence on my life," she replied venomously.

"Affected your life? What on earth are you talking about? What do you mean?" he asked.

For her part, Zelda looked like she wanted to crawl into a hole in the ground, he believed.

A gray cat with a leopard-skin pattern chose the moment to appear on the doorstep, meowing loudly.

Promptly Cruz pointed at the cat. "Beautiful animal. Is that your cat?"

"No. Murphy was just living here when I moved in. Living up to his name."

Astonished, Cruz raised his eyebrows. "And so, you just kept him?"

"Believe me, I did my best to get rid of him. I put up notices, notified the police, and tried to track down the former tenants, all to no avail."

"Did you ask Kat for help?"

Kat ran the local animal shelter and took care of all the stray four-legged friends.

"Of course, I did. But Kat was no help. She did offer to advertise him on her website. But she refused to take him in. She felt he might as well wait for a new home with me. I'm now a foster."

"Makes sense, Cruz said. "I mean, that's true, actually."

"Oh yeah?" She raised one of her finely arched eyebrows and looked directly at him for the first time, a clear challenge filling her gaze. "You're welcome to take him home. No joke."

He didn't believe she would willingly give him up, not from the look on her face. She was grandstanding, Cruz realized.

The gray cat with the striking fur markings stalked over toward Cruz and sniffed his shoes. Cruz bent down and stroked his silky fur. "It's almost as though he knows what we're talking about."

Cruz waited for the inevitable hissing and subsequent pawing but nothing of the sort happened. The traitor purred loudly and dropped to the ground in front of his feet. Probably so Cruz could more easily reach all his favorite petting spots. Unbelievable, this cat. "I might actually take him with me. He seems to like me."

Zelda averted her eyes. "Forget it. He's staying here with me. Whether he wants to or not." She glared at the disloyal cat. "Better remember who's opening your tuna can in two hours."

Murphy yawned, unimpressed.

Cruz continued to run his fingertips over the silky fur. The weak spring sun warmed his face. Surprised, he realized that he felt quite peaceful, despite the fact that Zelda gave off about the same energy as an angry porcupine. It had been like that before, he remembered. He dated her because he had liked her and most of all, he always felt comfortable around her. It was exciting how a brief encounter could suddenly bring up long-buried memories.

Determined, he pushed open the garden gate and sat down on the doorstep. Murphy followed him and stroked his legs before elegantly pushing himself off the ground and leaping onto his lap.

"What do you think you're doing?" asked Zelda, alarmed.

Cruz, who had leaned his head against the doorframe gave

her a wink from one eye. "Are you talking to me? Or do you mean the cat?"

"With you, of course. Murphy is a lost cause."

"I'll just make myself comfortable here."

Zelda was speechless. Something that didn't happen to her very often, God knows. What was she doing now with a pseudo-spirit in her garden? She blinked. A ghost. That was the answer to the problem currently making itself comfortable on her doorstep. She would just ignore it and him. That was what you did when a ghost haunted you, right? She could, of course, call a priest to perform an exorcism. But at this point, that seemed like too much trouble. Ignoring him was good enough.

For the next few minutes, that worked just fine. Zelda stubbornly continued to work the soil, even though she realized that she was at least two months early with her gardening plans. Seemed the Rockies were quite different from Arizona after all. What a surprise. But that was typical of her. She sighed. Once she made up her mind, there wasn't much that could turn her back on her plans.

Her mind wandered back to that summer fourteen years ago. That had been her problem even then. Growing up in an extremely strict home, she had always tried to be a good girl. But then Cruz burst into her life with his charm and flashing eyes. For the first time, a boy seemed to see something in her other than a chubby girl with no friends. Most of the popular girls of that time had fawned over him. Was it any wonder that she had fallen head over heels in love with him? Once she had admitted it to herself, there had been no stopping her. She would've walked through fire for him. All the more painful once she had the realization the same had not been true for him.

Zelda hacked the innocent earth. Small clods of dirt splattered in all directions. If he'd claimed not to have died—which she still didn't quite believe, for the moment it suited her just fine to think him a product of her overactive imagination—why had he never written to her? Never called? He was just like all the other men. Out of sight, out of mind. She ignored the fact that she had recently met several men to whom this did not apply at all.

Unfortunately, the fragile peace did not last long.

Cruz spoke, his hand still buried deep in Murphy's fur. "You didn't answer my question."

"What question?" grumbled Zelda. Of course, she knew which one he meant. Obviously, he still wanted to know how his unexpected demise, or his departure, as he called it, had affected her life. Was there something like a denial of the facts among ghosts, too? She assumed it must be quite frustrating to realize that one was dead.

"How my sudden departure affected your life." He gave her a lazy smile that seemed to be in perfect harmony with the sun's rays on his face and the cat on his lap.

At the sight of him, Zelda's heart leapt. Toward her number one enemy. That wasn't such a surprise, though. After all, her heart had also decided she should keep Murphy. She just couldn't depend on the flighty organ. To forestall any further missteps of her heart, she opted for brutal honesty.

"You want to know what my life was like after that fateful day?" Zelda rose from the ground and straightened up bolt upright. "Not enough that the boy I had been traveling with was pronounced dead. And not because of a tragic accident or illness. Nope. You had to get yourself shot in a drug deal gone bad. From this, all the inhabitants of Independence concluded that I must at least be pregnant by you because afterward I couldn't stop crying."

"Pregnant? But we never had..."

Cruz was lost. Despite his momentary shock, it didn't escape him how beautiful Zelda looked when she was angry. The sun drew bright lights in her wild mane. She placed her hands at her narrow waist, which showed off her round hips and shapely bosom. She radiated a vitality that captivated him, the same as it did back then.

"You know that, and I know that." She still hadn't. With anyone.

She winced inwardly as she stumbled over her own lie. At least with no one that counted. She'd been so successful in repressing that unpleasant chapter in her life that it wasn't true anymore. The few failed attempts with one of her fellow students at college didn't count. None of those awkward, hasty encounters of two sweaty bodies in the dark had held anywhere near the magic that a single kiss between her and Cruz had. After a few times, she'd given up hope that it would ever get better and called off the affair, if you even wanted to call it that. And somehow, she never got back into dating. How embarrassing was that? Thirty-two and not a hint of a sex life. *Maybe I should sign up for the Guinness Book of World Records*, she thought. But that didn't matter and was none of Cruz's business.

"No one else gave a damn about that detail," she said. "The gossip and my never-ending grief eventually got so great that my parents saw no other way out than to move with me to Arizona. Far away from the source of the shame I had brought upon the family."

"But that's absurd!" he said.

"Is it? Is it?" She saw no reason to admit that for a long time she had thought so, too. Meanwhile, from an adult's perspective, she could understand that her parents had only done what they thought was best for their daughter. Admittedly, she would have understood even more if they hadn't constantly made her feel guilty over the years. But basically, she forgave her parents.

"Nine months later at the latest, it must have become clear to everyone that it was nonsense."

Cruz was apparently still stuck on that part of her pregnancy. *Typical,* she thought.

"Makes sense, though. You can believe me," she said. "My parents were very relieved when month after month went by without my belly getting any bigger. Even the assurance of a gynecologist they dragged me to couldn't completely get rid of them worrying about it."

"Then why the move?" Cruz asked.

Exhausted by her emotional outburst, Zelda slumped her shoulders. With heavy steps, she walked toward the house and plopped down on the doorstep next to Cruz. Murphy hissed indignantly. Clearly, she had fallen short of his personal comfort distance once again. Too bad for him. She couldn't take care of everything.

"You know my parents. Nothing is more important than the family's good reputation. Besides, I was miserable. I actually did nothing but cry for several weeks."

Cruz kept silent for a moment, his chin down. He squeezed Murphy, who was less than pleased. With a growl, the cat wriggled out from under Cruz's hand and jumped off his knees. A few feet away, Murphy sat down and began to clean himself.

"I'm sorry about that," Cruz finally said. "I had no idea

about any of this. Of course, that doesn't help you now..." He shrugged. Gave her a sidelong glance.

Zelda waved wearily. "That was all a long time ago now. But there's one thing I'd like to know." She looked at him, making sure he was paying attention. "How come you never got in touch? Did our time together mean so little to you?" Her voice trembled a little at the last question. It wasn't easy for her to ask but if she was going to cast out demons, she might as well go all out.

"I did."

"You... did?" Zelda stared at him in disbelief.

"Yes. I wrote you a card with my new address. However, I suspect you had already moved away by then. When I didn't hear from you in response, I figured you didn't feel like keeping in touch with me. Of course, that put quite a dent in my ego. But in the end, we were both very young. Long-distance relationships are difficult enough for adults."

"So, you just got on with your life," she stated.

Cruz lifted a shoulder and smiled.

"What can I say. Our move to California came very abruptly for our family, too. I still had my high school graduation ahead of me and was busy making new friends. That turned out to be not so easy. No one knew where I belonged. Was I a hillbilly? A Latino? Both?" He grinned. "You could say I'm guilty as charged. I'm just sorry you mourned me for nothing, but I had nothing to do with that."

Zelda bit her lower lip as she tried to make sense of what she'd heard. "What did you move for, anyway?"

Cruz frowned. "You know, I was wondering the same thing earlier for the first time in years. I remember my parents always dodged the question. I didn't care about it too much back then. As we've already established, eighteen-year-old boys have a relatively short attention span for things that aren't directly related to their lives."

"And now?" probed Zelda.

"I'd actually like to know more about it." He frowned. "Especially now that I've heard from you what else happened at the time. Why do you think?"

"Well," she replied. "Somehow everything seems..." she searched for a suitable description, "... too easy for all those incidents to be pure coincidence. Your unexpected departure, the rumor about your death and the drug dealers, the rumors about me..."

"What else could it be other than a chain of unfortunate circumstances?" he asked.

"I don't know." Zelda said.

"I can tell you have an idea," Cruz said.

Crap. Did he really still know her that well? After all these years? Impossible, she thought while her heart beat got faster. What was that about? Surely her heart should have learned the painful lesson that Cruz was nothing but trouble. To nip any romantic impulses in the bud, she decided to answer his question truthfully. Should he subsequently consider her a crank, so much the better. Then hopefully he would keep his distance and she could go back to pretending he was dead. She took a deep breath. "You'd almost think someone wanted to make sure we and our families left town. And would never, ever come back."

Dumbfounded, Cruz blinked and shook his head. "Drive our families out of Independence? And who, pray tell, would have wanted to do that?"

"I don't know," Zelda answered.

"Neither your family nor mine was important enough to need to be gotten rid of." He laughed. "Just look at my family. We never had enough money. No wonder someone got the idea I was into dealing drugs. Believe me, it wouldn't have taken anything too dramatic to drive us away. A check for a few hundred dollars would have been enough. Who knows, that's probably exactly what happened. I'm sorry people then drew the wrong conclusions about you. But I had nothing to do with that."

Cruz slid back and forth uncomfortably on the doorstep.

Zelda gave him a tired smile. "It's all right. I didn't expect you to believe me." She patted the dust off her pants. "It was just a crazy idea. Take care. And if you ever get a cold, you know where to find me."

It was almost amusing again to watch Cruz jump at the chance to escape when she had offered him a polite way out. With a relieved mutter about some meeting he had to prepare for, he rose and left.

Just as she had expected. Instead of being happy to see him, she felt a quiet disappointment about how easy it had been for him to run away from her. Again.

On silent paws, Murphy crept to her side and pressed against her leg. She pretended not to notice, otherwise the cat would be gone. She sighed. He was just the same as all the other males in her life. Maybe she should finally accept Paige's offer to introduce her to some of the firefighters in Independence.

CHAPTER THREE

In the following days, Cruz immersed himself in work, a deliberate distraction from the intriguing conversation with Zelda and thoughts of the enchanting woman herself. His supposed crush, supposedly set aside fourteen years ago, resurfaced unexpectedly. Pausing from signing contracts, he gazed out the window at the harsh winter scene in the Rockies, pondering why he had returned to Independence instead of thriving in Florida; there, he wouldn't be forced to keep the ice scraper handy in his car eight out of every twelve months.

When living in California, he'd felt compelled to return to the Rockies. Whether it was his roots or simply an affinity for the mountains and the rugged outdoors, he couldn't say. He knew the decision to return to Independence had been the right one.

Cruz thought about Zelda. She seemed unsure whether she really felt comfortable in Colorado. The question of what had actually happened back then remained unanswered. He didn't know why the answer was suddenly important. After all, he'd lived fine in blessed ignorance for the last fourteen years. Hard to imagine any answers would change that. But he had to admit his natural curiosity was aroused. After all, it wasn't every day one was accidentally declared dead.

His gaze wandered to the phone. Should he call his mother and ask her for her take? He dismissed the idea in a blink, doubting she'd shed any light on the matter. Besides, she'd had a stressful few years, with the divorce and all that entailed. She'd been remarried for a year, to a successful film producer in California, and was enjoying a very different life. He wholeheartedly enjoyed newfound happiness and was reluctant to disturb her hard-earned peace with silly questions about his romantic past. His father had died of liver failure shortly after the divorce. The receipt for the years of alcohol abuse from which his wife and children had suffered. Cruz could not ask him for any clarity. His siblings, two sisters and a brother, were younger than he was. They knew even less than he did.

Frustrated, he dropped back into his comfortable office chair. Who'd know about the events from that time? The Diner Sisters, who ran the Rocky Mountain Diner together, were the logical choice. The diner had been in existence for over twenty years. In addition to the fact that they served hearty and inexpensive food, they offered a sympathetic ear to every guest, which had contributed a lot to the popularity of the restaurant. All the threads of the local gossip channels ran through them. However, Cruz doubted Zelda would appreciate it if both their names were on everyone's lips again. That'd be inevitable if he asked Miss Minnie and Miss Daisy for advice.

Cruz chewed on his not-so-cheap ballpoint pen. He needed someone who'd keep quiet about the whole thing. The sheriff, he thought. Jake Carter had only been sheriff in Independence for a few years, but if a body had indeed been found and misidentified as Cruz Ruis back in the day, there had to be records.

Satisfied to have brainstormed a practical approach to the problem, he sent Jake a short text.

> Wanna grab lunch soon? Got some things I'd love to chat about.

Since he often played pool with him, they knew each other well. Jake certainly wouldn't mind answering a few questions for him.

Cruz turned back to his work. Unfortunately, he forgot that the questions about his past hadn't been the only thing to occupy his attention. Zelda's face appeared in his thoughts. *I wonder if she still has the ability to light up an entire room with her laughter. A few days ago, she obviously had no reason to be cheerful. I wonder why she came back when she clearly had very ambivalent feelings about Independence?* Or did she actually blame him for everything that had happened fourteen years ago? If so, that was all the more reason to find out the truth. Not that it mattered what she thought of him. Personally, he didn't care. But Independence wasn't big enough to successfully avoid each other. It'd be more pleasant to clear things up for the last time. He suppressed the fact that seeing Zelda again soon filled him with anxiety. *It's just nostalgia, that's all. Nothing else. Impossible to still have feelings for her after all this time. Right?*

After another hectic day at the pharmacy, Zelda closed the massive wooden door to her little kingdom. The onset of winter had caught half the population of Independence on the wrong foot and caused a nasty wave of colds and flus. No wonder, she thought, amused. No sooner had the temperatures climbed just above freezing than the locals felt short-sleeved T-shirts and shorts were the only acceptable clothing. Of course, she felt for her customers and wished them a speedy recovery. Still, she couldn't help but think her own tactic of wearing a hat and scarf until the temperatures climbed into the low double digits was smarter. She would be careful not to make her secret widely known. Not if it brought her high sales. If Jaz Carter, the owner of the yoga studio, was right about her karma theory, she'd eventually have to atone for her money-grubbing thoughts; they didn't exactly show compassion. She'd worry about that when the situation arose. Until then, Zelda assumed the town still owed her something for having treated her like a fallen girl.

Many of her friends, and not least her parents, wondered why she'd even considered moving back. She probably wouldn't have, either, if the VGI committee that had approached her with the proposal to open a dispensary hadn't consisted of the very women who had stood by her back then. Brenda Carter had urged her five children to stand by her in school. The Diner Sisters had tried their utmost to keep the gossip in check, albeit with moderate success. Jaz's grandmother, Rose McArthy, repeatedly invited her to her home under the pretext of needing help canning vegetables. She knew quite well the mood at home must have been stifling for a girl who was herself in mourning.

The memories, coupled with her feeling that something needed to change in her life, had prompted Zelda to seize the opportunity. She struggled with her decision occasionally, but that was her problem. Who would blame her if she was happy about every cough syrup or nasal spray sold? At least she was able to make a living and deliver successful quarterly reports to VGI.

Outside, she hurried to wrap the thick, yard-long scarf around her neck. The wind was so biting it even found a way through her polar down jacket. Indecisive, she looked from the pharmacy toward her car. Should she drive home? Somehow, doing so wasn't particularly enticing.

Other than an anti-social hangover, snuggling up alone seemed a depressing option. No one was waiting for her at home. Even the prospect of an evening of her favorite TV show and a big tub of ice cream left her feeling hollow. Zelda tried to think of some options. Maybe she'd visit Charlie Triton. Charlie had surprisingly taken over the bookstore next to the yoga studio two weeks back.

Originally, Mrs. Jensen had opened the store and a good part of the population had been delighted there'd finally be books to buy in Independence. However, it soon became clear that Mrs. Jensen's taste was very different that those of her clientele. Mrs. Jensen's goal was to bring a little culture to the mountain village. She favored hard-to-digest literary yarns, abstract art, anything highly praised by the literati. Customers, on the other hand, including Zelda, had been looking forward to an appealing mix of light fiction, outdoor guidebooks, cookbooks, and little knickknacks like bookmarks, stuffed animals, and trinkets from various local artists. It didn't take long for the different expectations to become obvious. People stayed away from the bookstore. Mrs. Jensen, disappointed, quit her lease after two months and moved back to Denver, where, she claimed, people appreciated her exquisite taste.

Even though everyone was secretly relieved, it did present the VGI with the problem of suddenly having a bookstore but no shopkeeper. They'd feverishly tried to find a replacement. Through Brenda Carter's youngest daughter Tyler, they found Charlie, a single mother with a twelve-year-old son named

Ethan. The previous summer, after a week-long hiking trip, she'd suddenly decided to stay in Independence until further notice. In the meantime, her savings, on which she and Ethan had apparently lived until that point, were gone. She also had a degree in English, so the job as a bookseller was tailor-made for her. Ethan could join her in the store after school, so she didn't have to worry about childcare, if he wasn't out with his many new friends.

After the ten-minute walk through the icy wind, Zelda felt relieved when she finally arrived at the bookstore and stepped into the homey warmth, an ancient brass chime sounding above the door.

"I'll be right there," Charlie called from the back of the shop.

Zelda unwrapped her scarf and draped it to dry over the back of one of the ancient, creaky leather recliner chairs Charlie'd hauled in when she moved into the apartment above the store.

"They have no place in the apartment," she'd said. "Here they fit beautifully. Maybe someone would like to take a peek at a book? And enjoy a cup of coffee with it? Or maybe I'll start a book club. Who knows. Add a hot chocolate... Perfect!" Charlie ran her fingers through her matchstick-short hair and dropped theatrically into one of the armchairs.

Zelda discovered her friend had dyed her hair purple from blonde after she watched her emerge from the depths of the store.

"What does your son say about your ever-changing hair colors?" Zelda asked after greeting Charlie with a hug.

"He brings me the color chart every Sunday," Charlie replied with an amused smirk. "I think he'd fall over in shock if I dyed it dark brown and left it that way."

"Pretty cool for a twelve-year-old."

"Sure. I think so, too. But then again, I might not be completely unbiased." Charlie grinned. "Admittedly, he doesn't know me any different. He probably thinks I belong to a rare species of rainbow horses."

Zelda laughed and took a seat on one of the armchairs. "Heavenly. I admit that these armchairs were a real stroke of genius on your part." She put her feet up and closed her eyes.

"Is everyone sick again?" asked Charlie, who recognized the signs of a rigorous day at the pharmacy. Zelda often came by after closing time to keep her company. Since she was open an extra two hours later, and it was often very quiet, it was a perfect fit. Of course, she hoped the clientele would increase. At the moment she was satisfied. Meanwhile, she had time to design her new dream according to her wishes.

"Of course. It's to be expected after these few quiet days we've had. People just don't seem to understand that single digit temperatures aren't a signal to break out their summer wardrobe."

"But it's tempting."

"If you're looking for a cold, then yes."

"Spoilsport. Want some hot chocolate? I tried a new recipe with cinnamon and vanilla."

"Mmm... Actually, I shouldn't. The three pounds I put on during Christmas are still on my hips."

"Forget your hips and live dangerously," Charlie teased, disappearing behind a curtain in the tiny kitchen that was part of the store.

"Easy for you to say," Zelda muttered, thinking about the pants she couldn't get over her hips this morning. Vaguely, she heard the chimes above the door, but didn't turn around.

"I'll gladly trade my hips for your breasts," Charlie, who had obviously heard her anyway, called from the kitchen. "I'll be right there for you," she added for the new customer.

Before Zelda could turn around and take a look at the newcomer, he unexpectedly interfered in the conversation. "Please don't exchange any of your curves."

The words were only mumbled, but Zelda recognized the voice. Surprised, she shot up from her chair and turned around with a flushed face. "Cruz! What are you doing here?" In her bookstore? It was her retreat. He had no business there, damn it! It was bad enough he was constantly haunting her thoughts.

Cruz raised both eyebrows. "Isn't this a bookstore?"

"Yes," Zelda replied reluctantly. "It is. I just didn't expect to find you here. I didn't think..."

"... that I can read?"

Zelda felt her face shrink. "Yes, of course. I knew you would. That you could read, I mean. Oh, just forget it." Too tired from her day and annoyed with herself for letting Cruz upset her so easily, she plopped back onto the cushions. Let him do what he wanted. It was none of her business.

"Are you scaring away my customers?" inquired Charlie with a smile as she stepped back into the salesroom brandishing two cups of hot chocolate.

"I wish," Zelda muttered. As if she were that lucky.

Cruz smirked in amusement at her prickly personality. Now it would only be nice if her hostility was directed at someone else. But that was probably too much to ask since he had the gall to still be alive.

"Are you looking for something in particular?" asked Charlie.

"Uh, yeah. Actually, I came to ask you if there was such a thing as old newspapers here."

Charlie frowned. "You mean, like, an archive?"

"Exactly."

"I'm sorry. As far as I know, no. I haven't unpacked all

the boxes yet, but I think you'd be more likely to find something like that in a library." She shrugged. "My goal is more to have the latest mystery and romance novels in stock. Unless you're looking for something historical? About the creation of Independence?"

Cruz nodded. "No. I didn't really want to go that far back." He cast a sidelong glance at Zelda. "The time I'm interested in is fourteen years ago."

"Ha! I knew it!" Zelda sat up straight. "Do you agree with me?"

Cruz stepped from one foot to the other. "I wouldn't go that far. But I have to admit I've become curious and would like to know what really happened back then."

"Do I need to understand what you're talking about?" Charlie asked.

"No," Zelda assured her. "I'll explain later." Or not.

"Okay." Charlie turned back to Cruz. "Why don't you try the school library? Or else maybe in Breckenridge. Independence doesn't have a public library, unfortunately."

"Good for business, I'm sure," Cruz said with a twinkle in his eye. "Thanks for the tip. I'll tackle that first thing tomorrow." He said goodbye with a wave and left the store.

For a moment, she only heard the crackling of the fire burning in the stove.

Charlie dropped into the other recliner across from her. "So, go ahead. I want to hear the whole story. From beginning to end."

"What story?" Zelda made a pitiful attempt to avoid the questioning.

Charlie rolled her eyes. "Remember, I have a twelve-year-old son. I can recognize evasive maneuvers in my sleep. The heat you and the hottie generated here was unbearable. I almost opened a window."

Zelda groaned and buried her face in her hands. It was nice that Charlie had no idea about their old drama. But it would be only been a matter of time before she found out, so she might as well the tale herself. She peeked from behind her fingers. "It's a long story, though."

"Perfect," Charlie said, sliding deeper into her recliner. "I love long stories."

CHAPTER FOUR

The next day, when Cruz entered the high school building during his lunch break and walked toward the secretary's office, he instantly felt thirteen again. At least he was there voluntarily and not because he had done something wrong.

Within minutes, the enthusiastic secretary had explained to him where he could find the library. The English teacher, who was apparently in charge of the library, was also pleased to see him. Remorse set in as he thought of some music cassettes and comic books he'd forgotten to return a good fourteen years ago. He decided he'd better not mention them. Presumably, the statute of limitations had long expired on those offenses, anyway. Besides, the library hadn't been half as big back then. Surely all the missing copies had long since been replaced, he reassured himself.

Suddenly he noticed the librarian was looking at him. He put on his most charming smile. "Sorry, I was just daydreaming. Old boyhood memories."

The librarian blushed and smiled back.

Zelda was sure going to the library would give her the recharging time she so desperately wanted. Low and behold, as soon as she entered the lobby, she couldn't help but roll her eyes.

Cruz, the old charmer, stood right there, chatting away with yet another blushing woman. No wonder he got along so well with her cat. She suspected him of sweet-talking all the cats within a one-mile radius. *Good thing he's neutered, she thought, smiling to herself.* Unfortunately, she couldn't prevent her own treacherous heart from jumping at his smile, either, which annoyed her.

"I'm looking for newspapers from 2003," Cruz told the woman.

"We," Zelda quickly added, pushing in front of Cruz.

Two pairs of eyes stared at her. Cruz's look was one of surprise. The librarian wrinkled her nose as if Zelda were something Murphy had dragged in during the night. Dead, disgusting, and most of all, totally unwanted. Zelda could understand. It wasn't every day she was exposed to a megawatt smile like Cruz's. Her sudden presence dimmed the experience considerably. But she couldn't worry about that. She wasn't going to pass up the chance to watch Cruz do his research.

After it became clear that Zelda wasn't going to vanish, the librarian's shoulders slumped in disappointment. With a resigned look on her face, she turned and led them to one of the computers. Next to the keyboard was a laminated card. She tapped it with one of her purple-painted fingernails.

"These are the credentials," she said, businesslike. "The newspaper articles are in the marked folder. If you're looking for events before the turn of the millennium, we'd have to go to microfilm."

"That shouldn't be necessary," Cruz asserted.

Zelda was only listening with half an ear. She took a seat in front of the computer and logged in. Of course, she had already searched the internet for the events of that time. Perhaps either she'd entered the wrong keywords, or the incident had simply happened so long ago that it was buried under the flood of information on the internet.

"Couldn't you have at least waited until the librarian said goodbye?" hissed Cruz in her ear as he pulled up a chair, pushing her a little to the side.

"What for?" replied Zelda. "She wasn't interested in my attention anyway."

"Still, it would have been polite."

Zelda rolled her eyes. "Since when did you mutate into the epitome of good behavior?"

"Since I'm a businessman and have to watch my reputation?" he replied, irritated.

"See, that's the beauty of running the only pharmacy for miles around. People have no choice but to come to me. No matter if they think I'm nice or not."

Cruz's eyes almost fell out of his head. Was this really the same Zelda he had once known so well? "Whatever happened to that shy, well-adjusted girl who couldn't hurt a fly?"

"She's grown up," she replied. Impatiently, she clicked through the countless newspaper articles. In the search box, she entered *murder*, *shooting*, and *burned body.* Yet somehow, her search terms seemed to be useless. "I guess I'd best try your date of death and work my way back from there," she muttered

"I don't have a death anniversary," Cruz said.

"So you say," Zelda replied impassively.

"How is it that now you're conducting this search?" He shook his head. "If I remember correctly, it was my idea. Don't you trust me?"

"Yes, of course. I just thought you might need some support. After all, it's not every day that you discover your own obituary in the newspaper," she replied sweetly.

"Well, that makes me feel a whole lot better," Cruz muttered through clenched teeth.

They both lied through their teeth, a skill each did extraordinarily well.

An hour later, Zelda pushed herself off the desk in frustration. They'd found nothing. Nothing at all. "You've got to be kidding me," she said. At least they were in their own area of the library, out of earshot of the nosey librarians and other patrons.

Cruz, on the other hand, leaned back in his chair, satisfied. "I knew it."

"What do you know?"

"That I'm not dead."

Zelda rolled her eyes and scrunched up her mouth. "Says you."

"And the newspaper," Cruz pointed out.

Unfortunately, they had nothing to counter their predicament. Independence didn't have its own newspaper at the time, and neither the *Denver Post* nor any other of the local papers of Breckenridge or the larger towns in the area mentioned the case. It seemed the crime had never occurred.

Zelda shivered; fear spread through her. Fear for her own sanity. After Cruz stood before her, extremely alive, with no way to prove her version of events, a small voice inside her raised doubts. *Did I imagine it all? Just my overactive teenage imagination, so to speak? It's well known that teenagers sometimes don't think very clearly*, she thought.

Cruz cleared his throat. "Well, I'm right after all. Even though there's been rumors about my supposed death, there's just no proof. Not even an article or an obituary." He slid back and forth in his chair. "It raises more questions than answers, doesn't it?"

"What?"

He hesitated. "Is it wise to give in to conspiracy theories? Wouldn't it be smarter to just let it rest? We can move on. Who cares about the past, anyway?"

Zelda lost patience. She stood up, yanked her jacket off the back of the chair, and slung the strap of her purse over her shoulder. "Go ahead. Go ahead and rub it in my face." She slipped on her jacket. "Just don't expect me to stick around."

"But..." Cruz protested.

Zelda stormed away, sure to dodge around one of the large bookshelves so she'd be out of his sight as soon as was humanly possible.

She heard him laughing behind her. *The nerve. He thinks this is funny. Thinks I'm funny. He isn't taking this seriously at all. I just can't stand his arrogance. Why did he come back here? To torture me?*

Cruz shook his head. The fruitless search had raised new questions. He would have no choice but to talk to Jake. Yesterday, the sheriff had been busy. Cruz had asked Polly Miners to let him know when Jake would have a moment at some point. The former police officer, who had been assisting the sheriff since her release from active duty, promised him she would do just that.

He sighed. It could be today, tomorrow, or even next week

until Jake got back to him. So, he'd have no choice but to wait patiently.

After the frustration of her morning research and another long day at the pharmacy, Zelda headed to the convenience store. She needed to replenish her stock of ready-made meals. At home, the refrigerator was empty. Ice cream had to be prioritized, she realized, as she pushed her shopping cart past the refrigerated section. Defiantly, she reached for all her favorites. Raspberry. Cookies and cream. And, of course, chocolate. Finally, she had hoisted everything into the cart. At that moment, Jaz Carter stopped beside her. Her daughter Cammie stood proudly on wobbly legs inside the cart, clinging to the grate.

"Hi, Zelda, long time no see."

"Hello, you two. Yikes, you've got a really big lady with you."

"Yes," Jaz agreed, with a loving look at her daughter. "Since she's been able to walk, she refuses to sit in a car seat."

The little girl began to sway. With a practiced grip, Jaz stretched and shoved the purchases together at the other end. Not a second later, Cammie plopped down on her rear end.

"That looks like a lot of practice," Zelda remarked, impressed.

"Trust me, the practice sets in incredibly fast after your child sits down on a carton of eggs the first time."

Zelda smiled as she imagined the situation. Eager to keep the conversation going a little longer, she said to Jaz, "You seem to be one of the few who made it through the renewed onset of winter without catching a cold."

"Yoga. It helps," Jaz replied. "What about you? Are you planning an ice cream party?" she asked after glancing at Zelda's purchases.

Zelda squinted into her cart. "Uh, yeah. Sort of," she fibbed. After all, she could not admit that all those cartons of ice cream were just for her. At least not to Jaz, who was known for her healthy lifestyle. The woman even held healthy cooking classes when she wasn't teaching yoga.

To her surprise, Jaz clapped her hands in delight. "Perfect! Promise you'll invite me?"

"To the ice cream party?" asked Zelda in wonder. "You mean you're eating this nasty, sugary, fatty stuff?"

"You bet! You bet." Jaz put a hand on her belly. "Since I got pregnant again, I could live on the stuff."

"Not just you," Zelda muttered. However, she was not pregnant. She saw Jaz in a different light. Not quite so perfect and unapproachable.

Zelda followed Jaz through the store. Together they ended up in front of the vegetable counter, which offered a surprisingly large selection compared to the tiny size of the store.

As she watched Jaz pack vegetable after vegetable into her shopping cart, and even her young daughter reached out enthusiastically for an eggplant, she impulsively made the decision to finally put her good resolution from the beginning of the year into action and improve her diet. She had to start sometime. So why not today? Keeping one eye on the contents of Jaz's shopping cart, she simply grabbed anything that looked similar.

"Impressive," Jaz said. "Taking on a healthy diet is imperative to feeling great. Maybe you can stop by and take a yoga class one afternoon?"

"Sure," Zelda said. "Maybe." She knew she'd need more

than yoga to make her feel better about Cruz's untimely return.

They approached the checkout stand and Jaz kept Cammie busy loading the groceries.

As nice as it was to see, it also made Zelda feel a little lonely. Her mind raced. What if she and Cruz had stayed together? Maybe they'd have a daughter of their own by now.

"Have fun cooking," Jaz called, breaking Zelda from her daydream.

Zelda blushed. "Oh. You, too! Thanks," she murmured, waving at Cammie. "See you sometime soon."

"But hopefully not at the pharmacy."

"I hope not, either," Zelda said, watching them roll away.

Now, willy-nilly, she had to plan an ice cream party, she thought as she drove home through the driving snow. Was it considered a party if she only invited Jaz? She didn't have many friends in Independence. She was not entirely innocent in that happening, she admitted. When she wasn't working, she'd been so busy thinking about the past that she turned down most of the invitations she received since her return. Pretty short-sighted if she was planning to build a life again. Was Cruz right about that? Would she be better off letting bygones be bygones?

Juggling the shopping bag and her purse in one hand, she unlocked the door. She promptly tripped over Murphy, who squeezed between her feet as soon as the door was open a crack. Cursing, she staggered into the house. The cat watched her, unimpressed as she put her things down. Murphy let her know by meowing loudly he was on the verge of starvation.

"It's okay, it's okay." Without taking off her coat, she opened a cupboard and took out a can of cat food.

Only after Murphy was sitting in front of his bowl, stuffing his belly, did she remove her winter clothes and slip off her shoes.

She stowed the ice cream safely in the freezer. She turned to the rest of her purchases. When she had unpacked everything, she stared at the plethora of vegetables. The entire kitchen counter was filled with healthy items. If she was honest, she had no idea what to do with it all. Carefully, she poked a bell pepper. She could eat it raw. That was probably the best strategy. Cooking had never been her strong point. Briefly, she considered just stashing everything in the fridge and tackling the problem another day. She just wanted to eat something and put her feet up.

She felt bad. With such a strategy, the greens would be guaranteed to hang around in the fridge for the next few weeks and turn to mush.

In a rare fit of petting neediness, Murphy left the spot in front of his now empty bowl and stroked around her legs. She bent down to pet him. He promptly hissed in disgust and stalked away.

She sighed and straightened up. Touching was taboo again. Her gaze fell on the vegetables. Unfortunately, they hadn't disappeared into thin air in the last two seconds, nor had any brownies come by to take their place. Crap! She'd have to deal with it.

Instead, she went into the living room and flopped down on the sofa. Her laptop was still on the coffee table from her past research the night before. She pulled it toward her and opened a browser. Everything could be found on the internet, even recipes.

She found plenty, many including photos.

But when she tried to read them, none of it made sense. What did the terms mean? How do you butterfly a pepper? What is the difference between simmer and cook? She'd need a translator.

Frustrated, she shut her computer again ten minutes later. She was too stupid to cook. The recipes might as well have been written in Swahili. She squinted toward the kitchen, where the vegetables waited patiently for her. Should she try one of the recipes on YouTube? At least they had videos. Indecisively, she chewed on her lower lip. Maybe she should call Jaz? She might have some tips for her.

Annoyed at the impossible situation, she swallowed her pride and dialed Jaz's number.

"Hello, Jaz."

"Zelda! What a surprise. Have you set a date for the ice cream party yet?"

"Uh, no. But soon! I'm calling about something else entirely. Do you have plans for tonight?" Stupid question. Surely, she had plans. After all, she had a husband, a child, and various animals. In short, a life. Not like her. "Forget the question. I'm sure you have to cook."

Jaz laughed. "For once, I don't. Jake is working until midnight. Cammie and I do have to eat sometime, but there's no rush. Why do you ask?"

Although Jaz couldn't see her through the phone, Zelda closed her eyes in shame. "You must think I'm a complete idiot. Earlier, when I saw you at the convenience store, I was so impressed by your vegetable selection that I spontaneously made the decision to finally eat a little healthier. So, I bought all kinds of stuff."

"I saw. That's excellent."

"That may be. It's just..."

"What?"

"I have no idea what to do with it," Zelda finally blurted out.

"You mean you don't have a recipe?" asked Jaz.

"I have several. Only they're written in some foreign language. I have no idea what is meant by sauté, deglaze, blanch, or whatever all the words are. What I need is an instant pot cooking class. Your next cooking class is not until next week, unfortunately, as I saw on your site. I don't think my vegetables will survive that long."

"I don't think so, either. Don't worry. I'm on my way."

"On the road?" echoed Zelda. "What do you mean? You want to come here?"

"Sure. Why not. Did you buy enough groceries to feed Cammie and me?"

"I don't know. I probably did. I bought everything you did," Zelda replied. "I can't possibly eat that much, now that I think about it."

She was flabbergasted by Jaz's willingness to drop everything.

"Actually, I was just calling for some tips. It was not my intention to cause you such trouble."

"Not a problem. Don't take offense, but I hardly think a few individual tips over the phone will be enough."

"Probably not," Zelda admitted.

"Besides, I think it's nice we'll finally have time to talk to each other. After all, it's been a while since we've done that. So, see you in a bit. We'll be at your place in about half an hour."

"Wow. Thank you."

"You bet," Jaz said.

Completely overwhelmed, Zelda disconnected. Nervous anticipation spread through her. She hurriedly began putting away old newspapers and fluffed the cushions on the sofa.

Indignant, Murphy jumped from his favorite spot on the sofa and took off, tail twitching. He probably snuck into her bedroom to attack the curtains. Next to her calves, those were his favorite victims when he was in a bad mood. He'd probably only left her calves alone because she'd picked up the hated vacuum cleaner. Who would have thought that one day she would have to rely on the protection of a vacuum cleaner, she reflected aloud and giggled. Elated, she continued with the housework.

CHAPTER FIVE

Thirty minutes later, a large Jeep drove up and parked on the side of the road. Murphy, who had calmed down somewhat in the meantime after she'd bribed him with some cat treats, jumped onto the windowsill and hissed.

"They're just visitors," Zelda assured her disgruntled cat. "You'll probably like them more than me again," she added, thinking of how affectionate he had been toward Cruz. She stood beside him and stroked his silky, mottled gray fur. For once, he even allowed being touched. Together, they watched as Jaz got out of her Jeep. She had hidden her chin-length blonde hair under a wool cap. A wide, gray wool coat completed her winter outfit. She opened the back door and took out her daughter. In her enterprising way, Cammie rushed toward the small garden gate. Jaz, on the other hand, leaned into the car again. She pulled out a cloth bag and slung it over her shoulder.

"Mommy," Cammie called, rattling the garden gate.

"I'll be right there," Jaz called over her shoulder and walked around the car to the trunk.

What else did she have with her? Zelda wondered. Her

whole kitchen? The question was answered when the trunk was opened, and a huge black dog jumped out. Oh, right. Jaz had a dog, after all. What was his name again? Rambo or something like that. A king poodle if she wasn't mistaken. How nice. "Unlike cats," she said to Murphy, "I actually like dogs." She peered at the upset cat at her side. He didn't seem to share her enthusiasm for the unexpected visitor. Fur bristling, he hopped up on the windowsill and hissed angrily.

"Behave yourself," she instructed him and went to the front door to let her visitors in.

"You have a Bengal cat," Jaz noted a little later when she spotted him on the top shelf of the bookshelf. "You don't often see rare pedigreed cats like that around here."

Cammie whooped when she spotted the gray tiger, waving enthusiastically in his direction. Murphy blinked in disgust. Cammie didn't let that faze her. Her cat, Jimmy, was her best friend. So surely that applied to Murphy, too. The latter didn't seem very impressed by Cammie's logic and stayed where he was for now. The little girl didn't mind and instead began to explore the small house together with the dog, who sniffed around everywhere.

"Oh, is he still here?" called Zelda from the entryway where she was hanging up their coats. "I was sure he'd hide under the bed after he made such a fuss when he saw the dog. I was even hoping he would move out on the spot. That would have been a nice side effect."

"He probably wants to make sure I take Rambo back with me when I leave, too."

Zelda laughed. "Quite possibly. He's not a particularly social cat, but he's smart as a whip."

"I can well imagine that. Do you really want to get rid of him?"

Zelda grimaced. "A few weeks ago, I would have answered your question with *immediately, at any time,* and *do you want to take him right away?* By now, we've come to terms with each other. After all, he got here before me. I tried to find out who he belonged to but, unfortunately, without success."

"You could have taken him to Kat at the shelter. You know the safe haven? On the other end of Independence? She's my sister-in-law. At least almost. She and Jake's brother Sam are taking their sweet time getting married."

"Believe me, I tried that. But Kat claimed I could foster him just as well as she could." After a brief pause, she added with a furrowed brow, "She can be pretty persuasive, your quasi-sister-in-law. So, I took my cat carrier home, along with its ill-tempered occupant."

"Typical Kat." The affection she felt for her husband's brother's partner was plain to hear. Jaz clapped her hands together. "Shall we get started?"

"You mean cook? Or you cook and I watch?" replied Zelda, with a laugh. "That would be far less dangerous. You know, your daughter?" She pointed to Cammie, who was busy pulling tissues out of a box. "I'm sure you wouldn't want her to be victim of a household accident. Believe me, they happen around me with high regularity."

Jaz laughed. "You need to do everything yourself. After all, you don't want to have to drop S O S signs every time you cook a little vegetable."

"Put that way, it really does sound a bit ridiculous," Zelda said. She took a deep breath and followed Jaz death-defyingly into the kitchen. In the meantime, Cammie had pulled out the last handkerchief and was trying to hypnotize Murphy into leaving his perch on the bookshelf. Murphy blinked and yawned.

Under Jaz's expert guidance, Zelda chopped a mountain of vegetables for the next half hour.

"You can slice the mushrooms. For most recipes, that's quite enough. But since today's vegetable skillet can fit large zucchini or squash halves, you need to turn the mushrooms ninety degrees once and do the same thing again." She turned to the next vegetable. "Peel the carrots and slice them finely." With the precision of a sergeant, she pointed to the leeks. "Cut those into rings. Like this." With a few practiced moves, Jaz demonstrated. "I like to peel the peppers with a peeler before cooking. Here, let me do that for you for a minute."

"Can't the shell stay on?" grumbled Zelda, while her poor brain tried to remember as much as possible.

"In principle, yes. But there are people who don't like the hard shell. After always having to convince my husband that vegetables are definitely an edible alternative to his steak, I'd rather not take any chances."

"I get it," Zelda grinned. She was amazed to find that the peeling, chopping, and slicing had a calming effect. All the stress of the day fell away.

"I brought you some spices because I didn't know what you had at home."

Zelda raised her eyebrows. "I have pepper and salt. Is that enough?"

"In principle, also yes," Jaz admitted. "However, it gets even better when you add some exotic spices."

Doubting, Zelda glanced at the bag. Cayenne pepper. Paprika. Cumin. "Isn't this all insanely spicy? I'm not sure I'm going to like it."

"Depends on how much of it you use. Here." She pressed the cumin into Zelda's hand. "Spread about a teaspoon of it over the vegetables. Follow it with the herb salt and cayenne pepper."

Zelda carefully seasoned the colorful mixture in the pan. She frowned. "Was that about a teaspoon now? Crap. I probably should have measured it out. Why didn't I measure it?"

Jaz chuckled. "Deep breath. You were restrained with the spice. The worst thing that can happen to you is that you have to re-season."

She pressed a wooden ladle into Zelda's hand. "Stir and taste."

"Aye, aye, sir," Zelda grumbled. Carefully, she blew on the vegetable mixture on the spoon. Impatiently, she stuck the tip of her tongue out at it. "Ouch! Hot!"

"Egg," repeated Cammie, who found this totally hilarious. Well entertained, she hopped up and down, chuckling.

"Hot," Zelda repeated. "But also delicious," she noted with surprise when it finally reached a tolerable temperature.

"Told you," Jaz commented with a smile.

"Okay, okay. You may continue to conduct your cooking classes. I hereby officially grant you the necessary permission."

Jaz grinned and picked up her daughter who was trying to climb up her leg.

"She has the same tendencies as my cat," Zelda remarked. "He uses my pants as a climbing aid, too."

"Ouch. That must hurt, with his claws," Jaz commented.

"You could say that. It's gotten better, though. There's still hope he'll stop it altogether at some point. At least that's what Kat promises me. I rather think he's learned to better assess his chances of success and is waiting until I'm distracted," Zelda explained. "Are we done?"

"Not quite. You had some broccoli somewhere, didn't you?"

"Broccoli?" Her head was buzzing from all the more or less unknown greens.

"Yes. You know. Green and looks like a little tree."

Zelda slapped her hand to her forehead. "Broccoli. Sure. It's in the fridge."

She took it out, cut off the heads and added them to the vegetable mixture.

A liter of vegetable broth and five minutes of cooking later, the meal was ready. Zelda mixed the vegetables with the rice she'd put on at the beginning.

"It's wonderful when it's done. It's a very different feeling than opening the microwave after two minutes."

"Absolutely. And imagine how healthy it is," Jaz grinned, sitting down at the table with Cammie on her lap.

"As long as it tastes as good as it smells, it gets to be as healthy as it wants to be," Zelda murmured, placing the plates on the table.

The next morning, Zelda got up feeling motivated. With Jaz's help, she'd compiled a list of women she'd invite to her ice cream party. All she needed was a date, and she could send out the invitations.

"I really enjoyed last night," Zelda said to Murphy. "Maybe not everyone in Independence is impossible after all." Yesterday she had asked Jaz about her memories of their last encounter. But after some back and forth it had turned out that Jaz had not been in Independence that summer.

"Sorry, I can't help you there. That was the summer my parents dragged me to Europe," she'd said.

"Dragged to Europe? I can think of worse."

"Oh, you know how teenagers are. They live in some

48

parallel universe. Now, in retrospect, I wouldn't want to miss out on that amazing experience, of course. Seeing all the places you usually only read about in history books was great. But at the time, I would have preferred to go to my grandmother's house."

"I can imagine."

"I'm sorry I'm not more help to you."

"No problem," Zelda had waved it off. "I was just curious, that's all."

"Maybe you should talk to Jake. My husband would certainly know more about it than I do. True, he wasn't the sheriff at the time. But momma Brenda Carter is usually well-informed about everything that happens in Independence. So, it's safe to assume her kids were in on it, too."

"Probably," Zelda said. "Then maybe I'd better talk to Brenda?"

Jaz shrugged. "You can do that, of course. On the other hand, Jake has a better chance of researching the case file in the police archives."

"The case file," Zelda repeated. "You're brilliant. Why didn't I think of that before?"

"Not everyone can be as brilliant as me," Jaz had replied with a twinkle in her eye.

Zelda hummed along to the melody on the radio. The reception here in the mountains was often lousy, but this morning she was in such a good mood that she just had to listen to music. Who would have thought that her inability to cook would result in an evening of delicious food, good company, the resumption of a friendship, and countless opportunities opening up?

It wasn't just the fact that she now knew how to make a delicious meal out of a bunch of stubborn vegetables; cooking reminded her of how she'd been completely fascinated by herbal medicine when she'd began her pharmacy studies. Unfortunately, they'd only touched on the subject during a single semester. Over the years and the flood of exams, her interest had been lost. But yesterday there had been the idea to learn more about the medicinal plants in the area. Instead of always just handing out the usual remedies, it would be exciting to be able to offer a few homemade, natural remedies.

Last night, after Jaz and her kiddo left, she ordered specialist literature online. She just needed someone local who knew about the plants and how they worked. She couldn't wait to dive into the reading. In her exuberance, she'd even clicked on the button for express delivery. She ducked her head a little as she thought of the painfully high extra fee. But it had been worth it as it'd been a long time since she felt such enthusiasm for a project. Except for the mystery that surrounded the incidents from fourteen years ago. Surprised, she realized the subject of Cruz didn't excite her nearly as much as it had the past few weeks.

A load of vegetables was healthy not only for her body but also for her psyche, she noted. Besides, with her new idea, the upcoming party to plan, and her rash promise to drop by Jaz's yoga studio one day, she didn't have time to chase such pipe dreams.

Yoga. She grabbed her soft belly. What had she been thinking? Her body was female. "Femininely rounded," she added with hard-won acceptance. After countless, fruitless attempts at dieting, she had long ago realized she'd never be one of those slim, athletic types. "So what if I'm not?" she thought defiantly. "Maybe a little yoga wouldn't hurt." Jaz assured her it was all about the experience, not performance. Still, she pushed the yoga lesson to the bottom of her mental to-do list, even if it made her conscience twinge.

Cruz stood at the window of the police station. Jake had called him early that morning and suggested they meet at the station. Outside, a couple of kids were throwing snow at each other. As is usually the case, the snow in this region of the Rocky Mountains was too powdery to form decent snowballs. That didn't stop the boys from having a real battle, though.

"I remember the case well," Jake said just behind Cruz's back. "Everyone was talking about it. After all, that's why everyone was so amazed when you returned a few years ago. Some of the residents were seriously concerned that you were a restless spirit and decided to haunt Independence, in revenge, as it were, for the injustice done to you back then. And your lover."

Cruz left his observation post at the window and turned to the sheriff. "Revenge? Injustice? Lover? That sounds a lot like the synopsis of one of those cozy romance novels."

Jake grinned. "Just don't let my wife hear your judgmental tone. She devours those books." He broke off and let his gaze wander into the distance. "And I must admit romance novels contain many an interesting, er, *suggestion*."

Cruz shook himself. "Whoa. That was definitely more than I wanted to know. Can we maybe get back to my demise? I like that topic better."

Now it was Jake who shook his head in amusement. "I've never heard anyone say that."

"Well, most people never face the problem of everyone else thinking they're dead," Cruz replied.

"Again, you're right about that. As I said, some people were so concerned that they wanted to organize a pastor who specialized in exorcising ghosts."

"Uh-oh. What happened next?"

Jake frowned. "If I remember correctly, your... aunt? Or was it your great-aunt? Adela, I mean. She lives in the old cabin by the lake."

Overwhelmed, Cruz lowered himself into the visitor's chair. "Adela. Indeed. I confess I haven't thought about her in ages. Is she still alive?"

He was ashamed, but they had never been close. He remembered how she always ruled over the family with an iron fist. They almost never saw her, even then. But her presence permeated the entire family. What Adela said was the law. She had been the only one who could get his worthless father to get up and look for work. Presumably, he should be grateful to her for that. Unfortunately, the verbal poison she sprayed in the process had put an even greater strain on the family's already very negative mood.

"She's still alive. It's no wonder you've not seen her since. She lives a very secluded life. Only a handful of people exist whom she accepts as visitors. Everyone else is chased away with her shotgun. In any case," he continued, "when the first concerns were raised about an exorcism after your return, she threatened to hex them all if they didn't leave you alone."

"People believed that?" Cruz asked.

Jake shrugged. "Looks like it. You have to remember, though, that the group of people to be convinced was, after all, willing to put their faith in a priest exorcising ghosts. From there, it's not a big step to believe in witchcraft, too."

"Strange," Cruz muttered. "Why has she never contacted me?"

"Don't know, but that still doesn't explain why you were declared dead in the first place."

"No, it doesn't," Cruz replied, deep in thought.

"You're saying you guys just left for California in a hurry in the middle of the night?"

Cruz looked up. "Yup. At the time, it was just another example of my father's strange choices. New job, new luck, as long as we were on the West Coast within, what, forty-eight hours? At least that's how I remember it. I'm probably not the most reliable historian, though. You've got to remember that I was still an impressionable youth myself at the time and had never gotten farther than Denver by then." He ran a hand through his short hair. "For me, it was all a great adventure."

Jake tapped the stack of files on his desk. "As soon as I finish my current cases, I'll disappear into the basement and try to find the relevant records, I promise. After all, according to my wife, you're not the only one interested," he added.

Cruz groaned. "Let me guess—Zelda."

Jake grinned. "That's right. That would be the 'lover'. All that's missing now is the revenge motive."

"And that would be?" asked Cruz, against his better judgment.

"Well, love, of course. What else?"

CHAPTER SIX

Zelda could hardly believe that lunchtime had already passed when she looked at the clock for the first time. A dash of good humor, and time flew by. Amused at her own thoughts, she called out to Shannon, who was loitering somewhere in the stockroom under the pretense of taking inventory. More likely, she was typing her fingers sore on her cell phone. She sighed. At some point, she would have to look for a more motivated employee. But that could wait.

"I'm getting lunch," she let the young woman know. "If anyone needs a prescription filled, have them come back in the afternoon. If it's urgent, you'll find me at the diner."

She believed a professional pharmacist should always be present. But as she had found out, the laws were interpreted generously in a small town, and the residents were flexible. Understandable, she thought. After all, the next-nearest pharmacy wasn't exactly around the corner. At the beginning, she had a hard time with the lax handling. But since then, she realized the low number of residents didn't justify two fully trained pharmacists. The prescription drugs were under lock and key and only she had a key. She assumed that satisfied the law.

"I know," came back the bored reply.

Zelda could barely suppress an annoyed eye roll. There was no reason to stoop to the level of a creature stuck in her teens, no matter how tempting.

Once outside and on her way, Zelda lifted her face to the snowflakes. Cold, but beautiful, she noted, making her way to the diner. A few people stopped and greeted her kindly. She didn't mind anyone who took the opportunity to tell her about their latest aches and pains.

Her own business, customers who trusted her, the ability to set her own hours... paradise.

In Arizona, she'd never been more than their daughter. It hadn't been a bad life, but overall it added up to just too little.

Zelda had been so wrapped up in her own past that she hadn't even gotten to really enjoy her new status. She had to think about how to thank Jaz. Maybe she should offer her services as a babysitter? Once the new baby arrived, she'd have her hands full.

At the diner, she was greeted by the familiar smell of fried food and coffee. She made her way to the counter while nodding to the occasional familiar face.

"Someone's in a good mood," Miss Minnie observed, bringing her a cup of coffee without being asked.

"True. Why wouldn't I? It's snowing," she announced, as if this was a whole new experience for her.

"It's snowing," Miss Minnie repeated incredulously. "Daisy!" she barked over her shoulder.

A few seconds later, her sister, Miss Daisy, stepped through the swinging doors that separated the guest room from the kitchen. She held a dishtowel in her hands and dried her hands. "Where's the fire?"

"Our new addition here is in a good mood."

Astonished, Miss Daisy looked back and forth between her sister and Zelda. "And that's worth mentioning because?" Her voice made it clear that she doubted her sister's state of mind.

"She claims the snow is to blame for her good mood."

"Oh." Her eyes fell on Zelda. The obvious concern about the state of mind transferred seamlessly from her sister to her. "Are you not feeling well?" she asked, concerned.

Before Zelda could assure her that she was doing exceptionally well, Miss Minnie's face took on a sly expression. "I think it has more to do with the fact that she spent half the day with Cruz yesterday."

"That's right. I read that, too. Honestly, I thought it was a rumor."

The Diner Sisters crossed their arms in front of their chests and stared at Zelda.

"Um, do you expect me to report to you now?" Zelda asked. "How do you even know about that?"

"Social media," Miss Minnie replied with relish. "However, the report was incomplete. Did you guys kiss? Make out? More?"

The blood rose to Zelda's head at the thought of kissing Cruz. Out of embarrassment, of course. Not because it made her all hot. That probably went without saying. To distract them from the reactions of her treacherous body, she muttered, "Whoever came up with this idiotic idea of a social media page should be run out of town."

"That would be us," Miss Minnie opined.

"Oh." Zelda folded her mouth shut again and ducked her head. Foot. In. Mouth. *Oof.* "I probably should have saved that observation until after dinner."

Miss Daisy laughed harshly. "Don't worry. We've got

thick skin. We'll feed you and your sassy mouth anyway." With those words, she disappeared into the kitchen.

Zelda wanted to shout after her that she just wanted a salad, since she was filled still with good intentions after being with Jaz. She changed her mind at the last moment though; Miss Daisy might have dismissed her comment about the social media page, but Zelda had a feeling if someone spurned her cooking skills, that was one subject she couldn't take a joke.

"Smart girl," muttered Miss Minnie, correctly interpreting her facial expression. "Now, out with it. What's the matter?"

When Zelda opened her mouth to make some irrelevant remark, Miss Minnie raised her finger.

"If you start in on the weather again, I'll personally see to it that you only get water and bread for the next few weeks. And not just at the diner."

For many years, the diner had been the only restaurant in Independence. With the increase in the number of residents, however, this had changed. In the meantime, there was Sweets, a café run by a distant relative of the Diner Sisters, and the Arcade, a pizzeria with an adjoining arcade.

"My sister may be soft-hearted. I'm not," she added when Zelda still wouldn't come clean.

"With these interrogation methods, it's no wonder you're always so well informed," Zelda muttered.

"Didn't you know?" Miss Minnie looked like she was about to burst with pride. "Bets are already on."

The diner had a little black book that was looked after by the Diner Sisters. Bets could be placed on anything: upcoming births, the weather, the coming harvest, hunting luck, but especially on romances and all their various stages. The winner got his bet back and additionally won a dinner for two. The rest went into a fund managed by the mayor.

The fund came into play when the normal social benefits were not enough. These included scholarships for promising, destitute students or medical treatment for people with no or insufficient health insurance. In exceptional cases, the money was used to cover extraordinary expenses of the municipality.

Even though the fund served an important, social purpose, it was difficult to object to the bets.

And Zelda realized it didn't change the horrible feeling inside her. Once before, she'd become the protagonist of all sorts of rumors. She had no intention of going through the whole thing again, thank you very much.

Miss Minnie must have seen her stress; she reached over the counter and patted her hand. "It's all quite harmless," she hastened to assure her. "Just, I wonder if you'll get together again and all that."

"No comment," Zelda repeated woodenly. Where had her good mood gone? It had been there a moment ago. But the thought of being the target of hidden glances and whispered words again made her stomach turn. Why couldn't people just leave her the hell alone?

"If I had known he wasn't dead and living *here*, of all places, I never would have taken you up on your offer to run the pharmacy," she blurted out. Miss Minnie had been one of the founding members of VGI and part of the persuasion committee. So, she felt quite justified in holding them personally responsible for her current plight.

Zelda wondered if she wasn't fooling herself. She had never had anything against Cruz. On the contrary. She had missed him as much as she would miss an amputated body part. Only since she had found out that all her mourning during the last years had been in vain, had she developed such negative feelings toward him. Nothing had changed about the fact that Cruz was as much a victim of the events of that time as she was.

Miss Minnie raised a scrutinizing eyebrow. Voices in the background caused her to shift her attention and look over Zelda's head toward the door.

A sly smile came to her lips, and she said, "The ghost from your past is gracing us with his presence right now. He looks pretty lively, though, and good enough to eat."

Zelda hid her face behind her hands. "That's the problem."

"He's coming your way. I'd better give you some privacy."

Zelda snorted. Hearing Miss Minnie utter the word *privacy* was something of an oxymoron. Where had her promising day gone? Vaguely she could remember having had quite a few plans, too. The plants! How could she have forgotten them? Suddenly, part of her good mood returned.

"Miss Minnie, wait."

The patroness of the diner paused in mid-motion. "I thought you'd be glad to get rid of me?"

"Yes, yes, in a moment," Zelda assured her. "I just have one more question. Can you recommend someone who knows about medicinal plants? Specifically local plants?"

Surprised at the sudden change of subject, Miss Minnie frowned. "Medicinal plants?"

"Yes. I'm thinking of making my own ointments and tinctures at the pharmacy."

"Hmm. I can't think of anyone right now. Quinn Davies at the wildlife refuge might be able to help."

Quinn. Of course. The game warden had helped her out of a jam shortly after her arrival, when she had carelessly tangled with an elk. Since then, a loose friendship had developed.

Miss Minnie thought for a moment longer. "Or..." she hesitated and broke off.

"Yes?" Zelda waited so eagerly for an answer that she didn't notice Cruz stepping up behind her.

"Adela Ruis," Miss Minnie said. "Cruz's aunt. Or great-aunt. She's... not very hospitable, though."

"Adela? Why is everyone talking about her today?" Cruz asked no one in particular, then turned to Zelda. "And for your information, Adela is not only not very hospitable, but also completely nuts."

"You see her often?" asked Zelda, interested in teasing an invitation out of him. If he wasn't going to do her the favor of being dead and staying dead, he might as well make himself useful. Of course, her question had nothing at all to do with the potent cocktail of hormones that was automatically released and heated her blood every time he showed up. After all, she had long since left her crushes of yesteryear behind. She was totally above that.

She was so engrossed in lying to herself that it took a moment to realize that Cruz was talking to her. "You stay away from her, you hear?"

"What?"

"The old witch is not right in the head," Cruz said. "You shouldn't go anywhere near her."

"Oh yeah, and since when do you get to tell me what to do and what not to do?"

"Believe me, I'm not joking. If you're lucky, she'll just sic one of her dogs on you."

"And if I'm unlucky?" asked Zelda, who didn't believe a word he said.

"Give you a load of buckshot in the butt," he replied.

"Ouch!"

"Exactly. Ouch. That's why you better ask Quinn or buy one of those botany guides."

How nice, Zelda thought, that men always felt they knew how the world worked. However, she had learned from her father, among others, that there wasn't much point in getting involved needlessly in a discussion. Better to give the impression of agreeing with them and then just doing whatever you wanted.

Zelda took a deep breath and nodded. "Sure. Whatever." Luckily for her, Miss Daisy was just coming through the revolving door with her lunch and set the plate down. "I have to cook now and serve people while you make nice conversation?" she barked at her sister.

Miss Minnie laughed. "Don't worry. I'm coming."

"*Bon appétit*," Zelda murmured, reaching for her fork.

Cruz didn't seem to have come to eat. He blinked and said. "I was just with Jake. Jake's the sheriff."

Zelda rolled her eyes and shoved a bite into her mouth. "I know."

"I asked him to look in the files to see what really happened back then."

"Okay."

"Okay? Is that all you have to say? I expected a little more enthusiasm," he said.

She swallowed and dabbed her mouth with the napkin.

Cruz followed her movements as if hypnotized. He looked like he … wanted to kiss her. But why? What was she doing that was so attractive? Was she reading him wrong?

Zelda tried to ignore the heat that was building between them. She was imagining the desire she thought she saw flashing in his eyes but pushed it away. "Good idea to talk to Jake. But I've actually concluded that you were right. What does it matter what happened back then? Fortunately, you're alive, and we live in the same place again. End of story."

Cruz raised his head and looked deeply into her eyes. "End of story? Are you sure about that?"

Completely thrown by the intensity of his voice and his words, she could only stare at him. So much for her resolution to meet him cool and detached.

Cruz leaned forward a little. She could feel his breath dancing over her skin; she got goosebumps.

"If you ask me, the story is just beginning." Surprisingly gentle, he brushed his lips feather-lightly across her cheek before pushing himself off the counter and leaving.

Zelda raised a hand to the spot. Had he really just kissed her? She looked after him with mixed feelings and an excited flutter in her stomach. She didn't know what to make of it. She sighed. That morning, the Zen lifestyle had seemed so easy, enjoying the here-and-now while making plans for tomorrow.

Plans that didn't involve a muscular, lithe guy with honey-colored skin, jet black hair, and a voice that made her heart flutter and then some.

Whatever, she thought defiantly. She would certainly not let him stop her from visiting one of the few herbalists in the area. Crazy or not.

CHAPTER SEVEN

"Ice cream? Party? As in together? You're still asking? Of course, I'm coming!"

Quinn's laughter spilled out of the phone, seamlessly adding to the joy that rose in Zelda. Another person who couldn't seem to think of anything better than spending an evening with her. Kat, Paula, Tyler, Paige, and Lara had already accepted. Avery and Becca had not replied yet. Until Jaz's visit, she hadn't even realized how much she was suffering from her mostly self-imposed isolation. She was grateful to Jaz for so many things that Jaz probably wouldn't have to hire an out-of-town babysitter again until the children were grown. But that was a price she was happy to pay in exchange for not feeling so lonely anymore.

Especially now that Cruz was no longer just haunting her dreams but was constantly running into her live and in color, she realized how desperately she needed company.

"I must warn you, though," she felt obliged to inform Quinn. "While I invited the others for purely social reasons, I plan to plunder your botanical knowledge of the area."

"Uh, my botanical knowledge? I'm actually more into fauna than flora."

"Don't worry, I'm sure you know more than I do. That's enough for now."

"If you say so. But I still get ice cream?" Quinn hedged.

"Well, of course. Although, naturally I'm deeply offended that you're only coming to fill your belly."

"Oh, I also come to hear about your latest moose adventures," she said, alluding to the situation in which they had met.

Zelda groaned. "Don't remind me of that. But you can rest assured—I took your advice to heart and gave a wide berth to anything that remotely resembles a moose."

"Very wise. I've heard rumors that you have other interests at the moment?"

"Other interests?"

"Yes. A certain handsome man is said to haunt your life."

"Oh that."

"That doesn't sound very enthusiastic."

Zelda went to the window with the phone to her ear. The weather just didn't know what it wanted. After it had snowed like crazy the last few days, it was unusually warm again today. You could almost watch it start to thaw everywhere. "What am I supposed to be excited about?" she tried to stall for time.

"Well, I thought you used to be a couple?"

"With the emphasis on *used to be*," Zelda replied. "After all, that was ages ago. People and feelings change. Otherwise, you'd still have to be with, what was his name? Frank?" Frank had been Quinn's high school crush. He was divorced for the second time, had a beer belly, and was always getting into fights of some sort.

"Ugh. Okay. If that's how you put it... However, I would point out that Cruz has done exceptionally well, unlike Frank."

At Quinn's words, images of Cruz rose unbidden in her mind. Like every other damn time he was mentioned, her pulse quickened. Was there no cure for that? And then there was that kiss...

"Zelda?" came Quinn's voice through the phone.

Caught off guard, she vigorously pushed aside the memory of the fleeting touch of Cruz's lips on her skin. "It's possible. I didn't even notice," she lied, quickly changing the subject. "I'm looking forward to seeing you."

Quinn laughed. "Now that was a definite case of shut-the-mouth. I'll draw my own conclusions from that and adjust my bet accordingly."

"What? You bet on Cruz and me?"

"Sure thing."

"Even you're part of the gossip in this town," Zelda said, sighing.

"Don't worry about it. No one is spared. Oh yeah, before I forget. Social media has the latest speculation on..."

"Who? What?"

"Oh, nothing. Forget what I said. I've got to go. Bye!"

Zelda took the receiver from her ear when the dial tone sounded and frowned. Had Quinn actually hung up on her? Admittedly, she had been very clever. Of course, she was now burning with curiosity. With a resigned sigh, she flopped down on the sofa and pulled up the social media app on her phone.

Murphy, who, regardless of the fact that there was more than enough room for both of them, jumped away to the floor in a huff.

"Sorry," she mumbled as she pulled up Independence's page.

Does a spirit dwell among us?

Eyewitnesses report: Cruz kisses Zelda.

Below was a picture of her looking after Cruz as he left the diner, a dreamy expression in her eyes and a hand to her cheek. Although she was annoyed by the unauthorized picture of herself on the internet, she had to admit the shot was quite flattering. Compared to the picture of her sitting on her butt in front of the moose, with the caption *The Future Moose Whisperer of Independence*, this one was a real step up. Under the picture it said: *Zelda shocked. Was the kiss that good or was she just kissed by a ghost?*

The former, she thought silently. She did not dare to imagine what a real kiss would do to her, if even his fleeting touch had such an effect.

The post already had 294 likes and over fifty comments. Disgusted, she turned off her phone after reading the first ten. Did people really have nothing better to do than report on their imaginary love lives? If there was at least something to report, she thought sullenly.

Call him, the cheeky voice in the back of her head advised.

And then? Do I open the front door to him naked?

Good idea, said her adventurous alter ego. *At least then there will be no room for misunderstandings.*

Zelda rolled her eyes. Sometimes she felt like she had two completely different personalities. The part of her that would gladly pick up the phone and invite Cruz over for a jump in the sack, however, hadn't made an appearance in a long time. After the disastrous result fourteen years ago when she'd first gone overboard and defied her parents' strict rules, she'd kept those impulses carefully in check. During all that time when she had thought Cruz was dead, she'd found that easy. It was only since she was back, and Cruz was alive again, that her impulsive side rebelled more often, trying to make itself heard. If she wasn't careful, it was going to get her into hot water. *Or into bed with Cruz*, the voice said slyly. Aarrgh!

In order not to have to deal with these disturbing facts, and what they probably meant, she went into the kitchen. There, a half-starved cat waited impatiently for her to finally feed him. A wave of unexpected affection for her grouchy, four-legged roommate gripped her.

"You've been abandoned too, haven't you? No wonder you don't trust anyone."

She leaned down and stroked his back.

As if sensing the connection she suddenly felt, Murphy acquiesced to the touch. Nevertheless, he continued to stare intently at the kitchen counter. He probably thought the can would open purely because of his excellent hypnotic skills, she thought, amused. Not willing to shatter his illusions, she retrieved the can opener from the drawer and set to work. After all, the cat had taught her well.

At the same time, Cruz was sitting in his office, the photo of Zelda in his hand. He had wanted to go home, but then he'd discovered the picture on Facebook, and his fingers had taken on a life of their own. A few clicks later, the printer on the other side of the room spit out the picture. Not sure exactly how that had happened, he stood up and received the photo.

The expression on her face pleased him. Surprised, as if she didn't know exactly what had just happened. He would have loved to visit her on the spot and try his best to conjure up that amazement once again. Unfortunately, he was pretty sure the more likely scenario was being kicked out of the pharmacy.

A knock on the door jolted him. He looked up and discovered the sheriff sticking his head in the door.

"You seem to have made quite an impression," Jake teased him when he spotted the photo on the desk.

"I wish," Cruz grumbled. "But I'm guessing you didn't come here to talk about the latest social media news."

"You guess right. May I?" He pointed to the chair in front of the desk.

"Sure. Sit down."

"So the good news is, you're not dead. You were never reported dead, either."

"You don't say?" asked Cruz in surprise. "You mean the whole story comes from Zelda's overactive imagination?" Although he had initially thought just that, the thought bothered him.

"I wouldn't put it that way. After all, we all thought you died in a drug deal gone bad."

"True. I still wonder why though. After all, I never had anything to do with drugs. Of course, like most boys, I got into mischief. But I always kept my hands off alcohol and drugs. With my father's cautionary example at home, it was very easy for me to do that."

"I think that was one of the theories, too. That you went to the meeting place instead of your father and got murdered."

"Uh-huh." Cruz was silent for a while. "But then shouldn't there have been at least one death? Anybody? I mean, fine to make up or believe a story. But people would have to have noticed the absence of a body."

Jake cleared his throat. "There was. And about your size. Charred almost beyond recognition. The car he was in was set on fire after he'd been shot."

"Shot and set on fire?" inquired Cruz incredulously. "There's a full report on that, I assume."

"That's exactly the problem. There is no file on it, just a handwritten note on a piece of paper. The file on the case is missing," Jake replied grimly. "Here. I wrote down all the facts that are known. Polly, my right-hand woman at the office, helped me. She has an incredibly good memory. Plus, she was still on active duty at the time."

"Who was the dead man?"

Jake shrugged his shoulders. "I don't know. I can only guess. After all the talk in the previous months about a vagrant who'd been picked up several times, it's reasonable to assume that's how someone solved two problems in one prank."

"You mean he was killed on purpose?"

Jake nodded grimly.

"But why?"

Jake helplessly raised his shoulders and dropped them again. "That's the big question. The one that Zelda is obviously asking herself, too."

Right. Zelda. She had started it all. Cruz frowned. "Except that instead of the answers we'd hoped for, there's only been more questions."

"Looks like it."

"Where do we go from here?"

Jake moved his head deliberately from left to right. "You know I usually don't rest until I solve a mystery. In the end, that's one of the reasons I became a cop."

"Yeah?"

"In this case, I'm not sure it's advisable to keep looking for answers."

"Why? Because you feel like we're not going to find answers?"

"Not that. You can almost always find answers. I just don't think you'd like them."

Cruz took note of this statement with a stoic expression on his face. The thought had already crossed his mind. "I can't just stop now."

Jake sighed. "I thought so. The problem is that the people who were involved back then are probably still alive and, in all likelihood, still living in the area. There's no statute of limitations on murder."

"All the more reason why you should be interested in clearing this up," Cruz noted.

"Right. But if it means my friends are in danger, suddenly the case isn't so clear," Jake replied.

"Will you pass me the peppermint ice cream?" called Jaz to Zelda.

Zelda stood up, leaned over the table, and took the big bucket from Lara's hands.

"I put extra bowls on the table."

"Pure waste after I plan to eat the whole bucket myself," Lara declared, trying to reclaim her favorite.

"I stocked my freezer well, so there's plenty for everyone," Zelda reassured her.

"I already looked inside. It's empty."

"Really?" In disbelief, Zelda stared at the bucket in her hand. Peppermint with chocolate chips. The flavor was popular with pregnant women. Jaz and Lara had been fighting all evening over who got to have it.

"I can go out and get more. The convenience store is open until eleven," Avery offered.

"No, no, it's okay," Lara replied with a sorry look on her face. "Chocolate will do in a pinch."

"When is your due date?"

"I'd be happy to do it today. Or tomorrow. But according to my cruel doctor, the new earthling is still about four weeks away." It was clear she was tired with being pregnant.

"Cheeky," Zelda smirked.

"I agree," Lara grumbled. "Patience has never been one of my strong points. Yesterday I was trying to scrape Devil's hooves."

"So?" her sister-in-law Becca inquired with interest. She and her partner Adrian had only vaguely discussed the subject of children so far. Since he already had a son, with whom she got along very well, and she was currently training to be an equine physiotherapist, having her own offspring was not on the agenda so far. But it didn't hurt to be informed in case that should change.

"Well, I bent over for his leg and almost fell on my nose. At the last moment I was able to brace myself against his stomach. Out of sheer fright, I guess I put too much force into the balancing motion, so I sat on my butt instead."

"I'm sure Devil found that very amusing," Quinn chuckled.

"Hank, too. He watched the whole thing from the kitchen window. Afterward, he tried again to convince me to stay away from the horses for the last four weeks."

"Well, what did you answer?"

Lara patted her belly. "What do you suppose? The dwarf here must be calibrated for horses after all. You can't do that, not to pet a horse's hide for four weeks."

Becca nodded in agreement.

Jaz rolled her eyes. "I don't think he wanted to keep you

completely away from your beloved horses. He probably cares more about you not riding anymore."

"I haven't done that in three weeks," Lara reluctantly admitted.

"How did he convince you of that?" interjected Kat, surprised, into the discussion.

"He didn't. The midget in my belly did that all by himself when I hoisted myself up on Devil like an overweight walrus and almost rolled back down the other side. That's when I decided I'd probably be better off doing groundwork with the guy. It's really cute to see how careful he is with me."

"I always find it exciting to watch how animals react to change."

Zelda glanced at her unhappy cat. To his displeasure, there were several dogs present, so he had retreated back to his high perch. Tyler had brought her German shepherd Ranger, and Kat had shown up with Nikita, a huge dogue de Bordeaux. Rambo was there, too. Ears flat against his head, Murphy watched the hustle and bustle of people and unwanted dogs with disdain.

Rainbow, the young bloodhound dog who belonged to Becca, was the only one who had tried to climb the high shelf. Zelda could have sworn that the cat had grinned as the young dog barked desperately at the wall. After failing miserably, she resorted to asking the other dogs to play in turn. Unfortunately, she was only somewhat lucky with Rambo. The others stoically ignored her overtures and would not be deterred from their naps.

"Speaking of changes: Have you been able to unravel the mystery of Cruz's supposed demise yet?" Quinn.

"I've decided to let the old stories go," Zelda replied, feeling quite proud of the fact that she felt only a slight twinge. She may not have reached true Zen status yet, but she was getting close.

"Probably for the best," Jaz said. "From what I've heard from my husband, there isn't even a file."

Avery, who had long worked for the DEA and FBI as an undercover agent, perked up. "No file? That means there was no dead body, either?"

Jaz, suddenly the center of attention, shoved down the last spoonful of peppermint ice cream. "Yes, there was," she muttered. "I guess there was one dead guy. He was identified as Cruz at the time. I don't know any more than that."

"Somebody has to know about this," Avery said. "Sloppy police work was always a thorn in our side."

Paige, who had previously worked as an investigative journalist, spoke up. "I'm sure Polly Miners knows more." All eyes turned to her, looking in wonder. "What? you know me. Mystery stories fascinate me. When Zelda showed up and I realized she thought Cruz was dead all these years, I did some research."

"I'm sure Ace is thrilled," Avery murmured.

"Ace doesn't know anything about it. After all, there's nothing to know. My work was purely scientific. I didn't leave my desk to do it."

"What did you find out?" Zen or not, that's what Zelda wanted to hear right now.

Paige shrugged. "Not much. Polly Miners is the only one still working for the sheriff's office today. You can probably learn the most from her."

"Jake already talked to her," Jaz took the floor again. "According to her, the sheriff at the time took care of the case himself. That's probably why no one noticed the file was missing. Or that anything was fishy about the whole story."

Forgetting all Zen-like thoughts, Zelda leaned forward. "I

have to talk to that sheriff," she said. "Does he still live in Independence?"

Jaz and Avery gave each other a worried look, while Paige reached into her bag and pulled out her tablet. "I forwarded you the address. He's living outside of Independence now, in a cabin across the river. But I have to warn you, he's a pretty strange fellow."

"Listen to what Paige is saying," Avery said. "He's crazy and lives a very reclusive life in constant anticipation of the end of the world, or at least the next world war."

"Oh. Whatever. That doesn't bother me. Can I talk to him?"

"If he doesn't shoot you first, maybe," Jaz replied.

"Oh." Zelda didn't quite know how to classify the information. First Adela and then the former sheriff. He was the second person in a few days who was said that he'd shoot first and ask questions later.

"I wouldn't put too much stock in that," Paula said. "I had that reputation for quite a while, too."

"You still do," Tyler said to her sister.

"Not true at all," Jaz defended her friend.

Paula laughed. "Just kidding. Seriously? I don't care. But you see what I mean? Anyone who doesn't immediately go into a frenzy of enthusiasm when company shows up is immediately put under general suspicion of being a maverick."

Zelda, who knew the gossip mechanisms of the small community extremely well, could imagine. Even she, as an avowed pacifist, was sometimes tempted to keep unwanted visitors at bay through force of arms. "Well, I'll just have to find an opportunity to talk to the sheriff to solve the mystery once and for all," she stated excitedly.

Avery and Jaz exchanged a worried look. "I'm not sure

it's going to be that easy. Promise me you'll let me know when you go out to see him," Jaz asked.

"Okay... But what's going to happen to me? Except a load of buckshot in my butt, of course," Zelda tried to lighten the serious mood a little.

"Just promise me, that's all."

"Sure. I can do that. There. Enough speculation about possible motives. Who wants more ice cream?"

CHAPTER EIGHT

Zelda hadn't slept a wink all night. Although she had tried her best, Paige's words had not left her mind. If she really wanted answers, she needed to talk to the former sheriff. Perkins was his name. Thomas Perkins. A meaningless name. Could he really be involved in a conspiracy? And why?

She straightened up in bed and looked out the window. The curtains were open so she could see the snow-capped peaks bathed in pink light from the rising sun. Murphy was curled up at the foot of her bed, asleep. I wonder if he slept there every night. She didn't know. She usually didn't get up until an hour later. Then he was always demonstratively waiting in the kitchen in front of his food bowl. She bent over and stroked his silky fur. Without opening an eye, he began to purr.

"Are you still asleep?" she asked softly.

Abruptly the purring stopped, and he opened one eye, then the second. After several surprised blinks, he hissed. With a jump, he moved away from her reach. Zelda smirked. "I thought you were wrong."

Instead of answering her, Murphy began to concentrate on grooming his fur.

"You can't fool me any longer," she said as she walked past him into the bathroom. The cat didn't dignify her with a glance. Nevertheless, she was more convinced than ever that he understood every word.

Only half an hour later, Zelda was on her way to the diner. She couldn't show up unannounced at a stranger's house and pester them with questions. She had no idea whether Adela Ruis and Thomas Perkins were churchgoers. On the contrary, she strongly doubted it. But in her home, Sunday had been sacred. She'd gone to church in the morning, while the afternoon belonged to the family. Her concerns, be it a desire for native herbal knowledge or a search for answers concerning her past, definitely did not fall into that category. She would treat herself to a hearty breakfast and then study the books Quinn had kindly brought her yesterday.

Zelda had barely taken her seat when Cruz entered the diner and headed purposefully for her alcove. Of course, Miss Minnie was promptly there with her coffee pot.

"Nice to see you two renewing your friendship," she quipped as she poured them both a cup of coffee.

"I can imagine that. If it becomes known that we shared a table, the little black book will probably catch fire," Zelda grumbled.

"Really?" laughed Cruz. "There are bets on us?"

"Of course," Miss Minnie said. "I put my money on you." She patted his hand.

Zelda rolled her eyes as she saw him grin in satisfaction at this information. "Forget it!"

"What?" he asked innocently. "I didn't say anything."

"Don't encourage them," she grumbled.

"Breakfast?" interrupted Miss Minnie.

Zelda was about to explode. Instead, she thought about the ice cream party from the night before. "Just an egg white scramble and some fruit for me, please."

Cruz stared at her as if she'd grown horns. "I, on the other hand, would like a real breakfast, including French toast, cinnamon rolls, eggs, bacon, and hashbrowns."

Miss Minnie nodded, while Zelda's eyes grew bigger.

Oh great. Now she'd be nibbling on her healthy breakfast while Cruz was eating all sorts of delicacies, Zelda thought. To distract herself from this unpleasant thought, she blurted out the first thing that came to mind. "Are you spying on me?"

"In a manner of speaking," Cruz replied.

Not expecting this answer, Zelda let herself sink back onto the bench in shock.

"No, of course not in *that way*," Cruz explained. I was on my way to the office when I saw you drive into the town square. Since I hadn't had breakfast either, I thought we could do so together."

"Because we're best friends, after all," she replied.

Cruz studied her for a few seconds. "We used to be," he said. "At least I thought we were."

Ashamed, Zelda lowered her eyes. Once more, she had to remind herself he wasn't the enemy. Agreeing, she tilted her head. "Maybe that's true, I'm not sure anymore." She let her gaze wander out the window.

Cruz cleared his throat. "I can imagine that. Listen, I was just talking to Jake yesterday. There does seem to be some inconsistencies in the story of what happened."

"I know," she interrupted. "Jaz told me that although a

dead body was found, no investigation was done." She chewed on her lower lip. "I've honestly tried to let the whole thing go, as you—and others—have advised. But I just can't." She studied the shape of her cup before finally looking up and straight into eyes. "Maybe if I get some answers, I'll finally manage to stop blaming you for everything."

Her voice sounded stiff, as if it had taken effort to admit that out loud. Before he could say anything back, Miss Minnie arrived with a large tray and placed all kinds of delicacies in front of Cruz and Zelda.

Zelda examined her plate. Fruit and scrambled eggs. Oh well. It was always better than nothing. Of course, she finished long before Cruz. She said, "Maybe I should just leave. At least then I'd no longer be exposed to the temptation to steal your breakfast right off your plate."

"Take whatever you want," Cruz grinned. Seemingly unconcerned, he speared some eggs and bacon, along with a piece of French toast, onto his fork and held it in front of Zelda's nose.

"You've always been the devil on my shoulder, you know that?" Zelda couldn't resist the wonderful smell of bacon and snatched the offered bite. "After all, it's only a forkful. This certainly doesn't count. Isn't there a rule somewhere that food fed to you has no calories?"

She ate it. When she realized that she had actually just been fed by Cruz in the middle of the diner, she turned bright red. Embarrassed, she looked around the room and caught some of the early risers present hastily averting their eyes. "Oh, great. No need to bother the local paparazzi. I managed to keep the rumor mill bubbling all by myself."

"Forget it and eat!" Cruz said. "I don't want to be the subject of gossip, either. But there's no way I'm going to base my life on what others think of me. Or us."

Zelda opened her mouth to protest. But before she could say peep, Cruz offered another irresistible morsel, which she ate gleefully. "That was pretty sneaky."

Cruz grinned at her. "Good, right?"

"That's the problem," she grumbled, swiping a strip of bacon from his plate.

"I don't know what you're so worried about!"

"You can't imagine?" she murmured, enviously surveying his well-toned body. He was made up of solid muscles. Muscles she'd love to explore. Her mouth went dry, and she swallowed. Where had that thought come from? Too much sugar? Or too little? She reached for the second half of the cinnamon bun on his plate. "Better not to take any chances that this goes to waste."

Cruz raised an eyebrow. "Have you acquired a taste for it?"

"What does it mean to have a taste for it? Falling back into bad habits is more like it." She let the icing melt on her tongue with relish. If she was going to sin, at least she'd enjoy it, she thought.

She sensed Cruz's gaze, deliberately taking his time. "If this is what your bad habits look like, please keep it up." He lowered his voice a little. "It'd be a shame if you lost those lovely curves."

Cruz's gaze made Zelda embarrassed. The compliment was like a balm for her soul, even if she found it hard to believe.

She didn't know what to say. He was really very nice to look at. Her hormones, dancing samba in her stomach as if drunk, erupted into cries of jubilation. *What is wrong with me?*

To distract herself from the chaos Cruz had unleashed inside her with his few well-aimed words, she said, "Sorry, but I have my doubts. You don't look like you appreciate curves. At least, I can't detect any on you."

"You noticed my figure, eh?" he replied, satisfied.

When she rolled her eyes, he leaned forward. "I like women with curves." He reached out and stroked one of the unruly curls behind her ear.

Zelda held her breath.

"I especially like your curves." After those words, he leaned back and abruptly changed the subject. "What are your plans for today?"

Zelda was dizzy. Whether from holding her breath too long, Cruz's touch, or his words, she didn't know. In any case, she was grateful for the change of subject. "I don't have any definite plans today. Maybe I'll take a walk if it doesn't snow. Tomorrow morning, on the other hand, the pharmacy's closed."

Surprised, Cruz looked at her. "Why is that?"

Zelda said, "I thought I'd drive up to Perkins, the former..."

"... Sheriff," Cruz completed her sentence.

"Exactly," she said.

"Do you think that he'll talk?" he asked.

"Probably. I just want to ask him a few questions."

Cruz ran his hand through his short hair. "Just ask a few questions? To an ex-cop who, for all we know, is dirty? Besides, they say he's paranoid. You think he's going to kindly invite you in for tea and tell you his life story?"

Zelda said, "Of course you don't think I'm capable of handling this. I can and will. I'll manage to elicit some answers from him. We have to start somewhere, after all. And since you seem satisfied with the non-answers Jake gave you, I guess it's up to me."

"You're not going there!"

81

"Oh yeah?" she said. "Since when are you my keeper?"

"I'm not, of course. But at least let me come with you. I'm just worried."

Zelda took her time with the answer while considering his suggestion. True, she was angry with him. There was nothing that would drive her up the wall faster than a man telling her what to do and what not to do. On the other hand, she herself was not entirely comfortable with the idea of confronting Perkins alone. Reluctantly, she finally nodded and stood up.

"All right. You can come with me. Tomorrow at eight in the morning. If you're not on time, I'll leave without you."

"Don't worry. I'll be there. Even if I have to postpone my entire schedule to do so."

She hesitated and smiled at him. "Thanks for breakfast."

Cruz smirked. "Always happy to."

Unwilling to let him see that he could make her laugh so easily, she left the diner. "Tomorrow morning. If you're not early, you're late."

"Understood."

Immediately after Zelda left, another guest, who had been sitting in the alcove behind them, unnoticed by Zelda and Cruz, threw a few bills on the table. His heart was pounding with excitement. He had not had such important news to deliver for a long time. Surely his father would be happy to have such information. He couldn't wait to deliver the news. He clenched a hand into a fist. He couldn't just ignore him.

Excited, he inconspicuously made his way through the other guests and toward the door.

After a few steps he was outside and at his ancient pickup truck.

He got in, started the engine.

A U-turn later, he was on the main road and on his way to his father's cabin.

Thomas Perkins frowned as he spotted the car slowly and steadily making its way up the hill. The vehicle disappeared around a bend, and he had to wait until it reappeared in his field of vision. Walt? What was his worthless son doing here? In these road conditions? The last time he'd shown up was when that damn Zelda had returned to Independence. As if he cared. Why couldn't people just stay where they were?

He put his hands on his hips and raised his face, tanned by wind and weather, toward the unwanted visitor. If Walt had expected a friendly welcome and a cup of coffee, he was wrong. He needed nothing. Not from anyone. Not even from his son. The only thing that mattered was the treasure. He was very close to finding it. He was sure.

High above, a bird of prey circled and emitted a shrill cry. It sounded like mocking laughter. Perkins raised his fist to the sky and shook it. "You just wait and see. I'm going to find him. Then I'll show everybody."

He had big plans for the gold. He would form his own independent state. With the treasure, he would have all the resources at his fingertips. Money. Weapons. Followers. Then his rules would apply.

"Dad?"

He'd been so absorbed by the sight of the bird and daydreaming about his glorious future that he had not noticed Walt's arrival.

"What are you doing here?" he barked, turning away to pick up the jacket he'd removed from the bench.

"Visiting you." Walt stepped from one foot to the other.

Unlike his father, who was still fit and wiry at nearly seventy, Walt had a gut. His skin was pale, except for his red nose. Too much office work, too much beer, and far too little exercise.

"Consider your duty herewith done. Now get the hell out of here."

Everything in Walt screamed to do just that. To run straight to the safety of his car and never look back. Let the old man go to hell! But then he remembered the important information he'd brought with him. He straightened his shoulders. Today would be different. Today was the day his father would finally look at him differently. Probably that'd make him a loser—that he was still looking for approval at over forty years old. But today the wait would be over.

"Let's go in," he suggested.

"What for? I like it out here."

"But I don't. I'm cold. And I have something important to tell you," Walt said. "So, let's do what I want for once."

His father shrugged and reached for the axe again. "Do it here."

Walt admitted defeat. He didn't know what had given him the crazy idea that he could stand up to his father. He swallowed his pride—it wasn't much anyway, as his father had seen to that long ago—and addressed his back as he spoke. "Zelda and Cruz have been talking again lately."

A vague grunt was the only indication his father was even listening.

"They want to talk to you. Tomorrow."

Perkins paused. "Talk? To me?" He laughed. "They'll

have to find me first to do that," he said. No one, except a few insiders, knew where his cabin was. Just the way he wanted it.

"They will. They know your address," Walt warned.

At last, Perkins turned to his son. His face was a single thundercloud. "Couldn't keep your mouth shut again, huh?"

Startled, Walt stumbled back a few steps. "Me, are you out of your mind? I would never tell them anything."

Perkins grabbed him by the shirt collar. "Who else would have said something?"

Walt broke free and took a step forward. "Jake Carter."

"The miserable son of a bitch!" exploded Perkins. "Mixing in things that are none of his business."

"Well..." Walt said. "They've gone to the sheriff. They want to uncover the back story that led to their breakup back in the day."

"He was shot. She was pregnant and left in disgrace. End of story."

Walt looked at his father as if he was not quite right in the head. The statement was wrong in so many ways that he was literally at a loss for words. If anyone knew what really happened, it was his father.

"Uh, clearly, he wasn't shot. Otherwise, he'd hardly be walking around alive and asking questions. Questions about his supposed death."

"Did they find out anything?"

"On the contrary. They found nothing at all."

A grin spread across Perkin's face. "See. Told you."

"Even the sheriff couldn't find anything on the case. Which made them grown suspicious. The current theory is that you had a hand in it back then."

Perkins remained silent. Only his face grew redder.

"Aren't you glad now that I came to warn you?"

Perkins blinked. "I'm not interested in that. I'm only interested in the treasure. Soon... soon it will be mine. I'm close."

Shaking his head in disbelief, Walt looked at his father. "You're all about that damn French gold, aren't you? But that's nothing new," he groaned. "It'll be exciting to watch you continue your treasure hunt behind bars when they convict you. After all, there's no statute of limitations on murder."

He was done. From now on, he no longer had a father. That had been the last time he tried to get through to him. Eventually, the mountains would kill him. He didn't care what happened to him in the meantime. He'd done his duty.

Relieved, Perkins watched his son turn the all-terrain vehicle around and start down the valley. Finally, he was gone. His skin prickled uncomfortably, as it always did when he talked to people, no matter who.

I wonder if he had been telling the truth about Zelda and Cruz, he wondered. He'd probably just wanted to make himself important. If the two of them showed up, he'd take care of them. He was the only one who knew what'd really happened back then. Or at least the only one who counted. In the meantime, he'd redouble his efforts to find the treasure.

If only he had a complete map...

Damn two-faced witch.

Cursing loudly, he trudged to his cabin.

CHAPTER NINE

Monday morning, as Zelda was disposing of a half-chewed mouse—Murphy's latest gift—her phone rang. The display showed Jaz's phone number.

"Good morning," she said. "How are you?"

"Not great. I'm sick," Jaz said.

"I hear that in your voice, poor thing," Zelda said.

Jaz sniffed a bit. "Hate to ask, but I was wondering if you had time to watch Cammie today? I know you're working. Normally my grandmother or Brenda, Jake's mom, would fill in. But they're both out of town for VGI. It doesn't have to be all day. Just a couple of hours would be great. Then maybe I'll get some rest."

"Sure thing. I was going to take the morning off, anyway. It's perfect timing."

"Really? But didn't you have plans?"

Of course, she had plans. But somehow it seemed ridiculous to her to chase the ghosts of the past when she could help a friend. "No, no. I didn't have anything specific in mind. Just this and that. Cammie can keep me company."

"Really? You're a sweetheart."

Zelda glanced at the clock on the oven display. It was half past seven. "I'm just going to get ready and then head over to your place. I should be with you in about an hour."

Jaz heaved a relieved sigh. "Perfect. I haven't slept a wink all night. The idea of being able to sleep now instead of spending the morning with an overly active toddler is heavenly."

"That's great, then." Zelda laughed. "Do you need anything else? Is there anything I can bring you? Medicine? Tea? Food?"

"No, thank you. I have all that."

"Good, I'll see you in a bit."

Zelda hung up and sent Cruz a short text explaining the situation. She hoped he wouldn't be too angry. Maybe it was cowardly to just send him a message. After being so adamant yesterday about going out to see Perkins today, she was uncomfortable that she, of all people, was canceling.

Cruz was on his way to his car—no way was he going to show up late at Zelda's only to find that she had already left without him—when his phone beeped. While reaching for his jacket with one hand, he read the text. In mid-motion, he paused. Zelda couldn't because she was *what?* Watching Cammie? He frowned. I wonder if that was true. It could just as easily be that she'd decided overnight to drive out to the former sheriff's house alone.

He stared out the window. It promised to be another clear, cold day. Maybe he should stop by her place? He'd postponed his appointments anyway. He grinned. Why didn't he just bring Zelda and Cammie breakfast? That way he could see for himself that she really was otherwise occupied and hadn't simply shut him out of the research. Besides, it gave him a chance to see her. Over a glass of wine, which he had enjoyed yesterday on the steps of his house, he realized he would no longer be content to reminisce. The multi-layered feelings Zelda evoked in him were far too strong. His fingers flew across the display as he sent the short message.

Breakfast is on the way. See you soon...

He grinned as he imagined her expression as she read the text. Would she be pleased or angry? It didn't matter. As always, every facet of Zelda's personality fascinated him.

How does she see me? he thought, while he packed up his things. *Does she still sometimes think back to our time together?* He had to admit that in recent years she'd been nothing more than a pleasant memory. Like a faded photograph that you always carried with you and took out from time to time and looked at with a wistful smile. But the reunion had struck him like a bolt of lightning.

Zelda didn't see the text until she got out at her house with Cammie in her arms. Breakfast? Had the idiot misunderstood her message, she thought.

When she arrived at Jaz's, Jaz opened the door and pushed the child and a big bag into her hand with the words, "Here's everything you need." Then the door slammed shut again. Surprised to find themselves so suddenly in close proximity to each other, Zelda and Cammie eyed each other for a few seconds. Finally, Cammie broke out into a broad grin so that Zelda had no choice but to smile back.

Back home, Zelda opened the garden gate and set the little one down. Immediately Cammie wobbled off on her short legs. She headed straight for the garden tools, which lay half-forgotten under the snow. They wouldn't last long outside in the cold. *I wonder if Cammie could hurt herself with the pick and shovel?*

An image played in her head of her temporary charge lunging and ramming the metal tool into her noggin. She squeezed her eyes shut and shook her head to get rid of the unwanted image.

Cammie seemed very pleased with her find. She plopped down on her butt and started working the ground next to her with the shovel.

"Child labor?" a familiar voice murmured.

Her reptile brain, responsible for her escape impulses, knew the voice. Startled, she jumped to the side and turned around. Eye to eye with Cruz, she grabbed at her violently pounding heart. "You scared me! What are you sneaking up on me like that for?"

Cruz smirked. "I don't sneak up on people. I'm just leisurely strolling." He lifted a brown paper bag.

Zelda's mouth watered when she spotted the Sweets logo. Aileen, a young woman who was related to the Diner Sisters seven ways to Sunday, ran a small café in Independence where she sold French pâtisseries as well as excellent coffee and exotic teas.

"You're on foot?" Zelda asked, not taking her eyes off the paper bag. He'd brought it for her, hadn't he?

"Yes. After all, it's not five minutes away from your place."

"How un-American to walk and not drive such a short distance," she muttered as she considered how long she might have to wait to ask for breakfast without looking greedy.

"But an excellent tactic if you want to sneak up on people." He winked.

Zelda's knees softened when she saw his mischievous

expression. The man always managed to elicit the strangest reactions from her body. Just like before. Only better. *I wonder if his kisses have gotten better, too.* Unfortunately, she had no way to compare.

Just kiss him.

Zelda was tempted to wave her hand as if to scare away a fly. Maybe then the cheeky voice would fall silent. Instead, she stared at Cruz's lips.

Cruz slipped the paper bag under his arm.

She looked at him. She bet he mirrored her feelings. Maybe it wasn't a projection after all. He was about to take a step toward her when Cammie came running up laughing and gesturing toward the brown paper sack.

Phew, thought Zelda. *Saved by a barely two-year-old.* Even if she wasn't sure what she had been saved from. From Cruz? Herself?

She unlocked the door and let Cruz enter. "Didn't you get my text?"

Cruz wasn't fazed by her brusque tone. "Sure, I got it. I just thought you two lovely ladies might not have had breakfast yet." He got down on one knee until he was eye level with Cammie and let her take a peek inside the bag.

Delighted, the little girl clapped her hands. Cruz turned his head and peered mischievously up at Zelda. "I've already convinced half the people present. How about you?"

Her heart leapt. How could she resist him when he was so... so wonderful? "Unlike Cammie, I don't know what's in there yet," she said, trying to be aloof. However, her attempt failed rather miserably as she tried to squint into the paper bag at the same time.

"Don't worry," he laughed. "I'm sure something will be found for you, too. Maybe you have a coffee for us?"

She raised an eyebrow in amusement. "If you fill

Cammie's cup with coffee, you'll be responsible for her the rest of the day."

"Understood." He stood and measured her with a long look. "I meant for just you and me."

"Well then, come on in," she invited him. She didn't quite know how she had come to have a surprise guest. Her feelings were so mixed that it was difficult for her to play the cordial hostess.

"I can take the treats back there, too," he said, lifting the bag up, out of reach.

Immediately Cammie howled in protest.

Zelda grinned. "Too late! Come on. In you go."

Later, when Cammie, tired from all the excitement and curled up asleep on the sofa, they sat side by side on the little porch that ran along the south side of the house. Despite the persistent March sun, it was still chilly, so they wrapped themselves in wool blankets.

Zelda blew into her coffee and had her eyes fixed on the distance. Cruz, for his part, watched the woman who'd haunted him. "Have you ever thought about what our lives would have been like if we had both stayed here back then?" he asked.

"I never allowed myself to ask that question," she admitted. "It would have been too painful."

Cruz just sat and waited as she searched for the right words.

"The what-if game is unbearable when one of them is dead. If we'd just split up, at least I could have imagined we'd meet again someday." She grimaced. "Like we are now. But then, I didn't know you were alive."

He put his hand on hers. Surprised, she looked at him and then away. She left her hand where it'd been. Under his.

Zelda turned back to the majestic mountains: silent witnesses to their conversation. No judging.

"But how about now? You know I'm alive." He swallowed.

"I don't think we could have done it. Too much opposition. Me, the good girl, and you, the wild boy from the broken family," she said. "We were very young."

She raised both shoulders and dropped them. "I probably would have gotten pregnant before I finished school, and you would have married me. Within a year, we would have done nothing but fight."

"Pregnant? We would have had to sleep together first for that to happen." He sounded as sullen as if it had been only yesterday that she'd been stalling him.

Zelda laughed. "Come on, aren't you glad we skipped that? Well, not necessarily the sex. I'm sure that would have turned out just as well as all the things we did," she admitted. "But the rest of it."

Reluctantly, Cruz smiled. "You mean the part where I turn into a carbon copy of my dad, and you have two screaming toddlers hanging off your legs while you bring me a beer?"

"Exactly."

"I'll admit when we moved to California, I was still so head over heels, but I didn't have much time to miss you. It was my senior year. I was busy in the midst of a new place, new teachers, new classmates. It wasn't bad. For a while we even had a little money. Plus, it was exciting to see more of the world. That's why I called you." He turned to her. "Every day I said to myself, tomorrow. Tomorrow, I'll call her. Because I knew if I heard your voice, I'd be on the next bus

VIRGINIA FOX

to Colorado. So, I did my best to put calling you off until later."

"How flattering," she replied, her voice shaking. There was no real conviction behind it. If she was honest, she could understand him all too well. She would have felt the same. "What do you mean, would have been?" she asked. "The only difference for me was believing you were dead. The only place I couldn't follow you."

"I know," he said. "And we're going to get to the bottom of that. You and me. Together."

"You've always been the romantic one," she added.

Cruz shrugged. "I guess. But the more important question is what do we do with this opportunity now?"

"Chance?" she repeated, trying to buy time. She knew exactly what he meant. What she didn't know was whether she would dare to answer the question truthfully. She felt her feelings for him, new and old, mingling together and slowly wrapping around her. Much like a climbing rose, she realized with surprise. Beauty and the pain of thorns so close together. One could not be had without the other. Did she really wish she had never known him, never loved him, even if he had died in the end? And now? Now that it turned out that, against all odds, he was alive, did she really want to let fear keep ruling her life? If you wanted to enjoy a rose, you had to take the risk of getting pricked, after all.

Overwhelmed, she impulsively leaned forward and kissed him.

Fourteen years of pent-up feelings flowed out of her and into the kiss.

Cruz hesitated a split second, then put a hand on the back of her neck and pulled her closer.

Zelda felt like she was on a rocket ship to outer space.

CHAPTER TEN

Four hours later, Zelda wandered restlessly around her home. Lost in thought, she bent down and reached for Murphy. Puzzled, he blinked before hissing at her, letting her know loud and clear they were nowhere near the cuddling stage in their relationship. She stood back from the cat.

Cruz's reaction to her reaching out had been quite different, she thought. Her stomach contracted as she reviewed the kiss—or kisses. What would she have done if he'd reacted negatively?

She didn't want to imagine.

Zelda had to catch her breath, unfortunately, when they'd kissed, and had backed away. As if spellbound, she had stared into his eyes. The surprise she discovered in them, and the hunger for more, mirrored her own feelings. This discovery gave her the courage to smile. He smiled back.

Murphy, who'd come up behind them, meowing loudly, had interrupted the intimate moment. Worried, she'd gotten up and gone inside to see if everything was all right with Cammie. The little girl was no longer asleep and had been happily pulling books off the shelf and throwing them onto the floor.

Both her visitors were now gone. Tyler had picked up Cammie and taken her to the former dance studio. Since her friend Pat also did his martial arts training there, they had plenty of mats available. It was a safe place to romp.

Zelda looked out the window. As a responsible business-woman, she was supposed to go to the pharmacy for work. But she didn't feel like it. She was still too shaken up by the new development between her and Cruz to offer customers advice and assistance. Since she had not known how long Cammie would be with her, she had already taped a note to the door that morning informing people of her absence. From that point of view, she could use the unexpected free time elsewhere. Since a trip to Perkins was out of the question—Cruz would never forgive her if she went off without him—she decided to visit Adela instead.

He'd forbidden her to do that, as well, but while she could understand his logic regarding the sheriff's potential danger, it was absolutely ridiculous not being able to see his great-aunt.

Before she could change her mind, she packed a few muffins, stowed her notebook, and slipped into her jacket.

Only when she locked the door behind her did she realize she didn't know where Adela lived. Without an address, she'd never find her.

She threw her bag on the passenger seat, carefully placed the bag of muffins next to it, and got behind the wheel. She wondered who might know Adela's address. There was no way she was going to ask Cruz.

The Diner Sisters. They knew everything. She slid the key into the ignition and drove off.

"You want Adela's address?" asked Miss Minnie.

"Yes. You explained to me I couldn't find a better healer."

"That's right. You've certainly come to the right place," Miss Minnie said.

"I just need directions," she repeated, "Can you help me?"

"Isn't Cruz going?" Miss Minnie asked.

"No," she replied.

"Well, he won't be happy when he hears you went without him."

"As far as I know, Cruz has no intention of visiting her," she replied.

"He'll like it all the less if you go up to her alone."

"I don't remember asking him for permission. Whether Adela sees me is her decision alone," she replied.

Miss Minnie grinned and patted her hand. "That's right. Wait here a minute. I'll get a map. I can draw you the location of Adela's cabin. Will you bring her something?"

"I have muffins in the car."

"Very good. I'll give you something else hearty. She's thin as a bird. I'm always afraid she'll fly off the mountain with the next gust of wind."

"Is she not well?"

Miss Minnie shrugged. "She's just old. As old as the mountains she lives in. I don't know if anything else is bothering her." With a final click of her tongue, she disappeared behind the swinging doors

"I see." Zelda would be extra attentive and see if Adele was missing anything during her visit. Her pharmacy had plenty to offer, in case.

Kurt, Miss Daisy's biker boyfriend, emerged from the

kitchen. He didn't adhere to any dress code but his own. Instead of an obligatory apron, he wore his beaten-up leather vest, scuffed jeans, biker boots, and a red cotton scarf around his neck. "You need directions to Adela," he said, gruffly. Kurt spread a map on the counter. He circled the diner with a pen. "We're here. Take the main road until you pass Scrooge's trailer." He lifted his head. "You know where that is?"

Zelda nodded. Scrooge was the town's resident drunk. There were certainly several others in Independence who had drinking problems. But he was the only one who indulged his bad habit under the sharp gaze of the Diner Sisters. Day after day, he sat in the diner in front of his beer. Occasionally, he'd allow himself a nap in one of the reclining chairs in front of the fireplace. In the summer, Scrooge could be found on the porch, too. The sisters tolerated him because he never caused any trouble and he'd donated part of his fortune to a charity. No one knew his personal story. Or at least nobody talked about it. Which amounted to a miracle.

"She lives that far up?" Zelda said.

"Just above the tree line." A large X marked the end of the road, the location of Adela's cabin.

"Okay," she said. "I can find her."

"Better take a white flag with you, otherwise she's apt to shoot you as soon as you set foot on her land."

"I'll be careful," Zelda said.

Miss Minnie came out of the kitchen carrying a large dish covered with aluminum foil. "Miss Daisy's homemade lasagna. That should last her a while."

Zelda stared in disbelief. How was the old woman supposed to eat so much? She'd have enough for a week.

"Should I bring the casserole dish back?"

Miss Minnie waved. "No, no. I'm going up next week to bring her groceries. I can take it back then."

"Is there any more lasagna?" she asked. "I'm starving."

Miss Minnie shook her head. "Unfortunately, no. That's one of our special rations for cases like hers. The menu today is pulled pork with potato casserole and zucchini."

"Then I already know what I'm having for dinner."

"I'll save you some," Miss Minnie promised with a wink.

"If she ever comes down from that mountain again," Kurt remarked.

"Don't listen to that old sourpuss. It'll be fine."

Zelda swallowed. She hoped so, too. What an irony if she would meet her own untimely end on her quest for medicinal plants, of all things.

She lifted the still-warm casserole dish into the air. "Let's hope the bribe serves its purpose."

Before she could put her life in danger, she had to find it first, Zelda thought, annoyed. She had just turned her car around for the third time on a narrow, practically non-existent mountain road. Every time she managed to turn the nose of her car one hundred and eighty degrees without crashing into the abyss, she'd been glad. When Kurt had told her the way, everything seemed quite clear. But looking for the right unmarked turnoff was impossible! There were so many, it seemed. No choice but to try one after the other.

"Signs," she said. "A sign would be very helpful." Adela had probably dismantled all the signs and made them disappear into the nearest crevice. Zelda questioned the wisdom of her undertaking. One of the thick tomes she'd ordered surely was capable of answering her questions. First-hand knowledge was completely overrated.

Again, she passed a narrow spot. Involuntarily, she squeezed her eyes shut after seeing the drop-off. Abruptly she opened them, realizing what a horrible idea it was to drive blind.

With only a few inches separating her from the next ravine, it was probably not wise to close one's eyes, no matter what her guts had to say. Determined, she clutched the steering wheel tighter. Her hands were wet with sweat. Her knuckles went white. She gritted her teeth and drove at a snail's pace.

At last, the road bent away from the abyss and led deeper toward the trees, sparser at such an altitude. Bravely, her reliable car climbed the last few hundred feet, struggling through the snow. The land opened up and flattened out.

Zelda spotted an old, weathered cabin perched on the highest point. A large rock nestled against its rear. It was probably one of the few things on earth older than the rickety building. The wind blew across the sparse landscape, brownish grass tweeds poking up out of the snow.

She preferred not to know the temperature. It was cold as hell in Independence. Up there, completely exposed to the elements without the protection of the mountain's flanks, it was certainly much worse. She peered through the windshield at the sky. At least the sun was holding up.

"Stop wasting time," she scolded. Her voice sounded unexpectedly muffled. Her ears were having trouble equalizing pressure. She parked the car and turned it off. Gathering all her courage, she pushed open the car door and put one foot on the ground.

A shot rang out. Gravel splattered near her where the bullets hit.

Zelda was so startled that she pulled back her foot with a horrified squeal and threw herself across the center console onto the passenger seat. She remained there for several breaths. Nothing happened. Not a sound. At least she knew Kurt and the others who'd warned her about Adela weren't kidding.

Finally, she couldn't stand the tension any longer and carefully pushed herself up from the upholstery so she could peek over the dashboard. There was no one in sight. Only the cabin, which made the same sad impression as before. Wait. Something had changed.

Smoke was rising from the crooked chimney, driven in all directions by the gusts of wind. She frowned. Had the crazy woman actually shot at her, only to calmly disappear back into her cabin and start a fire?

For some reason, this annoyed her immensely. If someone was going to shoot at her, then she at least wanted to have more than just a few brief seconds of their time. Determined not to leave until the woman at least acknowledged her presence with words, she jammed the bag of muffins under her arm and reached for the casserole dish in the back seat. Thank goodness she hadn't transported them in the passenger seat, she thought. Otherwise, she would have ended up upside down in lasagna. In that sense, she had been lucky.

She took a deep breath, death-defyingly pushed open the car door and wriggled out of the car. Presumably the muffins suffered quite a bit from the rough treatment, but she didn't care. Being on the wrong side of a gun changed her priorities. *Very refreshing, actually.* Even if common sense didn't seem to have much say. Probably wasn't particularly wise to jump into the lion's den. But she was tired of reacting in her life and not being proactive. If she was going to die, at least she should die standing up, not lying down in the car.

By the time she arrived at the cabin, most of her anger had dissipated. *What was she doing here, anyway?* she wondered, setting the casserole dish down on the slanted bench standing against the wall of the house. Her hand free, she raised her arm to knock.

Before she came into contact with the wood, the door swung inward, almost causing her to fall headfirst into the house. Zelda tried to regain her balance and held on to the door frame.

Watchful black eyes flashed shrewdly behind glasses and sized her up. The loopy white hair, streaked with a few gray strands, was braided into a long pigtail that hung over her right shoulder. Wrinkled skin stretched over high cheekbones.

She must have looked stunning in her youth, Zelda thought.

Finally, the woman lost patience. "Zelda!"

Flustered by the fact that Adela knew her name, Zelda took a step back, startled.

Adela rolled her eyes theatrically. "No, I'm not psychic. I've known your name for years. Besides, Miss Minnie mentioned the last time she saw you that you'd probably stop by sometime."

Great. Miss Minnie could have told her that, too, Zelda thought miffed. "Then why the welcome in the form of buck-shot?" she blurted out. Even on good days, she found it difficult to keep her temper in check.

"I had to see if you had any backbone," she replied. "I don't have patience for cowards." Adela turned and disappeared into the dark interior of the cabin. With an impatient wave of her hand, she motioned for Zelda to follow.

Backbone? Was the woman not all there? She ducked her head. Stupid question. Everyone had warned her. To act astonished now was rather disingenuous.

"Are you coming? I have no intention of heating up the whole Rockies."

Zelda noticed the biting cold, cutting through her thick jacket and right into her bones. She grabbed the casserole dish and rushed into the lion's den. Uh, the lioness's. She had the feeling Adela would insist.

CHAPTER ELEVEN

The small room was not very high. Zelda who, at only 5'-2", was by no means tall, had to duck her head to avoid bumping into the countless bundles of dried herbs. The scent of sage mingled with the smoke and fire. Above the cooking area, she spotted an ancient blackened cauldron as her eyes adjusted to the dim light.

"Come, come. What are you waiting for?" Shaking her head, Adela pushed aside a few old newspapers, a dangerous-looking knife, and an old, small chest.

Zelda placed the lasagna on the vacated table space and set the bag of battered muffins next to it.

A black cat jumped elegantly from the windowsill and stroked the old woman's legs. Amazingly agile for her age, Adela bent down and stroked her fur.

Zelda leaned back and crossed her arms.

"Not a big cat person?" Adela asked.

"It's more that cats are not great friends of mine. I've found it's better if I keep my distance."

"Don't you have a cat?"

Had Miss Minnie brought her a complete resume? "I

don't own a cat. A male cat lives with me temporarily. But it's solely his decision how long he stays. So far, he seems to like it. At least, as long as I don't get any absurd ideas like petting him."

Adela grinned. "You don't own cats. They only honor you with their presence." She looked down at the black cat. "And how is my nephew?"

"Cruz?"

"How many of my nephews live in Independence?"

"How should I know," Zelda said. "Since I don't spend my time exclusively following the latest gossip, it's quite possible you have a complete family branch somewhere I'm not aware of. Aside from the fact that calling yourself a great-aunt is probably the understatement of the year."

Adela narrowed her eyes. "Did you just call me old?"

"Well, you are!" she said.

Adela studied her for another moment. Then she put her head back and laughed. "Well, at least we can agree on that."

Zelda squinted, worried. Perhaps she was suffering from hypoglycemia. "Want a piece of lasagna?" she asked, pushing the dish across the table.

Adela waved it off and wiped the corners of her mouth with her apron. "Later. Right now, have some tea and then I'll show you the plants."

Zelda nodded. Hopefully the tea was drinkable. She knew she'd have no choice but to drink it.

Adela plucked several leaves from one of the bundles above her head, dropped them into a cup, and used a ladle to pour boiling water from the pot into the cup. "Don't worry, there are no toad eyes in the kettle." She placed the cup of tea in front of Zelda. "Just spring water." She leaned forward. "And spider legs."

Zelda managed to stop herself from grimacing. "I'd

expect nothing less." She grinned and reached for the cup, inhaling the aroma. She needn't have worried. Wild mint and a second, very spicy smell hit her nose. She took a sip. Pleasantly surprised, she closed her eyes. "This is really good tea. Thank you."

Satisfied, Adela prepared a cup for herself.

Zelda noticed Adela added a third herb to hers, which she took from a special paper bag. "What's that?"

"It's why you came." She set the cup on the table and held out the bag. "This is sea dew. It has a strong stimulant effect and should be used with caution."

"It's being brought through the Medicines Act. At least, efforts in that direction were underway when I was a student."

Adela waved her off. "It helps me keep up with young whippersnappers like you. Plus, it eases my breathing problems."

"Eat something first." Zelda slid the lasagna closer.

"Later, I told you. I'm not hungry."

"Sea dew is known for its appetite-suppressing effect. Is that why you're taking it? You're very thin. If you get sick, you have no reserves."

"Don't look at me like that," snapped Adela. "One of the advantages of getting old is that no one can tell you what to do anymore. I'm certainly not going to spend my last days forcing myself to do anything."

"I understand," Zelda said. "It's just worrisome."

"I've survived much worse," Adela said. "You've avoiding talking about my nephew."

"Cruz is fine," she murmured.

"And you know that because..." Adela's eyes flashed.

Zelda blushed.

"Ah," Adela said. "You two are an item."

The old witch couldn't possibly know. Or could she?

"It's complicated."

"Isn't it always. But it's simple, too. But if he's in your graces, that's enough of an answer for me." With difficulty, she rose from her chair. With trembling hands, she reached up and pulled bundle after bundle from the rope stretched criss-cross under the ceiling.

The cat, silent as a ghost, crept up and watched.

Adela arranged the various plants into categories, asking Zelda to smell the leaves, study the flowers, and sort out unusable parts.

Soon they developed a rhythm and worked hand in hand.

"I was a fool," Adela interrupted.

Zelda looked up from the yarrow. "A fool? What do you mean?"

Adela's expression gave nothing away.

"I thought I could control my little world. My sister's son was worthless. Only booze in his head. No will to persevere." She looked away, into the distance, as if she were somewhere in the past. "I took no account of what effect my selfish actions would have."

Zelda frowned.

"You were too much of a distraction for that boy. Hard to believe a single question from me would have such an effect." She shook her head, as if she couldn't believe it, even though it'd been fourteen years.

"What question?" asked Zelda.

"If you were pregnant. After all, you were inconsolable after Cruz left."

"Left?" Zelda stared at the old woman. "You declared him dead. Of course I was inconsolable." She swallowed and tried to regain her composure. "I can't believe..."

She stared at the woman responsible for the trauma that'd defined the years of her life.

Adela pointed to the unsorted herbs. "Go on, then. The herbs aren't going to sort themselves."

Zelda resumed her work. "And that's it? That's all we're going to say about it?"

"As I said, I was a fool."

"And that makes up for everything?" asked Zelda.

"Of course not," Adela replied. "I don't need forgiveness. Not from you or anyone else. I just thought you deserved the truth."

Zelda felt dizzy. Maybe it was the smoke and the intense scent of the herbs. She pushed back the chair and jumped up. "I need some fresh air."

Zelda welcomed the cold wind on her face.

Perhaps things would be clear if she stood outside long enough, looking over the high plateau. The snow-capped mountains stood like great sentinels at the edge. A little ways away from the cabin lay the small, crystal-clear lake. The sun was low on the horizon, casting a play of light and shadow on the motionless surface of the water. Soon it would be dark. Despite the magnificent panorama, she couldn't stop thinking about Adela's revelations. For the first time, everything made sense. She understood the motivation. Family loyalty.

Without looking up, she noticed Adela stepping next to her. The old woman cleared her throat. "I'm sorry. Really."

"Thank you. I understand. Just tell me one thing..."

"Yes?"

"Did you kill the tramp?"

Adela shook her head. "That was a happy coincidence. Nothing more. I'm a healer. Not an assassin."

Zelda didn't know what to think. What a mess. "That's good to know. I wish I didn't have to go."

Adela nodded. "I understand. Will you come back?"

"Maybe," she answered. Until the confession, she'd enjoyed being with her very much.

Adela nodded. "I hope you do."

For a moment, Zelda believed Adela understood her. Deeply.

At the diner, the Diner Sisters greeted Zelda like a lost daughter. "You made it back without a bullet in your butt," Miss Minnie noted.

"It was close," she half-joked.

"Believe me, if Adela had not wanted you there, you would have known. That's just her idea of fun," Miss Daisy said.

"Ha ha," Zelda replied.

"You're now part of Adela's inner circle. That's a great honor," the other sister said.

"Can I get something to eat?" asked Zelda.

"Sure thing." Miss Daisy hurried toward the kitchen.

Miss Minnie wanted to follow, but Zelda, on impulse, held her by the sleeve.

"Tell me, is it true that Adela started the rumors about me back then?"

Miss Minnie squirmed. "I can't remember exactly."

"Adela told me."

"Then it must be true," Miss Minnie replied. "Does it matter? You know how it is. Someone asks an innocuous question and a few seconds later it's considered fact."

"I know," sighed Zelda. Another piece of the puzzle. She didn't know if she felt better or not.

Fortunately, Miss Daisy came right after with the food.

"Wow. That looks good."

"You look like you could use it. You're a little pale."

Zelda bowed her head and got to work.

When she was close to done, she heard a voice. "Hey!"

Surprised, she looked up. "Cruz?"

What the hell was he doing at the diner? How was she supposed to talk to him with an open mind when his great-aunt had just rocked her world? Was she supposed to tell him? She didn't want to drive a wedge between them.

"What's wrong?"

"What do you mean?"

"You tell me. You look like you've seen a ghost. And I don't mean me," he said and sat across from her. "What did you do this afternoon?"

Miss Minnie stepped up to the table and caught his question. "Well, she was with Adela, of course. Didn't you know?"

Cruz frowned. "Didn't I tell you to stay away from her?"

Zelda nodded. "You were right about that."

"Oh yeah? What happened?"

"She was kind," she said. "And honest. Maybe too honest."

"Is that why you look like someone ran over your cat?"

"I don't want to talk about it, okay? But if you'd like to eat here with me and have a little conversation about something else, I'd be happy to."

"Sure," he said. "I'd like nothing more."

CHAPTER TWELVE

The following days passed as if in a fog. Zelda worked, served customers, finally kicked out her unreliable employee and replaced her with Astrid Stone, a pharmacy student in her final semester. She didn't have as much time as the former employee, but she worked reliably when she was there and came with the highest recommendation from Brenda Carter.

She spent the evenings with Murphy on the sofa in front of the television. He seemed to become more accustomed to her presence, and it was comforting to know he was waiting for her at home each day.

When she first arrived in Independence, she'd avoided any contact with the outside world. She served her customers in the pharmacy but blocked personal questions.

Now Adela's confession had thrown her off. She couldn't get past knowing someone had deliberately orchestrated such events in her life, and that led to many other unanswered questions. She had to find answers, and to do that, she would have to expand her contact with people.

She felt unable to move forward. Jaz's approach of "living in the now" sounded good in theory, but she didn't know how to put it into practice. Something was going to have to change.

After several days of her mind spinning in circles, Zelda realized she needed to get off her butt and do something if she was serious about finding answers. The following day was Saturday. She'd drive out to Perkins and talk directly with him. She texted Cruz:

> Do you have time for a quick trip to the former sheriff tomorrow?

Murphy sat up next to her and yawned.

"You again. You always manage to put things in perspective." She stroked his forehead.

Murphy tended to hold still and would purr accidentally if she didn't pet him with her whole hand. And he'd linger nearby at feeding times. She eyed him. He was exceptionally clever.

She gave him a stern look.

"You almost got away with it," she said. "But believe me, in the future I'll have a better grip on myself."

Murphy blinked, unimpressed.

Great. Not even her cat took her seriously.

Her phone beeped. A message from Cruz.

> Pick you up at nine.

"Yes!" Zelda hopped up off the sofa. "He's coming with us. Did you hear that?"

The cat paused his ritual, laid his ears flat, and hissed.

"Okay, okay. It's not exactly a love letter, but after the cold shoulder I gave him this week, this is great."

Murphy leapt to the floor and disappeared toward the basement stairs where he had his personal cat flap.

Zelda looked after him in dismay. His behavior was so clear it was hard not to take personally. She sighed. He was right, after all. If anyone heard her talking to the cat, they'd probably have her committed.

Her thoughts galloped like a herd of frightened antelopes. How was she supposed to get through the hours until nine tomorrow morning without going crazy?

"Breathe," Jaz's words came. A sensible piece of advice.

Cruz leaned against the wall in the diner, letting the phone move from hand to hand. No response to his answer. In theory, he could have let Zelda wait. After he'd been so pleased that she hadn't pushed him away again, she'd done just that. Of course, he could have just walked by the pharmacy. But he had his pride. He suppressed a laugh. A pride that vanished into thin air as soon as Zelda so much as made a peep. Pathetic. Still, he couldn't stop a smile.

"Good news?" asked Ace, with whom he was playing a game of pool.

"In some ways," he dodged the question, pretending he had to concentrate on his pool cue.

Ace, of course, saw through him. "That was Zelda, admit it."

"That was Zelda," he confirmed, taking aim at the eight ball.

"Hot date?"

His cue promptly slipped on the white ball. "Not a hot date, I'm afraid."

"You're welcome," Ace said, ending the game by sinking the last ball. He straightened up and held out his hand. "That'll be five dollars."

"Two out of three?" asked Cruz.

"Sorry. No time. Paige and the dogs are waiting. I worked the night shift last week. We have some catching up to do. Dog walks. And other stuff." He winked.

"Lucky you," Cruz muttered.

"You said it," Ace replied, giving him a friendly pat on the back. "Maybe you'll get a dog, too?" he suggested.

"At most, that will lead to Zelda's cat putting me on his hit list. At the moment, at least he's happy when I show up. Not so sure about Zelda."

"Then you have no choice but to apply at the fire department. With enough training, we can make a good firefighter out of even a desk jockey like you. Women go for it."

Cruz didn't respond to the friendly taunt. After working out three times a week with the guys from the fire department at Pat's gym, it was clear that Cruz was exceptionally fit. "I wonder if Paige would agree with you on that."

Ace grinned. "I don't know what tipped the scales. Maybe it was my charm."

They laughed and said their goodbyes. Cruz watched his friend leave the diner; he felt a pang of envy. He was happy for Ace that he'd found happiness with Paige. He just wished he had someone waiting for him when he got home, too. Preferably Zelda.

For what felt like the fiftieth time, Zelda looked at her watch. Crap. It was thirteen minutes until nine o'clock. Unlike the fifteen minutes when she had last looked at her phone.

After a sleepless night, her nerves were stretched. Not exactly the best conditions for a calm and reasonable conversation. When she finally staggered out of bed at half past five, a strange face with bloodshot eyes had looked back at her in the mirror. With the help of eye drops and makeup, she removed the worst traces and felt at least halfway human.

It hadn't just been the worry about the conversation. If she was honest, she didn't know how to act toward Cruz. She found it easier to be angry with him. Probably because then she didn't have to face her own confused feelings. She was aware she sent mixed signals during their last two meetings.

It'd be exciting to see how Cruz met her. If he showed up. She bit her lower lip and risked another peak at her phone's display. Ten minutes left. With an impatient grunt, she flopped down on the sofa, earning a dirty look from Murphy. The cat was unhappy with her, as always. Annoyed by her restless pacing, he'd moved into the living room after trying in vain to sleep next to her.

"Don't worry. Your special friend will be here soon." She wrinkled her nose. "He may not like me right now. But I'm pretty sure that doesn't extend to you."

Murphy ignored her.

Just as well, she decided. The less interaction with men, the better.

Cruz was thinking similar thoughts as he drove to Zelda's house. How would she receive him? And perhaps more importantly, how would he react to her? He frowned. He hadn't quite forgiven her for last week's radio silence. He didn't want to spoil his free Saturday morning by being in a bad mood. He had taken the time to go to *Sweets* to get coffee and some freshly baked croissants. Since he could hardly show up with just his coffee, he'd brought one for Zelda, as well.

At least they finally had better weather. The wind had shifted and brought warm air to the plateau. The Chinook did its best to drive away the freshly fallen snow of the last weeks. The first leaves were sprouting, bathing the area in a cheerful bright green. If they were lucky, that was it for the snow. At least until the end of September. Even though he had grown up in Independence, he had to admit he still struggled with the long, harsh winters. The milder temperatures of California were much easier to endure.

He turned into Zelda's short driveway. Before he had turned off the engine, Zelda opened the door and stepped out with a hesitant smile.

Suddenly it was clear how the morning would go. It made no sense at all to hold on to his grudge. Whatever had prompted Zelda to hide the last few days seemed gone. It likely had nothing to do with him.

Zelda was obviously happy seeing him. As he walked toward her, he returned her smile. Her cheeks gently reddened.

"Ready for our joint investigation?"

She couldn't manage more than a nod. Seeing her again so suddenly, practically at the same place where they had kissed the last time, was a challenge. "Then let's go. Coffee and provisions are waiting in the car." With an inviting motion of his head, he turned back toward the vehicle.

"Uh, how? Just like that? Right now?"

Amused, he turned back to her. "Did you have something

else in mind?" he inquired, stretching. His gaze traveled downward until it rested on her lips.

Zelda's ears turned red. She squinted her eyes. "That's not what I was thinking…"

Cruz raised an eyebrow.

"At least not *only*."

He stepped toward her.

Her eyes got bigger the closer he got, and she didn't back away. He liked that. She didn't let her nervousness get the better of her. Clearly, her curiosity was greater. Or were her memories of the last kiss as good as his, so she wasn't averse to a repeat?

Cruz understood the latter well. He couldn't get the feeling of her lips on his, the taste of her mouth and her way of kissing out of his mind. Just as good as fourteen years back, if not better. Definitely better, he corrected himself. A morning in bed was also a much better idea than a visit to the former sheriff. And that was definitely where they would end up if the second round went like the first. Besides, there was no Cammie to throw a wrench in their plans.

Visions of Zelda naked on her bed, her dark hair spread out on the pillow...

He lowered his head and whispered, "Did you want to find out first if that last kiss was just a one-time miracle? Or if the spell will last?"

His hot breath brushed over her lips.

Zelda's whole body tingled in a very pleasant way. Involuntarily, she leaned toward him. But then she remembered her plans and Cruz's resistance. Was it just an elaborate strategy to distract her? Quite possibly, she admitted. Doubt had the same effect as a bucket of cold water. Sobered, she straightened up and pushed him aside.

Surprised, Cruz took a step away from her and frowned. "Did I just misunderstand something?"

Careful to be out of his reach—not because she didn't trust him, but because she didn't trust herself; even *her* willpower was not infinite—she winked. "No. Definitely not. I just decided we'd start that up at a different time. Work first, pleasure second." With an apologetic shrug, she opened the passenger door and got in.

Cruz looked at his feet, where Murphy was currently stroking his legs, purring loudly. "Are women always this complicated?"

"Worse," she said with a laugh.

At the sound of his voice, the cat looked up. Cruz swore he was winking. He adjusted his jeans and followed Zelda to the car. The sooner they got the useless visit over with, the sooner they could get back to kissing.

CHAPTER THIRTEEN

Perkins sat hunched over the treasure map. His brow was furrowed in deep creases. The drawing was not clear. Unfortunately. Then again, it made little sense to hide something and then draw a map. He hadn't thought it'd be so damn hard. As he had done countless times before, his finger followed the faded lines of the mountains and valleys.

Suddenly angry, he banged his fist on the table. The wobbly wooden thing swayed. Coffee spilled over the edge of his cup. At the last moment he saved the precious parchment from the black broth. Sweat stood on his forehead as he checked the map.

He cursed like a sailor. He'd almost wasted his last chance. Before he set about cleaning up the mess, he slipped the document into a clear plastic sleeve. Only then did he get up to fetch a rag.

That old witch was to blame. He was certain she'd tricked him. Either part of the map was missing, or she'd planted a fake. Perkins scrubbed the weathered wood harder. Either way, she would pay. First, he'd make one last attempt to find the treasure. Now that the warm chinook had returned, the snow would melt, clearing the way to the inaccessible area where he suspected it was hidden.

Perkins imagined the vast amounts of gold the French soldiers had left behind as they fled the Indians. More than enough to build his own small army. The area on the map was not called Treasure Mountain for nothing. He wasn't the first to search for the gold; many before him had failed. But he had the map. That's why he'd succeed where the others had been thwarted. If he had to take on Adela again, he would do it.

Alarmed by sudden bird cries, he raised his head. Something must have startled them. Something was usually synonymous with an unwanted visitor. Alert, he listened. Indeed. A car. Surely his useless son again. He pulled himself up. The boy had no idea what life was about. The warning he gave him last week turned out to be unfounded. He'd expected nothing less. But when junior set his mind on something, there was no talking him out of it. Was it any wonder he wanted as little to do with him as possible? When he finally established his own little empire, he'd make sure Walt stayed away from him. It would not make a good impression if it was known what a wimp his son was.

He wiped his hands on the damp rag and went outside.

"What are you doing here?" he asked as Walt stepped out of the vehicle.

"Can't I even visit my father?" asked Walt, crossing his arms in front of his chest.

Thomas raised his narrow, sinewy shoulders. "What for? We have nothing to talk about."

Walt winced. "Did you have a visitor?" he asked.

"Not that it's any of your business." Thomas bent down and began gathering up wood that was lying around. If he was going to be forced to talk to Walt, he might as well make himself useful while he did it. "But no one was here. So, you can go back home with peace of mind."

"Are you sure?" Walt asked.

"Of course I'm sure," Perkins said. "I'm old, not senile. Now go on. I've got work to do."

"Sure," Walt said. "Your sweetheart mother lode's waiting for you just as it has been for the last fourteen years. Yet you'll never find it." He ran his jacket sleeve over his sweaty temples. "Mom knew what she was doing when she ran away."

Unconsciously, Perkin's fingers curled around one of the freshly split logs. As the sharp edge dug painfully into his palm, he raised it into the air. "Get out of here before you get hurt."

Walt stumbled back and fled to the car. Only then did he dare to say something again. "Just you wait and see. I'm right." He spat on the ground next to the vehicle and got in.

Shaking his head, Perkins looked after him. He was going to come to a bad end one day. That's what his gut told him. He shrugged. Oh well. There was nothing he could do about it. Maybe it was better that way.

It did not occur to him that the bad end could also drag him down, too. That didn't come for another hour.

"Shit," it slipped out of Cruz's mouth as another vehicle came toward him on the narrow mountain road. At the last moment, he steered the car toward the edge of the forest. Without slowing, the other driver roared past.

Zelda contorted her head and looked in the direction of the rising dust cloud. "Is he nuts?"

"Looks like it." Cruz clutched the steering wheel. "That

was a damn close call. I thought Perkins was a loner who never had visitors?"

"I heard that, too."

"Whoever it was seems to have a death wish. If we hadn't swerved at the last moment, we'd both be in the ravine right now."

"Thank you."

"For what?"

"For saving us."

Her praise felt good. Still, he felt obliged to say, "That was pure luck."

Zelda shrugged. "Doesn't really matter, does it? Everyone needs a little luck," she said. "Thank you for not making this trip unnecessarily difficult."

Surprised, he looked at her. "What do you mean?"

"You have questions about my visit with Adela. You'll get answers too, I promise. Besides, it wasn't very nice of me never to return your calls last week. I'm sorry."

"Why didn't you?"

"After talking to Adela, reality caught up. The fact that you're alive, my mourning period, was all for nothing," she said. "The attraction between us. The kisses. It was just too much. The thought of having to put it into words overwhelmed me."

"Understood. I was pretty pissed you could push me away so easily. Like our last encounter meant nothing."

"Believe me, it did."

Cruz reached across the center console and stroked the back of her hand with his thumb. "Then I'm glad."

She smiled tentatively. "Same here."

"Shall we continue?"

Zelda nodded.

A few turns later, the other car braked. *That's them,* Walt thought. He realized what that meant. After all, he knew his father well enough to believe he'd been involved in something illegal. He broke out in a sweat. It wasn't the police. Two private citizens couldn't do much, could they? Not right away. But if they could get the sheriff to listen to them...

Walt couldn't care less what happened to his father. He could burn in hell for all he cared. But not until he had gained his father's respect. So, he'd take care of them. Immediately. He drove a little farther to the spot he had in mind. From there, it would be child's play to make it look like an accident.

He just had to wait.

"What is it now?" Perkins hollered at the crows. Another visitor? Since when was his cabin such a popular destination?

Had Walt come back? Strange. He would have thought the boy had taken enough for the next few days. But, well, there was more where that came from. If he wanted to get more unpleasant truths from his father, he wouldn't stop him. Maybe it'd finally give him some backbone. On the other hand, it was a damn nuisance. He had better things to do than to keep having such discussions.

The engine noise came closer. Irritated, he tilted his head. He recognized it as a diesel engine. Not his son's car. Who could it be? Whoever it was, he'd make sure they disappeared quickly.

On his way out, he grabbed his shotgun.

When the car finally arrived, he recognized the occupants.

It was Zelda. And Cruz. Damn! Walt'd had a hunch. He wasn't worried. Just curious. The two of them couldn't hurt him, no matter what his son might think. The only witness who could harm him was Adela. And she had her own reasons for keeping her mouth shut.

Surprised and a little impressed, he watched the car back up and turn around. They parked and got out. That exactly how he would have done it. Only way for a quick exit, should the situation require it.

Waiting, the shotgun leaning inconspicuously behind, he raised his chin.

"Mr. Perkins?"

It was Zelda Chastain. The name was burned into his brain. Who would have thought she would grow up to be such a hottie? Admiringly, he let his gaze glide over her curves.

Cruz stepped up behind her. If he couldn't keep his girlfriend in check, he was worth nothing, Perkins thought. No wonder. Even back in the day, the guy had been nothing but trouble. Not only him, but his father, too. He hadn't been sad when the family had turned their backs on Independence. Zelda's family leaving, too, though, wasn't part of the plan.

"Did you just have a visitor?" asked Cruz. He watched the old man attentively, spotting the rifle.

"What's it to you?"

"Nothing. But it would be good if you could advise your visitor to drive down the hill at a reasonable pace. We were almost run off the road."

"Some people can drive," Perkins replied. "Others can't." Secretly, he applauded his son. Seemed like the good-for-nothing had done something right for once. It was a pity he hadn't sent her into the ravine in the process.

Zelda put on her best smile and took a step forward. "Mr. Perkins," she said, extending her hand to him.

Only hesitantly did he grasp it, as if the gesture had become foreign to him.

"I'm Zelda Chastain. This," she gestured to Cruz, "is Cruz Ruis."

Perkins ignored the gesture and spat into the sparse grass that grew next to the cabin. He had his arms folded defensively in front of his chest. "And what are you doing here?"

Zelda glanced at Cruz, looking for help. Cruz shrugged his shoulders. "We have a few questions." She pointed to the cabin. "Do you want to maybe go inside?"

"Spit out what you have to say. And then get out." He raised his head defiantly. "I don't like visitors. Especially not visitors with questions."

"I can imagine," Cruz muttered.

"Fourteen years ago, Cruz was declared dead," she said. Zelda waited for Perkin's reaction, but none came. "Do you have anything to say about that?"

"What can I say? Obviously, he's cheated death. Congratulations. Now leave."

"Not so fast," Cruz said. "There's a problem with the paperwork."

Perkins grunted. "Who cares about formalities? You're alive. That should be enough for a guy like you."

"Someone died. Even if it wasn't Cruz, we still owe it to the dead person to find out the truth. When I think that there's someone out there, a mother, a brother, a friend, grieving just as I did for the past fourteen years." Zelda took a deep breath. "It breaks my heart."

Perkins let out a harsh laugh. "Don't worry. Nobody's mourning that bum."

Zelda's eyes narrowed. "So, you admit you knew it wasn't Cruz?"

"I admit nothing," barked Perkins. With a lightning-quick

movement, he reached behind him and brought the shotgun into position.

Startled, they both took a step back and stared into the muzzle.

"Now get the hell out of here." He waved the barrel of the rifle toward the car. "What word didn't you understand? Do I need to be clearer?"

"We're going," Cruz said. "Come on." He pulled Zelda along.

She followed without turning around. "I'll arrange for an investigation!"

Perkins took a step forward. "No one will believe you."

"Then you have nothing to worry about," Zelda replied.

Perkins saw red and pulled the trigger.

Zelda ducked.

Part of the buckshot scattered into her leg.

Cruz pulled Zelda away. "Ouch!" she said.

"Sorry," he muttered. "We have to get out of here."

Limping, Zelda followed him and he opened her door. He helped her inside and ran to the driver's side and got in. "Put your seat belt on!" He started the engine. Gravel splattered up beside the car.

Zelda tried to keep her nausea at bay. After the first turn, she felt her pant leg become wet. She squinted down into the footwell. The spot was dark. She felt a dull throbbing in her calf, which developed into a serious pain. Carefully, she reached down and pulled up her pant leg. Bravely, she blinked as she discovered the bleeding wound. Fortunately, she wasn't a whiner and could stand the sight of blood just fine although the wound burned like hell.

"Is that actually a popular sport around here?" she groaned between clenched teeth.

Cruz risked a quick glance before refocusing on the breakneck descent. "What?"

"Running off people with shotguns."

"Should we stop?" he asked.

Zelda shook her head. "No. It's probably just a graze."

At least she hoped there was no buckshot in her leg. Otherwise, she was in for a visit to the hospital. She was very skilled with a scalpel and tweezers, but unfortunately her name wasn't Rambo. Picking metal pellets out of her leg was beyond her skills.

"I knew this visit would be a stupid..."

"Not a word!"

"But..."

"You think I'm going to sit next to you while I bleed on your floor mats and listen to you tell me you were right?"

He didn't reply. He knew better than to argue, she bet. Zelda looked in the rearview mirror. "Cruz? There's someone behind us."

"I think it's our friend from earlier. I'm sure he's up to no good if he's been waiting."

"You don't think it's just a coincidence?"

Cruz tried keeping the car on the narrow path.

"No one else lives here for miles except Perkins. Perkins' visitor decided to wait us out. Hang on."

She gripped the handle tighter, pushed her healthy leg against the floor, and braced for the worst.

CHAPTER FOURTEEN

Walt's hunting instinct kicked in. Who would have thought that it would be so much fun to have a race on the mountain road? Actually, racing was the wrong expression. It was more of a cat-and-mouse game. The other driver was not an equal opponent. For one thing, he knew every curve and evasive action by heart. The other driver didn't. They had the bigger vehicle and wouldn't possibly keep up with the maneuverability of his Subaru. His car navigated the hill like a cat.

Farther down, he spied the spot he'd chosen for his purposes. Time to find out what they were made of.

He stepped on the gas pedal. The Subaru hit the left rear fender of the off-road vehicle.

As expected, the driver swerved right, toward the abyss.

Would he lose control of the vehicle right away?

That would be a shame, Walt thought. He was just starting to enjoy the game.

The impact surged through Zelda's spine. She cried out in fright. The abyss came closer and closer. Crashing seemed inevitable. She squeezed her eyes shut. She was not brave enough to face her own death.

At the last moment, Cruz managed to wrench the steering wheel and get the car back on track. His hands were drenched in sweat. She glanced in the rearview mirror, seeing the other driver had fallen behind. Good news.

"Looks like he was just trying to scare us."

"You sure?"

To the right was a steep drop. To the left, the trees were close together.

The other car sped and hit them again.

And again.

"He's trying to force us off the road!"

"We have to get out of here!"

Cruz gunned the gas.

The wheels spun on the gravel. They got a grip on the ground, and the car shot forward.

Zelda felt like she was on a roller coaster. Trees and rocks rushed past as the abyss loomed menacingly like a yawning black hole.

She spotted the gap in the trees on the side of the road.

"There," she called, pointing ahead. "Can we pull over?"

"All right. Get ready!"

Cruz headed for the narrow spot. He accelerated, keeping an eye on the distance.

Tree branches clinging to the rocks, scraped across the right fender. The wheels kicked up dirt and their pursuer was enveloped in a thick cloud of dust.

Good thing. Maybe that helped.

He reached for the handbrake when the left front tire went

into a deep gully. Instead of landing safely among the trees, the wheels locked and skidded on the unpaved surface.

Walt watched the car in front of him speed up even more. Did the idiots really think they could get away?

As the SUV swayed, he smiled and stepped on the gas. He had a chance.

If he caught it sideways while it was skidding...

Zelda screamed as her pursuer crashed into the side. The impact shook her. A jolt ran through the vehicle. Helplessly, she watched as they came closer to the dangerous precipice.

The other car pulled back, and she wondered where it went. Was he taking another run-up?

With relief, she saw him speed past them and head toward the valley.

Zelda realized it could only mean he'd achieved his goal.

As if in confirmation, the right tire of the car slid over the edge of the cliff. Only a puny tree kept them from falling into the depths.

She preferred not to rely on it supporting them. "Get out!" she yelled, fumbling with her seatbelt. "He could come back. Hurry!"

Her seat belt came off. She leaned over and grabbed Cruz's arm. They had to get out of here. Why wasn't he saying anything? Determined, she shook him.

Dazed, Cruz turned his head.

"Get out!" she urged him.

"What?"

Had he hit his head? She reached over and undid his seat belt and pushed open the driver's door. She had to lie prone over his legs to do so, but she managed.

"I like you on my lap," Cruz remarked.

"Not the time," she scolded. "Typical man. Now get out before I leave you here." She pushed his shoulder.

"Hey!" he protested.

The car groaned. With a jerk, it slid a few inches and tilted precariously.

If they didn't get out in the next few seconds, it'd too late. She grabbed a water bottle and unceremoniously emptied its contents into his face. "Snap out of it!"

He shook his head and crawled out of the vehicle. She grabbed her purse and hurried out behind him, clambering over the driver's seat and center console.

Zelda hit the ground hard. Only her head, which landed on Cruz's stomach, was spared. He grunted as she hit him, and she winced. Head injuries were not to be trifled with.

Breathing heavily, blood rushed in her ears. Or was that sound from the car? Zelda raised her head. The rear of the car leaned into the air, while the small tree, overwhelmed by the load, gave up the fight.

The vehicle reared up like a futuristic memorial and disappeared into the depths with a final crunch.

They heard a crash and squeal, and they felt the impact's vibration.

Zelda shuddered as she thought of how damn close that had been.

Exhausted, she dropped her head again.

Zelda noticed Cruz was neither moving nor talking. Concerned, she straightened up. Cruz lay motionless. A serious-looking swelling on his forehead was turning bluish. She took off her jacket and rested his head on it.

A sharp pain in her leg reminded her that she herself was also injured.

Gently, she pulled the tattered, bloody fabric up again. She saw the extent of the damage the buckshot had done. The edges of the wound were irregular. Carefully, so as not to increase the pain, she pulled the pant leg back down. Her medical knowledge wasn't sufficient enough to determine whether any of the shot was still lodged inside her. After all, the wound had stopped bleeding. The dizziness she felt was more likely the result from adrenaline and not due to a blood loss.

But Cruz worried her. She put two fingers to his neck. His pulse beat strong and stead. Relieved, she stood up. Time to call the police.

When Cruz regained consciousness, his head was pillowed on Zelda's jacket. Instantly he missed her closeness. How much time had passed? Awkwardly, he straightened up. A few feet ahead, on the edge of the precipice, Zelda limped up and down, her cell phone to her ear. Good, Cruz thought. Obviously, she had reception. Not common among all these mountains.

Zelda raised her head and looked in his direction. Relief spread across her face when she caught sight of him. As quickly as she could with her leg, she came to him and crouched down without taking the phone from her ear.

"How do you feel?" she whispered.

"It's like I just got away with it."

Zelda smiled, but instead of talking to him, she spoke into her phone.

"He's doing relatively well. At least he's talking again.

But we need an ambulance urgently. I think he has a concussion. Me? There's nothing wrong with me. I just got shot." Great excitement erupted on the other end of the line. She listened intently as she casually brushed Cruz's hair out of his face.

"I know you don't have proper ambulances." Zelda rolled her eyes as she listened to the person on the phone.

Cruz giggled. *Giggled?* He never giggled. Giggling was for girls. Yet he just couldn't stop. After a collision with an SUV, boys giggled, too, apparently.

Zelda raised an eyebrow when she heard the unfamiliar sound. The right corner of her mouth twitched as she watched his outburst of mirth.

Cruz couldn't stop laughing.

Zelda watched him anxiously. The head injury and the tension of the last half hour had probably been too much. She also suspected that his adrenaline was wearing off, just like hers, which was responsible for the trembling in her limbs. Biochemically, it was easy to explain. Experiencing it in one's own body was something else entirely. She shivered.

"I'm hanging up now. Cruz needs care. It's possible that shock is setting in. Yes, I'll be fine."

What else could she do, she asked herself silently, after she had finished the conversation. With her attention back on Cruz, she put the cell phone in her pocket.

"How are you?"

"Crappy," he replied. After a little pause for thought, he reluctantly added, "Except for the teeny tiny fact that I'm capable of feeling crappy at all. I suppose that belongs on the plus side."

"Plus side?"

"Well, on a plus-minus list where you list pros and cons of a situation or solution." A look came over his face, as if he realized he was rambling incoherently. Then he shut his mouth abruptly. With difficulty he got to his feet.

Zelda could not stand the sudden silence and his pain-distorted face. "Should you even be on your feet? I think you have a concussion."

"Says the woman who got shot," he replied dryly.

She squinted her eyes and wrinkled her nose. "I'm not the one who got hit in the head. You were almost unresponsive in the car if you remember."

Humor flashed in his eyes as he looked down at himself. His T-shirt as well as the front of his pants were completely soaked from the water she'd poured on him. He probably wouldn't forget that anytime soon, even if he wanted to.

Zelda felt the blood rush to her head. That was a good sign, wasn't it? If the blood loss from the gunshot wound had been too much, she certainly wouldn't have any reserves left for her head. She nodded affirmatively to herself.

"Talk to me," Cruz prompted her, putting a hand to her forehead in concern. "You just looked like you were having a full internal conversation. I feel left out," he teased her.

"I just wanted to spare you from my ramblings," she muttered.

"As I mentioned before, it's a privilege to be able to ramble at all. Or to listen," he replied.

"True again." She yawned, feeling her energy reserves dwindle. Those post-adrenaline effects were quite persistent. Where was the damn rescue?

"Listen, my head is fine. I was just a little slow on the uptake for a moment."

Despite her fatigue, Zelda snorted loudly. "A little slow? A snail would have jumped out of the car faster than you."

"Probably it also had to do with the shock. I was like frozen. Literally couldn't move."

Lulled by his pleasant voice, she closed her eyes.

"Wait. Don't fall asleep. I want to look at your leg."

She hissed, "No, don't touch it!" With a leap, she moved back.

"Come here." Not wanting to scare her away, he gently took her hand. "Okay, just sit with me."

"Are you dizzy?"

He nodded, although she didn't think it was entirely true.

Hopefully, the firefighters would hurry up with their makeshift all-terrain vehicle converted to an ambulance. As Jake had explained to her on the phone, Independence was too small to justify the purchase of a real ambulance. If there was time, the ambulance service from Breckenridge would come to Independence. In urgent cases like this, the fire department's vehicle would have to do. Zelda had seen it; it had top-of-the-line equipment. As far as she knew, it had been financed with money from the betting pool.

Impatiently, she listened for an engine. Nothing. Just the usual sounds of the forest. To distract herself, she kept thinking about the fire department's special vehicle. In her opinion, it was much more useful here in the mountains than a normal ambulance anyway, which would have no chance to cope with this road.

Finally, through the trees, they saw the flash of the red-painted vehicle. Together she and Cruz got up and stood at the edge to wait.

CHAPTER FIFTEEN

"So, can I finally go home?" Cruz impatiently asked the doctor in charge. What was her name? He glanced at her tag. Dr. Kristina Biel. A whole family of woodpeckers seemed to have taken up residence in his head, hammering incessantly and making it impossible for him to remember the simplest things. At least they had already made their statement to the police. One of the deputies had done so while they were in the hospital intake.

Dr. Biel raised both eyebrows and grinned. "You're not going anywhere. We're keeping you overnight."

"Overnight?" He hated hospitals. Although he didn't have any particularly bad memories of them. Just the idea of being under the same roof as countless other sick and injured people made him nauseous.

Zelda hobbled into the room on crutches, and the doctor gave her a nod.

"Unless you have a guardian who can care for you," Dr. Biel said to Cruz.

Guardian? Cruz thought. As if he was a child?

The doctor excused herself to get a chart, and Zelda told

him that, fortunately, her shotgun wound had turned out to be only a graze. The wound had been cleaned and thickly bound, and in her opinion, the crutches were unnecessary. The bones and musculature had remained intact. Thanks to the medication, she hardly felt any pain. But she had decided to use the crutches dutifully until she was home. There she could put them in a corner.

"So, how is he?" Zelda inquired as the doctor returned.

"He has a concussion. We'll keep him here overnight for observation."

"That's definitely for the best," Zelda agreed, shifting her weight a little more onto her healthy foot.

"This is not the best thing at all! *He's* here," Cruz said. "So, stop talking about me in the third person."

"Someone's in a bad mood," Zelda observed, limping over to his bed.

"I'll leave you two alone," Dr. Biel said. "Let me know when you're leaving."

Zelda nodded.

"What are you two? Best friends?" Cruz muttered when the doctor had disappeared.

"Hey, you better be nice to me if you're serious about not wanting to stay here overnight."

He gave her a suspicious look. "What do you mean?"

"If you want, you can sleep at my place tonight."

"You want me to sleep over?" Despite the hellish headache, the idea put him in a good mood. The thought of falling asleep snuggled close to Zelda was definitely better than the idea of staying in the hospital.

Something in his gaze must have told Zelda in which direction his thoughts had wandered, because she hastily added, "I have a guest room. Nothing special. But it'll do."

"And you sleep where?"

Without understanding, Zelda looked at him. "Well, in my bed, of course."

Cruz put on his best puppy dog look. "Isn't there room for me there?"

"Not today. Murphy has already made his claim," she replied.

With a groan, he let himself fall back into the pillow. "Today is definitely not my day. First the doctor insinuates I'm still living with my mother, and the next thing I know I'm losing to a cat."

"Well, what can I say. Life is hard," Zelda replied. "Anyway, try to get some rest for a bit longer. I'll talk to the doctor and see if she'll release you into my care."

"I wouldn't be so sure," Cruz grumbled. "She seemed extremely amused by my situation for some reason."

"I'll do my best," Zelda promised, and with the help of her crutches, slipped into the hallway.

Unaware of the drama unfolding just a few miles away, Perkins pored over his treasure map. He painstakingly compared the lines on the parchment to an actual trail map. Repeatedly, he lost focus and had to start over. With a loud curse, he pushed the papers away.

There was no point. He couldn't concentrate. The only thing to blame was the visit by that nosy Zelda and insolent Cruz. A sharp pain ran through him, and he clutched his chest. He breathed shallowly until the burning subsided. Then he shuffled to the kitchen cabinet, took out a pillbox, and poured two pills into his hand. Without any water, he swallowed them.

He admitted the unexpected visit had thrown him off

course. His health, the suspicions, all of it triggered a sense of urgency. As if he didn't already have not much time left to find the treasure.

Although Zelda hadn't said anything to indicate new evidence, he had the unmistakable feeling he was missing something.

Adela could be the weak link. Damn it. He knew he'd regret collaborating with her but hadn't a choice. If she decided to talk, he had a problem. There was no statute of limitations on murder. He didn't have time for problems. He had never been so close to finding the treasure. He felt it in his bones.

Filled with renewed determination, he pushed himself off the kitchen counter and reached for his shotgun, which he'd taken back to the cabin to clean and reload after the encounter.

On his way out, he grabbed an old, frayed baseball cap off the hook and put it on. A visit to the old witch was long over-due. She owned something of his. The complete version of the map. He was sure she had screwed him over back then, or he'd have succeeded in his quest long ago. Not much of a surprise, really. Women were not to be trusted, he believed, so that made their deal invalid in his eyes.

Coughing and sputtering, his old pickup truck came to life. He'd take the long way through the woods, he decided. That way he had a better chance of surprising her.

Two hours later he arrived back at his cabin without having achieved anything. Although he had waited for over an hour, Adela had not appeared. He'd only encountered two white goats, which were fenced in on a piece of meadow near the cabin. Where was she? She was as much a hermit as he was. Couldn't stand most people. In the summer months, she sometimes set out to forage for herbs. But at this time of year? Just above her cabin there was still snow. Nothing grew there but ice flowers. So, where was she? Frustrated, he pulled his secret stash of homebrew from the cupboard. Normally, he didn't drink much. But the day's events warranted a hearty swig.

The next morning, Zelda stood in her kitchen, the room filled with the aroma of cinnamon buns, her specialty. Who would have thought she'd have a house guest? She thought of Cruz's compact, muscular body lying upstairs in her guest room.

She found herself caught up in daydreams of him looking into her eyes, talking in his mellow voice: *Slept good in your guest bed. Think how well you'd sleep in my arms.*

Zelda could imagine that well. She remembered the nights they'd spent together under the stars. She didn't doubt a repeat of that experience would be just as beautiful. Probably more beautiful. In contrast to her, he had probably expanded his… remarkable abilities.

Nevertheless, she remained stout. Sure. Her female ego appreciated the flirting, but she wasn't sure yet if she wanted to keep acting on their attraction. On the other hand, kissing him had been heavenly. Did she really want to let the past rule her life? A past that had turned out to be quite different from what she'd thought. Wasn't it better to act on a second chance? What was life for if not to be lived?

Torn between old fear and expectant anticipation, she pushed herself off the kitchen counter and went to the coffee maker to pour herself another cup. In doing so, she had to step over Murphy, who had taken up residence in a sunspot in the middle of the kitchen floor. She grinned. If Cruz knew that Murphy had been out all night and she had had her bed to herself...

No matter. Should she actually decide to give in to temptation and sleep with Cruz, she'd like him to be fully conscious. Every two hours overnight she'd checked on him. She had tried to fall asleep again herself but had not counted on Murphy's sixth sense. As if he had an internal alarm system, the cat had returned from his nocturnal excursion hungry and loudly reminded her he was on the verge of starvation. To prevent waking up Cruz with his yelling, she'd gotten back up.

After feeding Murphy and brewing coffee, she'd been wide awake. So, she decided to make breakfast. She kept herself busy, otherwise she would not be able to resist the temptation to crawl under the covers with Cruz.

The kitchen clock beeped. She opened the oven door and pulled out the delicious smelling pastries. To cool them, she opened the window and placed the cinnamon buns with the tray on the windowsill. To be on the safe side, she set the timer again. Two minutes. Then they'd be lukewarm when she brought them back in.

She mixed the ingredients for the glaze. Double cream, powdered sugar, and vanilla extract. When she was done, she brought the fresh pastries in and poured the sweet delicacy over them.

Two strong arms closed around her waist from behind.

Zelda winced. "Cruz!"

The cat opened his eyes and stared accusingly at this troublemaker who'd walked in to block the sunspot on the floor, then got up and ran off into Zelda's bedroom with a hiss.

Cruz stretched his nose in the air and sniffed with relish, but without loosening his grip. "I didn't even know you could cook. It's a wonder you don't have bears in your backyard that you woke up from hibernation with that delicious smell."

Zelda laughed and thought back to her healthy cooking experiment. "I don't know how to cook. It's baking. With lots of sugar and fat. Plus, it's the only recipe I know."

"Just what you need after a sleepless night."

He hid his face in the hollow of her neck and sighed, and she felt as if she were exactly where she belonged. Namely in his arms.

Zelda closed her eyes and enjoyed his closeness. If she wasn't careful, she was still in danger of getting used to Cruz. She wrenched her eyes open again. Who was she kidding, anyway? The train had long since gone. She didn't want to imagine how empty her little house would feel when he went home after breakfast.

Cruz raised his head. "What's wrong?"

"Nothing," she replied. "I was just thinking about what the penalty is for kidnapping."

He let go and turned her to face him. She put her arms around his neck.

"Kidnapping?" he said. "Did you have someone specific in mind?"

Zelda dug her incisors into her lower lip and smiled. "Yes."

"And that would be?"

Zelda glanced at him. Should she really dare to tell him what she was thinking? Was she really going to let her fear rule her life? Her stomach fluttered. "Well, you, of course. But first? Let's eat."

Zelda approached the table with the plate of cinnamon buns and met Cruz's gaze, and her breath caught. His dark eyes radiated such intensity she had to gulp.

Her fingertips touched his hand. Sparks flew. An electric

current shot up her arm like lightning, and she shuddered. Under lowered lashes, she glanced at him. Had he felt it, too? Or was she the only one suffering from acute sensory overload?

Seeing the hungry expression on his face, she relaxed. She needn't have worried. She was definitely not alone with her... *yes what, actually*? Pent-up lust? A new experience for her. Until that moment, she thought she just didn't have a very big sex drive. She'd just been missing the right man. She hoped she wouldn't spontaneously burst into flames.

"What's on your mind?" he asked.

Zelda blushed and shoved a knife and fork at him for the sticky cinnamon buns.

"Oh, nothing. I was just analyzing a particular physics problem."

Cruz raised both eyebrows. "Can I help?"

"I hope so." Louder, she added, "First, eat. They're best when warm."

Breakfast was a sensual affair. Glowing looks alternated with not-so-casual touches. At one point, Zelda reached out and wiped a blob of frosting from the corner of Cruz's mouth. He caught her hand before she could pull it back and licked the glaze off her finger. A small longing sound escaped Zelda's lips. Hearing the sound, Cruz's eyes darkened.

Heat rose inside Zelda and spread. She felt beautiful and desirable. An intoxicating feeling.

Cruz bit her lightly on the tip of her finger. Involuntarily, her hand tightened. She could no longer stand the tension and growing anticipation.

She grabbed his shirt with both hands and pulled him toward her. "How's your head?" she whispered close to his lips.

"Excellent."

"Good."

Greedily she kissed him. She let her tongue dart in and out and explore the outer line of his lips; she nibbled lightly on his full lower lip.

Their lips met.

An eternity later, he lifted his head to gasp for air.

"If you're going to stop, you better tell me now."

"Stop? Are you insane?" she groaned.

"Thank God!"

"You sure ask a lot of questions," she teased.

"Your bed or the guest room?"

"Mine," she replied, and began pushing him in the appropriate direction while her hands struggled with the buttons on his shirt.

Promptly, Cruz bumped his heel on the dresser in the hallway. He lifted her up and carried her up the stairs.

"Hey, put me down. I'm way too heavy." They made it to her bedroom.

Cruz laughed. "Did you just think I'm a weakling?"

"What? No! But..."

"All's well, then," he said, dropping her onto the mattress. Poor Murphy, who'd already sought refuge here earlier from the kitchen, and had just fallen asleep in the bedding, hissed indignantly again, and fled away with a leap.

Neither of them gave the animal—or the open window—a glance.

They were too busy tearing each other's clothes off.

"Who's coming with me to see Zelda?" called Paula up the stairs. Her two daughters had barricaded themselves in their room upstairs after breakfast and were up to who knows what. They were probably plotting to take over the world, knowing them. It was high time they got some fresh air before they got themselves into trouble via the Internet. Admittedly, they'd already helped her muck out the horses, but that was a daily routine and didn't count.

Leslie, soon to be sixteen years old and the older of the two, had run away from home two years ago and sought refuge on her farm, or rather in her stable. Cautiously they had approached each other and overcame some difficulties together. In the meantime, she had officially adopted the wonderful girl. About the same time, she had met Nate, a veterinarian. He was the father of ten-year-old Shauna, who however, was often thought to be at least thirty. To everyone's delight, the two girls got along very well despite their age difference and spent almost every free minute together.

No one had been more surprised than Paula herself when she fell in love with the charming Nate. Actually, until then she had been firmly convinced that all that romance stuff was hokum and, above all, not for her.

Paula smiled as she thought about her patchwork family. Then she frowned. There was still no answer from upstairs. Great. They probably had music on again. Not very enthusiastically, she eyed the stairs. Yesterday, in a weak minute, she'd let her sister-in-law Jaz talk her into a yoga class.

She felt as if a truck had run over her. She had sore muscles in places where she hadn't even known there were muscles; she would get back at Jaz for that. She had a half-day ride in mind. Then it would be Jaz who suffered the next day. Unfortunately, she would have to postpone that until after Jaz had given birth. She didn't think Jake would take kindly to her taking Jaz for a ride. Either way, she now had to climb the stairs to the second floor.

Leslie and Shauna drew apart from the computer, caught off guard, when she opened the door to their room.

"Do I want to know why you two look so guilty?"

In unison, they shook their heads.

Paula decided to let the matter rest for now. Knowing these girls, they had again spread a rumor on Independence's social media page. Shauna had a soft spot for everything that had to do with journalism. Leslie took over the technical side and edited the videos and pictures.

Paula, wasn't above using their guilty consciences to her advantage. "We're going to see Zelda. She had something of an accident yesterday."

Shauna sked, "Accident?"

"At the car in ten minutes, okay?"

Shauna and Leslie nodded. "Of course," Leslie said.

They parked the car in the town center on the community square and made their way on foot through the park to Zelda's house. The girls walked behind Paula and goofed around with each other. As they turned into the street where Zelda lived, a loudly meowing cat approached. Paula bent down to pet the beautifully patterned animal.

"Well, handsome? Are you the Bengal cat who success-fully won Zelda's heart?"

A loud complaint followed in the form of angry meows.

"Can't you get back in?" Paula asked it. She liked every-thing that had fur. But cats and her usually stayed out of each other's way.

A gust of warm wind blew her chestnut curls into her face and carried strange sounds. Was someone screaming?

She grinned broadly as she realized what she was hearing.

146

Someone should point out to Zelda that she'd better close her windows during certain activities.

"They must have disturbed you during your well-deserved nap," Paula confided to the cat.

As if relieved she'd finally understood, Murphy stopped meowing and tentatively rubbed against her legs. Behind Paula, she heard the sound of girls' running shoes clapping on the asphalt.

"Is Zelda in danger? Do we have to help her?" Shauna asked, worried and out of breath.

Paula caught her by the sleeve just before the little girl rushed full speed ahead into the house.

Leslie said nothing, just stared wide-eyed and red-eared in the direction of the unfamiliar soundscape.

"Uh, no. Let's not disturb Zelda right now," Paula said.

"But..." Shauna said. "Can I at least record it? In case the sheriff needs proof later."

"No way," Paula said, covering her ears, trying to stifle a laugh. "We're going to the diner. I'm sure the Diner Sisters will have some information for you."

That satisfied Shauna. Leslie said nothing but caught up with her sister as she skipped toward the park. She probably knew pretty well what she had heard and did her best to pretend she hadn't.

"Bye, old chap," Paula said to the cat. "You're on your own again."

Murphy gave her a disdainful look, and his tail twitched in displeasure.

CHAPTER SIXTEEN

Adela paused in mid-motion and tilted her head to listen. Only when she was sure the engine noise was far away did she pick up the knife and proceed to finely chop the parsley and chili. A stew simmered over the fire. She'd not cooked it herself; Miss Minnie had brought it. To warm up the food, she had dumped the contents into the big kettle. All that was missing were a few herbs to put the final touches on the stew of beef and mushrooms. She loved her few friends for taking such good care of her. If she had to make the meals spicier, it was a small price to pay.

Cutting board in hand, she went to her fireplace and added the finely chopped herbs. With a large wooden spoon, she stirred.

She pricked up. The vehicle was closer. She had a good idea who was about to show up. The tracks she found the prior day were clear and unmistakable.

With a regretful last look into the pot, she thought it possible she'd whipped up the stew for nothing. She'd not invite any unwanted visitor for lunch. Whether she'd still eat later? She doubted it.

Adela reached for a dishtowel and dried her hands before stepping to the back wall of the cabin and pulling a loose board from its place on the wall. With shaky hands, she reached for the parchment that lay inside. She studied the map, convinced there was a curse on the treasure for all the mischief that it'd brought. But maybe that was just an old, foolish woman's attempt to excuse her own bad decisions, she thought, tucking the paper into the neckline of her faded dress.

A goat bleated, announcing the arrival of a stranger. The gravel crunched as a rickety pickup truck stopped. She took off her apron and hung it over a hook on the door. *Showtime. Should I bring my shotgun?* Adela decided against doing so. It wouldn't make a difference. She smoothed her unruly gray-white hair and stepped outside.

Thomas Perkins sat in his car. The smoke rising from the cabin proved he'd have better luck than last time. He pushed open his car door and got out.

At that moment, Adela stepped out, too. With a squeak, the door closed behind her.

Like two predators facing off, they stared each other down.

Adela was the first to break the silence. "What do you want, Perkins?"

"Clarify a few things,"

"I have nothing to settle with you. Now get off my property."

Her black eyes bored into his.

For a moment, he felt the urge to get in his vehicle and leave. Perkins blinked and shook his head. Damn witch. He wouldn't leave until he got what he came for. He reached for his shotgun, which was lying on the bed of his truck, and tucked it under his right arm.

Adela smiled.

Perkins returned her smile. She'd stop laughing after he was done.

She straightened her shoulders and strolled toward the sloping cliffs. The white mountain peaks shone in the afternoon sun; the slopes were dotted with bright green patches of sprouting aspens.

"Hey," Perkins shouted. "Hold it right there."

She stopped, turned.

"Who do you think you are? First you cheat me out of my fair share and now you sic Zelda and that no-good nephew on me."

"Did I?"

"How else would they get the idea to question what happened fourteen years ago? You and I are the only ones who know what really happened."

"And now you're scared it will come out that you shot that tramp in cold blood."

"It was you who immediately seized the opportunity."

She laughed. "You're just annoyed I even knew about it. Ever wonder how I found out?"

Indeed, he had. Incessantly. Until it had driven him almost into madness. Fortunately, he still had the treasure hunt. It had saved him from his obsession. "I'm not interested in that," he lied. "What interests me is the real treasure map." He took another step toward her and raised the barrel of his shotgun so that it pointed at her stomach.

"Treasure map?" she asked. "I gave it to you, didn't I?"

"You gave me the wrong one. Otherwise, I would have found the treasure a long time ago."

Adela reached into her neckline and pulled out a small folded paper.

Sneering, she held it up. "You mean this?"

Perkins stumbled. "Give it here or else..."

"Or else what? You're gonna shoot me? Go ahead. I've lived my life," she said.

"You're just saying that." He waved his shotgun.

She shook her head. "It's the truth."

"Then it doesn't matter if I take it," he said.

Still laughing, she stepped back and held the map just out of reach.

With a guttural scream, he rushed her.

Adela's eyes widened and she took a step back. The edge beneath her foot crumbled. Instead of throwing herself forward toward the ground, she let herself fall.

She didn't notice Perkins reaching for her, her gaze was fixed upward.

Blue sky and a few streaks of clouds were the only things she saw.

So, this is what it felt like to fly. To be free.

She closed her eyes.

Perkins watched Adela lose her footing. In a last-ditch effort to save the precious map, he lunged forward to pull the crazy old woman to safety.

He didn't give a damn what happened to her.

But the treasure map...

Perhaps his attempt would have been successful if he

hadn't stumbled. No sooner had his hand touched fabric than the toe of his boot caught on a stone, and he lost his balance. Horror filled him as he realized there was no turning back. Holding a corner of Adela's dress in his hand, they fell together into the depths.

His cry rang out against the rock walls. The goats on top of the plateau raised their heads and flicked their ears when they heard the loud thud. Then they turned their attention back to the sparse grass.

The next day, Zelda sat in the diner waiting for Cruz. She'd been walking around all morning with a stupid grin she couldn't manage to turn off. Several customers had called her out on her unusually good mood. They ribbed her with trivial remarks about the warming weather. Her new coworker Astrid had been more persistent. "Tell me what's going on," Astrid demanded.

"Oh, not much," Zelda said. "Or, if you must know, I spent the weekend with Cruz."

Astrid rubbed her hands together and shouted "Yes!"

Zelda didn't even want to know what Astrid had bet on.

"Someone looks pleased," another voice called over. "Had a hot night?"

"Miss Minnie! Really!"

"Don't be shy, girl. I need all the details. After all, I have to lead the bets. Besides, it's almost unnatural how good you look. Weren't you shot in the leg just barely forty-eight hours ago?"

Zelda groaned as she realized that her life was again the subject of public interest, and she hid her face behind her hands. "What if I'm silent as a grave?"

Miss Minnie chortled. "Don't worry. I'll find out the truth, all right. Someone always knows." Unfortunately, this was true, as Zelda knew too well. "However, I can't promise that a detail or two won't be added. So, it'd be much easier for all concerned if you would pour your heart out to me."

Zelda didn't think about it. If she wanted to be informed about everything, she should have to make a little effort.

She was so lost in her own thoughts that she didn't notice Cruz's presence until he placed his hands on her shoulders. Surprised, she turned her head and looked.

Cruz seized the opportunity and kissed her.

The scent of aftershave and fresh mountain air filled Zelda's senses. The touch of his lips on hers transported her back to the bedroom. Except for a few brief forays into the kitchen, they'd spent most of their time together in bed. Zelda still felt tipsy thinking about it. Involuntarily, her hands clawed at his shirt and pulled him closer.

At some point, Miss Minnie cleared her throat. The two of them pulled apart. At the other end of the counter, Scrooge sat with glazed eyes in front of his half-empty beer glass and clapped.

"Now that was definitely more information than I needed. We have rooms, too, you know," Miss Minnie said.

The second half of the building, which housed the diner, functioned as a bed-and-breakfast under Miss Daisy's management. Just a few months back, they'd added on and installed a spa. The thought of disappearing into one of the rooms for a few hours instead of back to work with Cruz was tempting.

Cruz laughed. "I'm sorry if I embarrassed you."

"That's all right. At least it saves me from the Inquisition."

"That bad?"

"You have no idea."

In the afternoon, there was nothing going on at the pharmacy. Of course, she could have sent Astrid home. But knowing that the student depended on the work hours, she left the place in her capable hands and got into her car.

After a stop at Aileen's, she made her way to Adela's. When she remembered she still hadn't told Cruz about her first visit to his great-aunt, a slight twinge of guilt hit her. She'd make up for it, she vowed. Would they see each other soon?

A song on her lips, she covered the weary path.

Zelda passed the bottleneck, and she was reminded about their near crash. She shuddered to think how narrowly they'd escaped with their lives. But she was alive. Cruz was alive. And she'd taken the first step toward a future not defined by fear.

Her car struggled up the hill as she thought about all that'd happened in the last six months. Finding out Cruz was still alive had been a shock, to say the least. Meeting him again and finding out the chemistry was still as explosive as ever turned out to be a delightful surprise.

She parked in the same spot as before. Better not get too close in case Adela's finger was on the trigger again. No need for any more bullet wounds, however superficial.

She was almost disappointed when she got out and nothing happened. Zelda spotted the pickup in the driveway. It was not Adela's. Maybe that explained the absence of flying bullets. Could she have a visitor? Briefly, she considered driving home. After all, she didn't want to disturb them.

On the other hand, Adela must have already heard her coming. It'd look strange if she left without saying hello.

In the meadow she discovered two white goats. One bleated. She hadn't encountered them during her last visit. The animals paid her no further attention and devoted themselves to eating again.

Hesitantly, Zelda walked past the goats toward the cabin. Something felt strange, as though she'd entered another dimension. She shook off the uncomfortable feeling and knocked.

With a soft creak, it swung open. The smell of a hearty stew wafted out. "Adela?" she called.

No answer.

She called again. Still no response. The uneasy feeling in the pit of her stomach grew stronger.

Should I call Cruz?

And explain to him what she was doing with Adela again? Better not. At least not *yet*, she thought, and ventured inside.

It was dark. The small window over the sink didn't let in much light. She made her way through the chairs and bags placed in the room without any discernible system and glanced at the cooking pot. Her mouth watered when she spotted the chunks of vegetables and meat in the sauce. She wondered if she could persuade Adela to share her dinner. After all, she'd deliberately missed the mark the last time she had shot at her. Surely that meant something. Judging by the rest of Adela's social behavior, it was probably tantamount to being friends-for-life.

Zelda reached for the wooden spoon, stirred a few times, and then raised it. She blew on it. She didn't feel like burning her tongue. Who knew when she'd need it again, she thought, grinning, Cruz's image in her mind. She carefully stuck out the tip of her tongue and tasted the concoction. She bristled when she noticed the stew was cold. Sure enough. The fire had burned down for some time. It didn't do any harm to the stew; countless flavors exploded. Heavens, it was delicious.

When she had savored and swallowed the last bite, she put the spoon back beside the pot. Without her potential hostess, it'd be rude to keep eating. She felt a little like Snow White. Adela would show up in a minute and ask who'd eaten from her little plate.

Zelda continued her search for Adela. Her eyes had become accustomed to the twilight. The bed in the far corner was untouched. A faded quilt lay on top. On the worn wooden table lay a small wooden board and a sharp kitchen knife. She inspected it closely. Tiny shreds of green herbs and some chili seeds stuck to its blade.

She shivered. Something wasn't right. The whole scene had something ghostly about it, as if Adela had just disappeared.

Except it was usually the living that made others disappear, not ghosts. Zelda remembered the vehicle in the driveway. Perhaps her visitor had turned out to be a killer? True, she had no idea who might be interested in killing Adela.

Nervous, she grabbed the kitchen knife and held it protectively in front of her as she stepped out of the cabin.

Nothing changed outside. The goats had wandered a bit up slope. Longer grasses bent in the wind. High above, a bird of prey circled and emitted a hoarse cry.

She wandered to the edge of the plateau. A movement in the corner of her eye drew her attention. A narrow strip of faded black fabric fluttered on the thin branches of a desert sage.

Aware of the steep rock face beneath her feet, she carefully got down on all fours and reached out for the scrap of cloth. Soon, she got hold of it.

Relieved, she scrambled to her feet and took a step back from the edge. Only when she thought she was at a safe distance from the abyss did she look into the depths. She scanned the rocks below and clutched the rescued cloth tighter.

A shapeless bundle far below confirmed her worst fears.

CHAPTER SEVENTEEN

Zelda sat in the diner holding a cup of hot chocolate, hoping to get rid of the cold that'd settled in her bones since her terrible discovery.

After finding a spot on the mountain where she had reception, she'd driven to the diner at Jake's direction. She'd wanted to help with the search, but he argued she had too little experience for rough terrain and it could be dangerous.

"Do you think there's any chance she survived the fall?" she asked the crowd, her voice weak.

All her new friends had shown up one by one to keep her company during the endless wait. Paula was there with her girls. She had just picked them up from school when Jaz's call reached her. Jaz had canceled her yoga class and was sitting on the other side of the alcove. Her black king poodle, Rambo, sat at Zelda's feet with his head resting on her lap. Charlie had left her son, Ethan, in charge of the store and had shown up with a *Simon's Cat* comic book.

"To pass the time," she'd said, as she placed it on her lap to read. Zelda smiled and thanked her, even though she couldn't imagine distracting herself with something so trivial.

Jaz and Paula exchanged a meaningful glance before Jaz turned to Zelda. She reached across the table, disengaged one of her hands from the cup, and squeezed it.

"The chance of anyone surviving a fall like that is extremely low. That's a drop of over three hundred feet."

Zelda nodded. That'd been clear. The tiny spark of hope in her chest hadn't let up until she'd asked the question. With her answer, her throat tightened. Tears welled up. Embarrassed, she wiped them away. "It's stupid. I didn't really know her at all."

"There are always people who remember us or touch us. No matter how long you knew them," Jaz replied.

Paula tried hard not to roll her eyes. She could understand that Zelda was shocked. Making such a discovery was never a pleasure. Adela had been a loner who hadn't given a damn about anyone else. When Jaz had told her about Zelda's visit to Adela, she'd asked her mother Brenda what she knew about the woman. Brenda had explained she didn't know a lot except she had never cared much for her own family. That was something Paula didn't understand. It was possible the woman had shown Zelda a different side of herself. That didn't make up for her past actions, though.

Jaz, who obviously knew her friend well enough to guess what was going on, leaned over to Zelda. "Just don't pay any attention to her. Paula doesn't like most people."

She gave her friend a disparaging look. For a second time, Paula tried hard not to roll her eyes.

"If it weren't for Nate and the two girls in her life, she'd be well on her way to becoming a second Adela herself," Jaz affirmed.

Charlie sat with big ears and eyes and absorbed all Jaz's gossip. Since she hadn't lived in Independence long, she found such personal insights exciting. Especially since her own personal life was non-existent. For a long time, she had longed only for peace. When they moved in last year, she knew she'd found it. Boring, Ethan might have called it, but besides his protests, they'd stayed. And it had been worth it. Ethan settled in well, and the difficulties from her previous life seemed gone. She felt safe and content. But lately, an inner turmoil was gripping her more often. She hoped she had not become too accustomed to the nomadic life. She would be reluctant to leave. Fortunately, the bookstore offered her a new challenge.

"Not true at all!" protested Paula, while the two girls listened.

"And who always opened the door with a shotgun in her hand?" Jaz asked.

"She still does that sometimes," Shauna said.

"Only if necessary," Leslie said.

Paula smiled and squeezed Leslie's shoulder affection-ately. Then her phone rang. Glad for the distraction, she answered the call. It was her brother Jake on the line.

"Hello, sheriff," she greeted him.

He sounded distracted as he spoke. "We found them."

"Is she..."

"Yes. Unfortunately." He took a deep breath. "Listen, can you do something for me?"

"Sure, what?"

"If Cruz shows up, convince him to stay where he is."

"Cruz?"

"Yes. I need to ask him some questions."

"But…" She glanced at Zelda, who immediately pricked up at the mention of her, well, what? *Her boyfriend? Lover?* "Why?"

"Simple. He's the closest and, as far as I know, the only relative she has," Jake said.

"Uh-huh."

Paula wasn't convinced that was the only reason, even if the statement sounded plausible. She was familiar enough with his job to knew he'd say nothing more. Just as she was about to hang up, he started talking again. "Paula?"

"Yes?"

"She wasn't alone. We found two bodies."

"Two?" she said.

"Perkins was down there, too."

"Shit! What a huge mess."

Jake sighed. "You can say that again."

Paula lowered the phone. Like dogs that had picked up a promising scent, her two daughters reared their heads. From the looks of it, they were bursting with curiosity.

Zelda leaned forward. "Was that Jake? And what does he want with Cruz?" She slapped her hands over her mouth. "Oh, dear. I'm such a bad person. Scratch my second question. What about Adele?"

"There, there," Jaz reassured her, patting her hand sympathetically.

"What you suspected. Unfortunately, she didn't survive the fall."

"Oh, no."

"And what was that about Cruz?"

"He's the next descendant," she said.

"Right. Makes sense."

Paula cleared her throat. "There's more. They found another body."

"Who?"

"Perkins, the former sheriff of Independence."

The others stared.

"Don't look at me like that. I'm just the messenger. That's all I know."

"Why did he call you and not me?" asked Jaz.

Paula mumbled something about police radio and gave her daughters a furtive sideways glance. Shauna and Leslie had gotten into the habit of listening to the police radio, even though she had forbidden it. Even Jake hadn't been successful in telling them to stop. Because of that, he liked to keep Paula in the loop, so she'd be prepared to know what the girls had overheard.

"I don't believe a word," Jaz grumbled. "Ever since I got pregnant again, he's been treating me like I'm a delicate little elf. He should know I have the constitution of an elephant."

"I wouldn't mind if my husband saw me as a delicate little elf," Paula said.

Jaz snorted. "Right. More likely, you'd lock Nate up on bread and water until he came to his senses."

"Elves are totally underestimated," Charlie said.

Paula and Jaz stared at her until Charlie threw her hands up.

"What? It's true. In my opinion, elves are a warlike people."

Jaz tilted her head. "Then Paula is definitely an elf."

Zelda didn't notice the elf discussion. Her brain was running at full speed. Could it be true? Adela and Perkins were dead? But why? Had her research triggered the horrible event? Aside from Adela's vague confession that she'd been conspiring with the sheriff at the time, there was no sign the two had maintained contact.

Until she had come along looking for answers.

"Oh, here you are," Cruz said from the doorway, snapping her out of her thoughts. "I've been searching all over for you."

Zelda looked. He was obviously coming straight from work. As always, he looked handsome in his suit. Though she was wearing jeans and flats, she saw no reason to dress up when she was on her feet all the time, wearing scrubs over her clothes. But she hoped her mascara and eye shadow were still where they belonged. She slapped herself inside. Two people were dead, and she was worried about her appearance?

"Where else would she be, in the face of a crisis?" asked Miss Minnie, pushing a full cup of coffee toward him as he reached her table. The brown brew sloshed over the table. Miss Minnie pulled a rag from the pocket at the front of her apron and wiped it up before hurrying away.

"True, actually," Jaz said.

"Sorry," Cruz said. "I was looking for you at the pharmacy." He looked at Zelda. "After all, no one informed me you were taking the afternoon off." He paused before continuing, "Maybe if I had, I would have taken the day off, too."

Zelda winced.

"What's wrong?" Paula asked.

"Can someone tell me what all the fuss is about?" asked Cruz.

Paula stood up and gave up the seat next to Zelda. "Sit down. We have some bad news."

Cruz dropped down on the bench next to Zelda. "I've already figured that much out."

Zelda took a deep breath. "I went back up to visit your great-aunt."

Cruz shrugged. "So what? Not that I'm thrilled. But you've made it clear to me that it's your decision. Which, unfortunately, you're right about. I highly doubt the mayor will call me about it, though." He looked around.

Zelda gulped and searched frantically for the right words. Of course, she couldn't find any. There were no right words. "Adela is dead."

"Dead?" he asked, "What do you mean *dead*?"

Zelda winced. "She fell," she said. "And..."

"There's an *and*?"

Jaz, seeing how hard Zelda was finding the conversation, jumped into the breach for her. "They found Adela at the bottom of the cliff with Perkins."

"Perkins?"

Toby, one of Jake's deputies, stepped up behind Cruz. "I have to ask you to come with me."

Cruz looked at him. "Me? But why?"

"You're Adela's only family here. Besides, we need your alibi for yesterday afternoon." Toby's voice sounded apologetic. Still, it was clear that he would carry out his order and take Cruz to the police station.

Everyone present turned to the deputy, horrified.

"For what period of time does he need an alibi?" Paula asked.

"That's Cruz's business," Toby replied.

"No, no, go ahead and tell me. Because I'd be interested in that, too," Cruz said. "What the hell is going on?"

"Yesterday afternoon."

Paula laughed uproariously. Miss Minnie, who had

164

approached their table with a tray of freshly baked cookies and had overheard the last few sentences, joined in.

"What's going on with those two?" asked Toby.

Zelda wanted to know, too. Of course, she knew where Cruz had been yesterday afternoon. But the others couldn't possibly know. Could they?

Charlie sat there, grinning ear to ear, while Jaz studied her fingernails.

Miss Minnie regained her composure, took a deep breath, and winked at Zelda. "Cruz has an airtight alibi. He was with Zelda yesterday."

Toby gave her a blank look. "Like, all day?"

All pairs of eyes swung in Zelda's direction.

Miss Minnie was the first to dare to ask. "Yes, tell me? All day?"

"Shauna? Leslie? Are you taking Rambo for a walk?"

Leslie jumped up as if she couldn't wait to escape the embarrassing adults. Shauna, on the other hand, not quite grasping what it was about. "Darn it. We always have to leave whenever it gets exciting."

Paula pointed to the door. "Out."

"Come on, Rambo," Leslie said to the big poodle. The black dog rose from his couch, stretched, and accompanied the two young ladies outside.

Zelda had turned bright red. "Tell me, is nothing sacred in Independence?"

Cruz shook his head.

"I'm beginning to think you've bugged my home," Zelda said. Her eyes flashed. An unruly curl fell into her forehead. Impatiently, she pushed it away.

"Now, now," Paula said. "If you're really that concerned about your privacy, you'd better close the windows before certain activities."

"Close the window?" asked Zelda. A light dawned on her. "Oh!"

Toby cleared his throat. "Is that right, Zelda? Were you with Cruz all day yesterday?"

Embarrassed, she nodded. "He spent the night at my place."

"Good, that's settled then," the deputy noted. "I would have hated to arrest you, Cruz."

"I'm relieved to hear that," Cruz said.

"I'd still be happy if you accompanied me to the station. You're Adela's last known relative, after all."

Cruz grabbed his keys off the table. "Sure."

He stood up, pressed a kiss to Zelda's cheek, and took advantage of her surprise to whisper something in her ear. "We're not done with each other yet. You still owe me an explanation."

Zelda wanted to say something back, but he had already turned to the others to say goodbye. She tried to interpret his expression, but he had put on his poker face. She sighed. She would have no choice but to wait until they had time to talk. Only then would she know if he blamed her for Adela's death, just as she blamed herself.

When Cruz left, eyes turned expectantly to Zelda. "What?" she said, knowing full well that what was about to come was inevitable.

"The wondrous benefits of a gossip-prone small town?" Paula asked.

"I don't believe it," Zelda said, hiding her face behind her hands. "Who'd think I'd ever be happy about the efficiency of the local rumor mill."

"Believe it. However, we want details now," Jaz said. The others nodded in agreement.

"I was afraid of that," Zelda muttered.

"After all, Miss Minnie has to keep up with the betting book," Charlie explained. "Then maybe I won't have to cook today?" she added with a hopeful look in Miss Minnie's direction.

Miss Minnie shook her head. "Forget it. You know perfectly well you bet on a different date."

"Was worth a shot."

Zelda had to laugh. Her friends were all insane. But they were her friends and the reason she was doing well, despite the terrible news.

CHAPTER EIGHTEEN

Three days passed without Zelda hearing from Cruz. Three days in which she had all the time in the world to imagine every kind of awful scenario. She could have called him, but she felt she had to leave it up to him when he was ready to talk to her again. It couldn't be easy for him to know it was she who had set in motion events that led to his great-aunt's death. Although she was eager to hear about the investigation, she held back and avoided pestering Jaz.

Of course, the local rumor mill ensured any news was constantly fed to her anyway, she recalled, as she watched Miss Daisy make her way through the Pharmacy's shelves of baby food and personal care products.

Finally, she arrived at Zelda's checkout. "It's terrible what happened to Adela."

Zelda nodded. "Yes, it's very terrible."

"Something like that was bound to happen."

"You think so?" asked Zelda. She was sure she hadn't thought of such a thing as foreseeable. Heavens, she wasn't even clear what that something that had supposedly been foreseeable even entailed.

"Why, of course," Miss Daisy declared.

Zelda felt reprimanded, as if by being out of the loop she'd violated her civic duty.

"I probably missed that. I haven't been back that long," she said.

"Why, yes," said Miss Daisy. "I'd forgotten about that." She leaned forward and her voice turned quieter. "Adela was sick. Cancer. She had been for years. She was getting worse. Adela was not one to wait for an invitation from the Grim Reaper."

Zelda's brain went into overdrive. It'd been a suicide? She could believe that Adela had been seriously ill. She'd looked it when Zelda had visited her. But she jumped into the abyss because of it? On the other hand, she had to agree with Miss Daisy; she was sure Adela would definitely have wanted to determine the time of her death herself. But what if Perkins had deprived her of this choice?

"Okay," she replied. "But how do you explain Perkins being there?"

Miss Daisy shrugged. "Maybe he came at a crucial time and tried to stop her. I can imagine that. Once a cop, always a cop, even if he'd become more of a maverick in recent years."

Zelda doubted that Perkins had been guided by noble motives. But she didn't want to speak ill of a dead man, even if her only encounter with him had been very unpleasant.

Miss Daisy remembered her shopping. She asked for cough syrup and put the shopping basket on the counter. Zelda was astonished when she discovered a pack of condoms inside, in addition to the hand cream. She put on her best poker face and didn't let on while she typed in the amount. When Zelda handed Miss Daisy the bag of groceries, she couldn't help herself from saying, "Have fun."

Miss Daisy grinned like a satisfied cat. "I sure will. You can be sure of that."

It was sobering to realize a woman at least twenty years older than her had an active sex life. Of course, she couldn't help but think of Cruz while on the subject. She cleared her throat to push the thoughts down. She'd have for that later.

"Astrid?" Zelda called.

"Yeah, what's up?" Astrid called from the back room.

"Can you please take over the register for the next half hour? I need some fresh air."

"Sure. No problem."

"Thank you."

Outside, Zelda lifted her face to the sun. The warm chinook blowing from the mountains stroked her face. She felt calmer.

Had Adela really been terminally ill? And perhaps jumped to her death voluntarily? They'd probably never know. Knowing her death had been the result of a free will assuaged her feeling of guilt, but not completely. Maybe Miss Daisy was right when she suspected Perkins had wanted to help.

Her thoughts raced. Guilt mixed with anger. Anger at Cruz. Couldn't he imagine she felt bad? She wished he'd call her and tell her what the police investigation had revealed. Instead, he was keeping her in the dark. Was that a promising start to a relationship?

Shaken, she stopped. *Relationship?* When had she started thinking they were in a relationship? A few hours together in bed was no reason to assume they were in a relationship, God knew. What if she was the only one who believed they were in a relationship? The idea hurt her heart. Oh dear. She loved him. Again. When had that happened?

She turned and made her way back. One thing was sure: she'd waited patiently long enough. As soon as the pharmacy closed, she'd get some answers, and get them from Cruz.

It was after nine o'clock, and Cruz was still in his office. He'd fallen behind on work due to the many interruptions of the past few days. A new start-up was waiting for his final assessment and recommendation to the mayor. Others needed to be completed.

He'd been on the phone several times with his auto insurance company, which was taking its time processing the case. If the delay continued, he'd have to buy a new truck, unsure what he'd get for the old SUV. That wasn't a problem per se. Cruz had saved enough so he could afford it but wasn't happy about the prospect.

With his car lying at the bottom of a canyon, collecting evidence proved difficult. The police had tried to get down to it without success. Despite the large-scale manhunt, there was no trace of the other driver. None of it looked promising.

Jake tried to comfort him. "Don't worry about it. From the looks of it, it was a stupid accident. Maybe the other guy lost control."

"Twice in a row?" Cruz asked. "The first time, when we were going up the hill and he was coming toward us, I can understand. But on the way back? He was waiting."

The sheriff shrugged. "Unfortunately, there are a lot of lunatics on the street."

"I was there. We were targeted," Cruz said.

"We'll keep our eyes open," Jake said. "But I wouldn't

get my hopes up. If the attacker has left the region, it's unlikely we'll catch him."

Cruz settled for the explanation.

Next, the medical examiner called with shocking news. Adela had suffered from terminal cancer. Since there were no signs of violence, the police assumed she jumped voluntarily.

Cruz had a hard time imagining that. However, what did he know about Adela? Even Zelda had the courage to visit her. Remorse plagued him. If he'd been closer, he might've been able to help. Send her to the doctor. Something.

"And what about Perkins?" he asked.

"What about him?"

"Those two weren't exactly best friends. We're supposed to believe the two of them jumped to their deaths together?"

"I'm sorry. I'm afraid I don't have an answer."

Very unsatisfied by the conversation, he had hung up.

Later, Cruz sat in front of the piece of parchment Adela had been clutching when she fell. Jake had hoped it was a suicide note but it was something different. He held an old treasure map. He remembered Adela always tried to motivate his father with the prospect of treasure. Or, rather, manipulate. If he believed Adela's story, it was not just any treasure: it was the fortune of Treasure Mountain. He stroked the faded parchment.

A knock on his office door startled Cruz. Who could that be?

Wilkinson sometimes worked late into the night. But he happened to know that the mayor had a date with Miss Minnie tonight. So, it couldn't be him.

"Come in?"

The door opened and Zelda entered.

Surprised, Cruz stood up. "What are you doing here?"

Zelda glared at him. His brusque and uninviting greeting

hurt her and made her angry at the same time. Who did he think she was?

"I wanted to see you. Do I need another reason?" she asked pointedly.

He winced imperceptibly as he recapped in his head what he'd just said.

"Sorry, sorry. Do you want to sit down?"

Stiffly, he pointed to the visitor's chair next to his desk.

Zelda's eyes narrowed. She ignored the offered chair and instead walked purposefully around the desk. "You know, I really try to be understanding of your situation and make concessions. But it's hard. Very hard, in fact."

Cruz shoved his hands into his pants pockets and teetered on his feet. What could he possibly say to that? He knew he should have called her. Countless times he had held the phone in his hand. But in the end, he hadn't dialed her number. He didn't quite know why. His reaction to Adela's death had caught him off guard. It wasn't that he suddenly missed his great-aunt. On the flip side, he missed Zelda. His emotions were on a roller coaster ride, and he had no idea what to do.

Zelda took another step closer. "Do you have anything to say? Strange, I thought that was your tongue in my throat last Sunday. Not to mention certain other body parts that were up close and personal. Forgive me for believing we were at least friends."

"Oh yeah," Cruz countered, her scent of oranges and mint rising. Did she have to smell that good? He couldn't think straight as it was. Her proximity confused him more. He took a step toward her. "Who was it who deliberately omitted to tell me about their visit to Adela?"

"I would have. But you're not talking to me."

Cruz would have liked to give her a quick-witted answer, but his attention was completely hogged by Zelda's proximity. A teasing strand of her hair tickled his cheek. On his lips, he could feel her hot breath. He lowered his gaze to her mouth, which was a tactical error. All his reservations and worries were blown away. He had to kiss her.

As if under a spell, she met his gaze.

When Cruz looked into her dark eyes, framed with long lashes, his willpower was gone. With a groan, he lowered his head and kissed her. Why had he thought keeping his distance was a good idea? He couldn't think of a single valid reason.

Although Zelda had hoped he would kiss her, it still surprised her when he did. She regained her composure. Heavens, could the man kiss. Her mind gave up sending warning signals, and her intuition took over. Her fingertips had a tactile memory and an amazing initiative—impatiently, she reached for his shirt and tugged. She couldn't wait to finally feel his velvety skin under her hands.

Cruz made a noise that sounded like a growl as her efforts were crowned with success. He lifted her up and placed her on the desk in front of him so that he stood between her thighs.

After minutes, or hours, Zelda could not have said, Cruz reluctantly broke away from her. Breathing heavily, he slid his hands into her hair and embraced her head gently. "That's probably not a good idea, with all the unspoken issues between us."

"Probably," she admitted a little breathlessly. "Do you have a better idea?"

The corners of his mouth twitched. "Honestly, no."

"Well, then..."

Deep inside, she felt the longing for his closeness rise to

the surface, sending sparks flying. It was a wonder they hadn't short-circuited yet. Before she could stop, a hoarse laugh escaped her.

Amused, he nudged her cheek with his nose. "What's so funny?"

"Oh, nothing," she replied.

"Come on. We just had our first fight over 'nothing'."

"Does that mean we're about to have hot make-up sex?"

Cruz grinned. "We're well on our way."

"Until you went and had to be reasonable," Zelda complained.

"Don't worry. Make-up sex can be made up too."

"I'd laughed because I was wondering why we haven't knocked out the power yet."

"So hot, huh?" he asked.

"Hey!" she protested, punching him in the shoulder. "You can't take all the credit."

"Definitely not," he said.

"What do we do now?"

"What do you say we get something to eat and talk it out?"

Zelda leaned her head against Cruz's shoulder. "That's a hundred percent a good idea," she said. "Let's go to my place. Otherwise, Murphy will probably destroy my curtains or do something equally destructive if I'm gone too lone."

He kissed her on the forehead. "Eating and talking. I wonder whose idiotic idea that was."

Zelda heard him, of course. "Definitely yours."

Cruz rolled his eyes and pushed her toward the door. "Then we'd better hurry," he said. "Don't you think?"

"Yeah. Let's get that part out of the way and get to the good part."

An hour later, they were sitting on the carpet in Zelda's living room. On the kitchen counter, two empty pizza boxes piled up. Cruz held a beer. Zelda's red wine glass was on the coffee table.

Murphy, the traitor, had stretched out on Cruz's lap and was purring like a world champion. Zelda suspected Cruz had bribed the cat with sausage from the pizza, but she wasn't sure. After all, she was the one who fed the velvet-pawed feline twice a day, and yet he acted like she was the worst cat owner ever. When they'd come home, he made a fuss as if she'd starved him for the last three days, not just missed his feeding time by an hour. Eventually, she'd convince him that she was purr-worthy, too. She sighed. In twenty years or so, maybe.

She told Cruz about her last encounter with Adela.

"She really implied that she set the whole thing up?" asked Cruz.

"Yes. At least, those were her words. The way I put it together, she wanted to get you and your family as far away as possible."

"Well, she did an excellent job of that. But for her to kill someone to do it..."

Zelda shook her head. "She denied that firmly. If I understood her correctly, she saw an opportunity and took it. She must have gotten wind that someone, I suspect it was that tramp, had died."

"Died? Or was killed," Cruz added.

"I think we can assume Perkins had a hand in that. At least that was Jake's assumption."

"True. But how did she get the old sheriff to go along with it?"

"I don't know. That's what I was trying to figure out."

"Seems like you were spot-on with your suspicions. Enough that Perkins felt the need to seek out my great-aunt."

"I know. I realized that much, too. No matter what happened up there, I didn't want that."

"Then what did you want?" he asked.

"Answers to my questions. Something that made sense of the chaos that ensued for me."

"Did you find what you were looking for?"

"On the contrary."

He squeezed her hand and put a pizza slice in her hand. "Eat. Otherwise, it'll get cold."

She accepted the offer and change of subject. "Were the police able to tell you anything about how it happened?"

Cruz turned to her and thought about what he should tell her. In the end, he decided to tell her everything. He had no desire to keep secrets. "They still don't know what happened between the two of them. However, the autopsy revealed Adela was seriously ill. Cancer. She wouldn't have had long to live either way."

"I was looking forward to learning more about herbs from her. Surprisingly, that part of my visit was really fun."

"I have a hard time believing that. But as far as her death... I think it was a blessing for her to go out like that, whether Perkins had a hand in it or not."

"I didn't know her well. But she also gave me the impression she was very self-determined."

"She had a map in her hand," he said abruptly.

"A map?"

"She was holding it while she fell."

"Of what?" asked Zelda.

Cruz shrugged. "Seems to be some kind of treasure map."

"The secret," Zelda snapped.

"The secret?"

"I forgot to mention that. At the end of my visit to her, she said we'd gotten too close to her secret. The secret that was supposed to give you and your siblings a golden future. That's a perfect fit for a hidden treasure, isn't it? Do you have the map here?"

Cruz shook his head. "No. It's still in my office."

"Oh. Too bad."

"It's not quite that simple. If you ask me, it's better we leave this alone."

"Why? What do you know about it?"

"Not much," Cruz admitted. "But what I do know, combined with both of our stories, doesn't necessarily put me in a gold-digging mood." He sighed. "I spoke with Ace, who knows quite a bit about the history of the area. He confirmed my suspicions that this is related to the Treasure Mountain treasure."

"Wow. Sounds impressive."

Cruz grimaced. "Wait till you hear the rest. Legend has it that somewhere in the Rocky Mountains lies buried a treasure of gold of immeasurable value. The only clue to the exact location is provided by an ancient map."

"Adela's map," Zelda said excitedly.

"Perhaps. Supposedly, over two hundred years ago, the only survivor of a failed expedition made the map. Since then, his descendants have been searching for the treasure. But every time they think they've finally deciphered the mystery, the curse of Treasure Mountain strikes again."

"A curse! This just keeps getting better and better."

"Have you been listening to me?" asked Cruz, irritated.

"Yeah. But surely such a paltry curse won't stop you from looking for it."

"Uh, yes?"

"Are you crazy? Surely this would be a chance to get something positive out of all this misfortune."

"I don't see it that way. Just what happened to me and you and now to Adela proves it's best to leave it alone."

"Okay, I admit Adela's death is sad. But we're still alive. Nothing happened to us, strictly speaking."

Cruz stared at her in disbelief. "Now that's quite a turnaround. Wasn't it you who suffered so much from what happened back then?"

"True," Zelda replied. "And maybe the treasure is the answer."

"Or the beginning of the next disaster," Cruz muttered.

"Do you really believe in a curse?"

"Of course not," he said.

"Then you won't mind if I take a look at the map," she replied slyly, smiling hopefully.

Cruz knew when to admit defeat.

"I look forward to it," she said, crawling over to him on all fours.

Murphy, who had been watching her approach critically, fled Cruz's lap and disappeared into the kitchen.

"Everything good between us again?" she asked, tilting her head.

Reluctantly, he nodded. He didn't like that she was so fixated on the treasure, but he could take care of that later.

"Where were we in your office?"

"Right," he replied, reaching for the hem of her sweatshirt to pull it over her head.

Zelda gasped softly.

When Cruz discovered only velvety skin and curves

179

underneath, he groaned. All thoughts of conspiracies were blown away. There was only Zelda and him and the heat that spread between them like a wildfire.

The anticipation gave him strength. He slid both hands under her buttocks, bent his legs, and stood up with her on his arm.

"Put me down. I'm way too heavy."

He gave her a playful pat on the butt. "Not at all. We need a bed. Now."

"Yes, we do."

CHAPTER NINETEEN

Walt stood in front of his father's cabin. He'd parked his new car a little ways down the road. After Saturday's stunt, he'd driven all the way to Denver and taken the old car straight to a junkyard. The entire drive he'd been afraid a police patrol would stop him, but he'd been lucky. The people at the junkyard hadn't asked any questions.

On foot, he had walked to the nearest used car dealer and bought an old Chevy. There'd be nothing to connect him to the incident on the mountain. At least something had gone smoothly. Unlike all the rest; Zelda and Cruz had escaped unscathed, while his father was dead. Gone.

Tormented, he bent down to pick up a large stone that hid the key to the cabin. For being so paranoid he hadn't shown much creativity when it came to home security.

His dad had relied on his reputation, Walt thought. His own repressed feelings were bubbling up. His relationship with his father had been very conflict-ridden. But at least, until yesterday, he had hope of proving to his old man he wasn't a failure. Anger rose, hot and impetuous, as he realized that was now no longer an option. And all because this stupid woman couldn't let bygones be bygones. He clenched his hands. The sharp edges of the key cut into his palms. He welcomed the pain, for it helped him return to the present.

One thing at a time. First, he had to take care of practical things like the funeral. Dying was expensive, as he had found out from the coroner.

Death from massive trauma. The diagnosis wasn't a great surprise. After all, the man had fallen over a hundred feet. No traces of extraneous impact. The old witch had probably lured the old fool over the edge with idiotic drivel about the treasure. His father had never told him of any relationship with her. Over the years, though, he'd put enough together he was pretty sure Adela had given him the map. Why the cranky old woman had ended up at the bottom of the canyon herself was beyond his comprehension, but no one knew better than him that plans could go awry.

He unlocked the door. The police had already been there. Out of habit, he pulled his stained sweater over his stomach. His father's harsh instructions rang in his ears. *Sit up straight. Straighten your clothes. You missed a spot shaving. Have you been sleeping under the bridge again? When are you going to do something about your gut?*

He shook himself to get rid of the uninvited memories. With one hand he pushed open the crooked wooden door and stepped into the cabin. It was unfamiliar in here, because his father had never invited him inside. He groped for the light switch, and as the single light bulb hanging from the ceiling turned on, he saw he hadn't missed much. The cabin consisted of a single room. A bed, a gas stove, and one chair.

The only two things that didn't match the Spartan décor were the massive weapons cabinet and the huge desk. His eyes lingered on the open gun cabinet. The police had confiscated all the guns. It had turned out his father had not permitted most of them. His father had big plans for the firearms, as according to the police, they had found evidence he'd intended to establish his own independent state. By force of arms, if necessary. He'd meticulously kept documents describing his plans in minute detail. Via computer, which the police had taken, he'd been in contact with like-minded people from various radical groups. How his father had financed all this was a mystery. Maybe he was lucky, and his father had stashed away a small fortune somewhere. That would be something, he thought.

Walt shook his head as he thought back to the conversation with the sheriff. When the cops had shown up at his door, he'd been sweating buckets. He'd been so sure the cops were onto him about the hit-and-run. When it became clear they were there because of his father's accident and not because of his attack on Cruz and Zelda, he had been relieved. He still was. But ever since he had heard about his father's death, he had also been angry. He didn't care about his father. He could burn in hell for all he cared. And he probably was that very moment. But he hadn't been done with his father, damn it! He had almost managed to finally gain the respect he had longed for. And now that chance was gone. Forever.

He didn't know how, but Zelda and Cruz would pay for it. Nobody got in his way with impunity. That much was certain.

He stepped closer to the table. A dust-free rectangle suggested where the laptop had sat. To the right were densely written papers arranged in two stacks. The police had deemed the documents irrelevant to their investigation.

Curious, he reached for the top folder. A yellowish piece of paper was inside. His heart beat faster. Could it really be... Indeed! It was the treasure map his father had always kept from him. Walt pulled the old paper out of its protective cover. Fascinated, he stared at the old drawing with its cryptic symbols. He let his eyes wander to the stack of other papers. Had his father recorded his findings? That'd be great. After all, he had always claimed lately to be on the verge of unraveling the mystery.

He pulled up the wobbly chair and delved into the map.

A few days later, Adela's funeral took place. Zelda arrived with Cruz. They stood on the hill behind the church and watched as a few women from the congregation held an impromptu service. Zelda grimaced. Church service was probably the wrong word. Although Adela had been a devout Catholic to the end, according to her loyal friends, she'd observed a somewhat idiosyncratic interpretation of Scripture. Because of this, the priest refused to say Mass. So, her closest confidants planned the funeral.

Zelda stepped from one foot to the other. The strong wind tugged at her hair, causing her to pull her black wool coat tighter around. Underneath, she wore a black dress and black, high-heeled boots. On impulse, she had completed the mourning ensemble with a scarf the color of flowering poppies. Her tribute to the dazzling personality of the deceased.

Cruz bristled when he saw it. She wasn't sure if he simply liked what he saw or if the bright splash of color irritated him. She suspected it was more the latter. She knew he liked *her*. That much had become clear. Even with all her curves and bumps, which was just fantastic for her self-esteem.

Was he now her... boyfriend? Lover? Crap. She had successfully avoided that conversation so far out of sheer cowardice. She shuddered as the possible outcomes of such a discussion flashed through her mind. She suspected he was not so sure that the color red was really appropriate for such an occasion. He was wearing a black suit, a snow-white shirt, and black cashmere coat. When she felt the soft wool under her fingertips, she didn't want to let him go.

Cruz must have sensed her shivering and pulled her closer.

Gratefully, she snuggled into his arm. She glanced at the surprisingly large group of mourners and noticed there were many familiar faces. She'd met more residents as a pharmacist than she realized.

After the ceremonial part was over, some came forward and told how Adela had helped them with an illness. Zelda pricked up her ears when the helpful cures were mentioned.

The general consensus was that Adela had been very gruff and aloof, but always extended a helping hand. Zelda could vividly imagine it: those seeking help first had to pass the shotgun test, though.

"Who would have thought," Cruz said.

"What do you mean?" asked Zelda.

He gestured toward the congregation "That my great-aunt was held in such high esteem."

"Didn't you know?"

"No. She was never like that with us. Like this..." He shrugged. "Listening to everyone, I get the impression she actually cared about people."

"She wasn't like that to you?"

Cruz shook his head. "Our family was always ruled with an iron fist. That's not to say family wasn't important to her. On the contrary."

"She just went about it the wrong way."

Cruz snorted. "I guess you can say that again. Especially now that we know she masterfully orchestrated the whole drama fourteen years ago."

"I think she realized what she had done," she said. "Her reclusive lifestyle and conflicting willingness to help others was her way of making amends."

"A more direct approach like an apology would have done more for me," he said.

"Understandable," Zelda said. Adela had apologized to her, even if indirectly. During her mourning for Cruz, she'd realized how precious time was spent with loved ones. She doubted he wanted to hear as much though, so she just silently squeezed his hand. There was time to philosophize later.

Cruz returned the gesture. Inside him, a wide variety of emotions were battling with each other. Grief for a relative he'd almost never known. Anger that the opportunity to get to know her all over again had been taken so suddenly. Jealousy that Zelda had spoken to her and he hadn't, even though he knew that was idiotic. After all, he hadn't even thought about his great-aunt in the past few years since he'd been back in Independence and had never tried to visit her. That was his fault. Nevertheless, it annoyed him. At the same time, he was grateful for Zelda's presence. She calmed him and gave him strength.

He pondered Perkins' questionable involvement in Adela's death. He'd love to ask the son of a bitch some questions. But it was too late for that.

Zelda moved and leaned against him. Her presence reminded him that sometimes there was a second chance. He rested his cheek against her temple and wrapped his other arm around her waist. Zelda raised her head and smiled up at him. Yes. Definitely. Second chances were priceless. So, he better put that idiotic jealousy out of his mind and focus on maintaining his newfound happiness with such an incredible woman.

Filled with determination, he waited with Zelda in his arms until most of the people left. Then he took her by the hand and followed the others.

On the way to the diner, where the Diner Sisters had prepared some delicacies and a drink for everyone, Zelda cast a furtive glance at the man at her side. Whereas before he'd made a bad impression, he suddenly radiated calm and composure. His thumb stroked the back of her hand, and he turned to her. Her heart skipped as she looked into his eyes. Something had changed. If she was to trust the hopeful acrobatics of the organ in her chest, this change could only mean something good. Unable to hide her good mood, she gave him a smile.

Cruz flinched, which turned into a smile. Somehow it seemed out of place to him at first, so soon after a funeral, but to hell with protocol. Life went on and was too short to be sad.

CHAPTER TWENTY

Cruz had barely unlocked the door to his office when Zelda impatiently stormed into the room. During the drink at the diner, they had gotten back to talking about the treasure. She couldn't wait to finally see the map with her own eyes.

Cruz followed her. He enjoyed watching her walk. Her swaying hips, the curls that fell wildly over her shoulders, the high-heeled shoes... He could think of all sorts of things they could do in his office. Studying a treasure map was not among them. Considering his wild ideas, he paused on his way to the desk and returned once more to the door to lock it.

Zelda arrived at his desk. When she heard the click of the key, she turned.

Cruz winked. "Better to be prepared, right?"

"I can't believe the direction your mind is taking," she laughed. She sat on the tabletop and crossed one leg over the other.

Cruz hurried toward her. She looked enchanting. The surprising thing was she didn't even seem aware. Her cheeks were flushed. The hem of her dress had ridden up past her knee, revealing a seductively rounded thigh. Farther up, mysterious shadows invited him to explore. He'd been an idiot to keep such a distance.

Cruz clasped her head with both hands to kiss her. "We have unfinished plans for this desk," he said. Impatiently, he ran his hand across the desk to make room. When the way was clear, he bent over her. With one hand on her back, he carefully lowered her onto the wide tabletop. "This is what I've been dreaming about."

"All this time?" she repeated. "Then why didn't you come to me?"

"I don't know. Apparently, men are idiots," he admitted.

Zelda drew in her breath sharply and stretched out an arm. Promptly, a small Post-it notepad fell to the ground.

The sound reminded Zelda of the original reason they'd come. "What about the treasure map?"

Treasure map. *Treasure map?* Cruz straightened up. "Obviously, I need to work on my technique."

"Your technique?"

"Well, how can you think of treasure after I'm about to seduce you into hot sex on my desk?"

"Multitasking," Zelda said, grinning. She straightened up and smoothed her skirt. "And since I've obviously succeeded in killing the mood, you might as well show me the map."

"Oh, I don't know. I'm sure with a little effort you'll bring the mood back to life," he said.

Zelda put a hand on his shoulder and pushed him away. "Come on now. The treasure map. I'll buy you dinner tonight and make it up to you."

Cruz conceded defeat. "Well, hopefully."

He pushed off the table, walked around it, and opened a drawer. At the top, carefully wrapped in a clear sleeve, was the yellowish parchment. He gave it to Zelda, and she studied the drawings.

"Are you finished?" asked Cruz after five minutes.

She looked up. "Finished? I'm nowhere near finished. May I make a copy of this?"

Cruz rolled his eyes. "You can keep the damn thing for all I care."

Zelda brightened. "Really? Are you sure?"

"I'm sure. Now come on. I remember a certain woman taking me out to dinner and stuff."

"And stuff?"

Cruz nodded.

She winked at him mischievously.

"Yeah. Stuff."

"Well, then..." She leaned forward and kissed him. "Let's not waste any more time."

"Best idea of the day," he said, holding the door open for her.

"Did you know the treasure was left behind by Napoleon's soldiers?"

Cruz groaned.

Zelda looked up. "Did you say something?"

Cruz hurried to cough. He didn't want to let on how much the "treasure hunt" topic was getting on his nerves. He imagined the evening a little different. True, they'd warmed up and eaten the bacon and bean soup from the diner. That would have been quite peaceful, if Zelda hadn't made assumptions about the map and its meaning. Eventually, he'd been so annoyed he suggested they postpone the questions. But no sooner had they finished eating than Zelda grabbed her laptop and disappeared into the internet.

He tried to help. "What were the French doing in the Rockies?"

He didn't care about the answer. He didn't care about the treasure. His treasure was sitting in front of him. Ignoring him. He sighed.

Zelda was so engrossed in her finds she didn't notice Cruz's lack of enthusiasm. She had always been like that. If something interested her, she no longer saw or heard anything outside her focus.

"These traditions confirm what you've already told me. Except here are the missing details. And without the curse, of course," she said.

"Yeah, yeah, all right. Tell me."

"Originally, the mountain was not called Treasure Mountain, but Citadel Mountain. According to legend, this changed with an expedition launched by Napoleon at the end of the eighteenth century. The latter urgently needed money to finance his ambitious military and political plans."

"And that's when he went looking for gold on the other side of the Atlantic, of all places?" asked Cruz.

Zelda shrugged. "Apparently so. After all, he sent out three hundred men and four hundred and fifty horses. He was very sure of success."

"Was he?"

"They weren't doing bad. Until they found the gold."

"Wait a minute," Cruz interrupted, "What route did they take to get to America?"

"They started in New Orleans."

"Logical, actually. It was a French expedition."

"Exactly. From there they moved across the area that is today Kansas westward to the Rocky Mountains."

"Where exactly did they find it?"

"The Wolf Creek Pass area."

"That's where Treasure Mountain is," Cruz noted.

"They found gold, and a lot of it. But with the find, their problems began."

"Problems?" Cruz sat up.

"The area was Indian territory, and they probably maintained a friendly relationship. But something seems to have caused the relationship between the two groups to deteriorate."

"What do you mean deteriorate?"

Zelda laughed. "If you believe the legend, it broke down to the point where the Indians sent out their warriors and chased the French out of the territory. The situation came to a head and the French had to leave the gold behind. They hid it and ran for their lives. However, few survived. The Indians were very thorough."

Cruz frowned. "Okay. I understand. But the survivors had to have been able to tell others were the gold was. Otherwise, the legend wouldn't exist."

"And there'd be no treasure map," Zelda said. "The historian of the group, a man named Le Blanc, managed to get back to New Orleans. Not only did he tell of the events that had occurred, but he produced two maps of the hidden treasure."

"Wow."

Zelda rubbed her hands together. "Incredible, isn't it?"

"Literally," Cruz said.

The story was exciting. That didn't mean Adela's map was one. On the contrary.

"What do you mean?" asked Zelda.

"Think about it. How long did it take you to find this information? Twenty minutes? Half an hour?"

"Yeah, something like that."

"The way I see it, the treasure either never existed or it

was found a long time ago, if it was possible to ever find. Treasure hunters are as old as mankind. You're not the first and you won't be the last to catch the fever."

Cruz leaned over to her and glanced at the open browser window on her screen. He quickly skimmed the parts Zelda had already told him about. At the bottom, he spotted a reference to a failed expedition. "Look," he pointed. "Years later, there was a second expedition to recover the gold."

"I saw," Zelda said.

"But they didn't find anything."

"Why do you think I didn't tell you about this?" she asked.

Cruz read the details of the failed expedition. Injured mules, deaths among the expedition members, and no treasure.

"The curse," Cruz said.

"Or poor preparation," Zelda countered. "At least the two mountain lakes and a creek were named after him. The Yule Lakes and Yule Creek."

"Small comfort when you've been hoping for treasure."

"Wait a minute..." Zelda reached for the map and a hiking guide. After some flipping through the hiking maps and checking with Adela's map, she said, "The lakes."

"What about them?"

Cruz returned to his place on the sofa and watched Murphy. The cat sat on the windowsill and looked out into the garden. The tip of his tail twitched as he absorbed the evening cat television program. Outside, the city had turned purple in the twilight. On the horizon, the last bright yellow streaks from the already-set sun could still be seen. Beautiful.

"Cruz?"

"What?" He'd been so absorbed in the beautiful view that he missed what she'd said.

"Are you even listening?"

"Of course."

"You remember the lake where Adela's cabin is?"

"Sure." He shrugged. "What about it?"

"This is one of the Yule Lakes," Zelda explained. "See for yourself." She pushed the map toward him.

Without reaching, Cruz stared at it, thunderstruck. That was not possible. Or was it? A dark foreboding gripped him. He swallowed and stood.

"Impossible. Even if it were, I don't want anything to do with that damn gold."

Cruz grabbed his coat and rushed to the door. He paused and turned to Zelda.

"I don't know why this treasure is so important to you. After all, it's only money. If your pharmacy is in trouble, then there are other possibilities. And another thing: If the treasure is in the immediate vicinity of the cabin, why didn't Adela ever recover it? Ever thought about that?"

Without waiting to see if Zelda had anything to say, he opened the door and disappeared.

Speechless, Zelda stared. Finally, she looked over at Murphy. "Did he actually just leave?" she asked the cat. "Without a goodbye kiss or any other word?"

Murphy lifted his front paw and began to clean his face.

"Wow. So much male understanding."

Somewhat lost, she stared at the hiking guide, the map, and her laptop. On the coffee table, she spotted the empty soup plates from the dinner. She'd imagined the outcome of the evening differently.

He probably did too, whispered the annoying voice in the back of her head. "Since when did you take his side?" she hissed back mentally. Too late. The first pangs of conscience had already crept in and spread. After all, she had intended to leave the subject alone.

Like a moth attracted to light, her eyes fell on the old map again. She would have loved to have gone off to look for the treasure. With her bare hands, if necessary. If she found the treasure, it'd all worth it.

She frowned as Cruz's last words echoed. Her pharmacy in trouble? What an arrogant guy. He believed she was motivated by greed. He didn't know her at all. She was concerned with the search. Finding the treasure would be like finishing the story from fourteen years ago. Okay, maybe more like over two hundred years ago, she corrected herself.

Maybe she really should go up the mountain, darkness be damned. The temptation was great. Involuntarily, she fumbled in her sweatshirt jacket for her car keys. Murphy jumped from the windowsill, marched up to her, and bumped his forehead against her legs.

She bent down and held out her hand. "Hey, handsome. You hungry?"

Murphy meowed loudly.

"Always trouble with the staff," she laughed, and followed him into the kitchen. On the way, she put her car keys on the windowsill; the sudden urge to look for the treasure was lost.

Murphy pricked up his ears when he heard the jingle of the keys on the wood. Satisfied, he blinked and turned his attention to his next goal: eating.

CHAPTER TWENTY-ONE

Walt carried out the next load of rocks and boulders beside the entrance to the crevice. With one hand he wiped the sweat from his flushed forehead. Promptly, fine dust got into his eyes. He cursed and rubbed.

He'd been searching for this damned treasure for two weeks. He'd quit his job and devoted himself to the treasure hunt. With the groundwork his old man had done, it should be child's play. But his search had not yet been crowned with success. His money was running out. If he didn't find something soon, he'd have to find work. The thought made him sick. Again, for peanuts, day after day. No, thanks.

He liked to imagine all the things he'd do with the gold. Travel. Expensive cars. Beautiful women. His mouth watered. The sight of the dirt at his feet jolted him back to reality.

As in the other places where he'd tried his luck, he had used dynamite first. Grateful for his father's hoarding tendencies, Walt found the dynamite in the shed. After a lifetime as an accountant, he faced a whole new set of challenges. He hadn't realized how much you had to know to be successful outside the legal world. He at least knew enough not to search the internet for explosives, where people could track such activities back to him. So he had been relieved to discover his old man had stashed the stuff in quantities. Probably in preparation for his militia. He was surprised the police hadn't confiscated the stuff too.

The dynamite was priceless. He saw no need to exhaust himself at the very beginning of his search. All the dirty work that followed the blasting was exhausting enough. In purely theoretical terms, the entrance to the hideout had to be large enough to accommodate the massive gold treasure. Since he had not discovered a cave large enough in the immediate vicinity of the hiding place indicated on the map, he had resorted to the theory that perhaps the entrance had been buried in the last few hundred years. Slowly he came to the same conclusion as his father: the map was not complete. And maybe it was wrong entirely.

Adela betrayed his father. Too bad the old witch was gone. He would have coaxed the truth out of her. By force, if necessary. The only question was: Who had the right map?

He threw his spade to the ground. The damn thing was probably in Adela's cabin. Thinking that he would need to search the woman's miserable dwelling, he suddenly remembered that she had a great-nephew. What was his name? Carlos? Definitely some foreign name, he thought. He had no idea whether he was an actual heir, but it seemed obvious he would be given the task of taking care of her estate.

A visit to the diner was the order of the day. He'd learn everything he needed to know there. It would be easier if Adela's cabin was untouched. No one would get in his way up there. But a nighttime visit to her great-nephew would not be a problem. A break-in probably couldn't be that hard. He grinned.

"Walt," Miss Minnie greeted her guest. "Long time no see. Because of your father, I suppose."

Walt nodded.

"A beer?"

"Sure."

When Miss Minnie returned, she commented, "I heard you quit?"

She knew that? he wondered. "Yes," he answered. "I need a change in life."

She patted his arm. "Everyone grieves differently."

He almost laughed out loud. As if he would mourn the old man. On the contrary. He was glad he had died. His father would never have shared the treasure. Fortunately, Miss Minnie didn't expect an answer and turned to other customers.

When she happened to be near him again, he asked, "Did Adela have any relatives?"

Surprised, she turned to him. "Didn't you know? Cruz Ruis is her great-nephew."

"I see." He just had to figure out who that was.

"He's sitting over there," Miss Minnie revealed.

Walt turned. Indeed, it was the guy he'd almost run off the road. Cruz Ruis. One of those foreigners. Surely, he was here illegally. All the more reason to take the real treasure map from him. He certainly had no right to the gold.

Cruz stood and said goodbye to his friends. Without taking his eyes off his prey, Walt reached into his pants pocket, pulled out a five-dollar bill, left it on the table, and stood.

Miss Minnie stared after him as he made his way to the door at the same time as Cruz. Strange. She hadn't even known they knew each other. Well. She couldn't know everything either. Still, it pained her. After all, she prided herself on always being well informed about everything. She shrugged her shoulders and continued her work.

Cruz didn't know what was going on. Since lunch, he felt like he was being watched. But every time he turned around, there was no one there. Or at least no one acting suspiciously. Just the usual passersby who populated Independence. Still, he was sure there was someone there who didn't belong.

His senses were honed in the gang-infested environment in California where he'd spent his senior year of high school. It paid to listen to his gut. After all, it had helped him avoid being pulled to the dark side. Despite his caution, he still had his struggles. In the end, his reputation guaranteed a relatively peaceful high school life.

His martial arts training with Pat ensured he retained his reflexes and intuition. Pat, who had a similar background, was involved with Tyler Carter, a former star ballerina. Tyler owned the building that housed Jaz's yoga school. On the ground floor, the unusual couple ran a dance school-slash-Aikido dojo. Depending on the time of day, classical music, hot rhythms, or meditation music rang out from the building. It was Pat he called, not Tyler. Perhaps it would have been more prudent to call the sheriff. But in case he was wrong, and it was a false alarm, he didn't want to burden the community's police.

Cruz locked his office and left the building. He'd managed to persuade Zelda to spend an evening with him for the first time in two weeks. She promised to postpone all treasure talk until dessert. It was up to him to arrange the evening to ensure she didn't bring up the subject. He had a few ideas. Fantasies flitted fleetingly through his mind all day.

As he stepped out into the street, he spotted Pat standing across the street, tying his shoes. Pat scratched his head, the agreed-upon sign he'd seen him. Cruz switched the briefcase to his other hand, his own signal to Pat to let him know the game could begin. He glanced behind at the street. There was no one standing out in any way. Still, the tingle on the back of his neck continued.

Soon he'd know more. He had no doubt that he and Pat would be able to track down the stalker in no time.

Slowing his pace, he stopped at one of the various shop windows slowly filling with life. He spotted a gift store that had apparently opened a few days ago, the bookstore he knew, and a barricaded store where a sign painted with brush and paint promised the imminent opening of a sports store. Not bad for a small town, Cruz thought. The tingle on the back of his neck grew stronger. Oops. He'd probably better concentrate on the task at hand.

Walt was sweating, even though the sun had set. Were his nerves going crazy? The first part of his plan had worked brilliantly. Tracking Cruz had been a piece of cake. Unfortunately, he hadn't gone home, but returned to his workplace. So he waited. And waited. Not wanting to risk missing Cruz, he hadn't eaten since that morning. No wonder he was in a bad mood. At least he had found entrance to an empty house where he was twice able to use the bathroom. The idea that he could be discovered at any time had given him quite a kick.

Probably a delayed reaction to being a policeman's son. No matter how corrupt he had been, Perkins had always demanded top tier behavior from his son, or else it'd mean a beating.

At the memory, his old familiar rage rose up. He spat on the sidewalk while keeping an eye on Cruz. Who the hell was working so late? In his own way, the guy was just as crazy as the old man. Cruz didn't seem to be in a hurry. He stopped at every damn store and studied the display in each window as if the crown jewels were on display. True, the slow pace made it easier to keep an eye on him. On the other hand, he had to be careful not to attract attention when he stopped in the middle of the sidewalk for seemingly no reason.

Nervously, he fingered the collar of his shirt, which seemed too tight, and cast a quick glance over his shoulder. Something was different. Like someone was stalking him. Bullshit, he thought. Why would someone be following him? There wasn't the slightest reason. For most people he was invisible anyway. He continued shadowing. The queasy feeling remained.

"Don't you think you're obsessing a little?" asked Charlie as she peered over Zelda's shoulder.

For the past two weeks, Zelda had spent every spare minute up on the mountain at Adolu's cabin, exploring the area during long hikes. When it got dark, she'd continue research with Charlie at the bookstore, where she scoured through every available map and treasure hunter's guide. At first Charlie had laughed about it, but slowly became concerned, making comments about this as being unhealthy.

She wasn't the only one. Jaz had made similar comments at yoga.

"Obsessing? What do you mean?" asked Zelda, annoyed.

"You don't have to hiss at me," her friend said. "But it's half past seven."

"So what?"

Charlie shook her head. "Didn't you tell me you had a date with Cruz tonight?"

Cruz. Zelda's head shot up and she looked from one wall of the cozy bookstore to the other. The store was empty except for her friend and her friend's son Ethan, who was sitting cross-legged in front of the fireplace doing homework.

"Crap. Is it really that late?" Zelda glanced at the papers in front of her.

"It is. So make sure you get home and get in the shower."

Zelda frowned. "Let me just finish this calculation, then..."

"Nothing there," Charlie said, closing the book on the table.

"Hey...!" protested Zelda.

"You'll thank me at your wedding," Charlie said.

"Which you won't be invited to if you keep being like this," Zelda grumbled.

"If I don't, there won't be a wedding at all."

"Maybe she doesn't want to get married," Ethan said.

Charlie rolled her eyes. "That was meant more as a reminder that there are things in life that are more important than gold."

Hurt, Zelda winced. Charlie didn't understand what the treasure meant. It was the cause of everything that happened back then. Why didn't her friend see it was an attempt to come to terms with her past? If she found the treasure, all the sacrifices, all her grief, and all the shame she'd experienced would be worth it. Suddenly, she felt very alone.

Zelda packed up her things and reached for the books on the table.

Perhaps she would have time at home to devote to her research.

"This stays here." Charlie unceremoniously took the stack of books.

She stared at her friend in disbelief. *No matter*, she thought. She could search one of the forums on the internet. Charlie couldn't stop her from that, could she?

"Do you think there's anything to the curse?" asked Ethan.

Charlie closed the door behind Zelda. "The curse?"

"Haven't you heard?" her son asked with the horrified incredulity of a budding teenager.

"No, I haven't," she said.

"According to the rumors, these treasure maps have only ever brought bad luck to everyone involved," Ethan said.

"Superstition. After all, no one has found it yet."

"It's more than that. Time and again, there are said to have been people who succumbed to the lure of gold."

"That rumor is nothing new, after all. This desire to find treasure is as old as humans."

"That may be. But this treasure, which is believed to lie under Treasure Mountain, is said to captivate people. They become addicted to finding the gold. The old sheriff did nothing else since he retired," he said. "And look how he ended up, a hermit, with no friends, only to find death at the bottom of a canyon, without a gold coin in sight."

"Oh dear," Charlie muttered. Of course, she didn't believe

in curses. They were nothing more than fairy tales. But she had to admit that it explained Zelda's feverish look and strange behavior.

"It wasn't much different with Adela," her son said. "Even if she resisted the pull of treasure hunting in recent years."

"How do you know this?"

"From school, of course. Curses are really exciting."

"As long as you stay away from curses..."

"Mom. I don't believe in that kind of thing.

"Are you coming up? I'll cook us something."

Like lightning, Ethan flipped his math notebook shut and jumped up.

Charlie watched him. Boys his age were always hungry. She felt like she had to buy the entire mini mart every other day. But she couldn't imagine a life any other way. As difficult as being a single mother could be, she wouldn't trade it for anything in the world.

Especially not for cursed treasure. She hoped Zelda would come to her senses. Otherwise, she would have to start an intervention. Jaz and the others would help.

Satisfied to have a plan in mind, she followed Ethan upstairs to the small apartment above the store.

CHAPTER TWENTY-TWO

Cruz's coat pocket vibrated. Finally, he thought, and pulled out his cell phone. About time Pat got in touch. At the slow pace he'd been going, he already felt like a tortoise on a long-awaited shopping trip. Pat's text message was short.

You definitely have a tail. Looks harmless. Male, stocky, gray casual jacket, bald head. Seems nervous. How do you want to proceed?

Cruz felt his pulse rate quicken at confirmation of his suspicions. All right, he thought. He'd find out what the idiot stupid enough to tail him wanted. He smiled.

But Zelda! He remembered her appointment.

Bakerstreet. I'll take care of it. You got my back?

He pocketed his phone and continued to Bakerstreet—a small alley off the main road. The ideal place for a private conversation.

Walt almost lost sight of Cruz when he sped up and hurried down the street. Where was he going? He pushed past two older women, almost threw a child off his scooter, and saw Cruz turn into a side alley. Was that his apartment back there? Panting, Walt hurried after his victim. Strange. He could have bet the guy in the posh suit lived at a fancier address. But looks could be deceiving, he thought. Out of breath, he hurried around the corner behind which the other man had disappeared.

Pressed against the wall behind a rain gutter, Cruz listened to the ambient sounds. Voices of passersby. Ubiquitous sparrows. The hiss of a wire. Heavy footsteps. A whistling sound like heavy breathing.

Patiently, he waited for the right moment. When he thought he could feel the hot breath of his pursuer, he stretched out his right leg. Perhaps not the most elegant of methods, but very effective.

Accompanied by a series of dazzling curses, the corpulent man fell lengthwise.

The dull thud that accompanied the impact of the body echoed in the narrow alley.

Cruz didn't wait and was at the guy in one leap, his foot on his neck. The guy didn't look very threatening. Had he even caught the right guy?

"Are you all right?" Pat's voice sounded from the background at that moment.

"Is that the guy?" asked Cruz over his shoulder.

"That's the one."

The man on the ground swung his arms, but Cruz's foot pressed him to the ground. Like a fish out of water, he gasped a few times before finally finding his voice. "Help! I've been attacked! Somebody help me!"

Cruz laughed. Pat joined in.

"Help! Police!" Walt cried.

"I'm looking forward to the conversation with the police," Cruz said. He reached down and lifted his pursuer's head so he could look him in the eye. "After all, you've been following me around all day, am I right?"

Walt shook his head.

Cruz loosened his grip. The pale light of the sparse street lighting fell on the man's face. He stumbled. "What's your name?" He pressed his foot a little harder against the man's neck.

"Walt. Walt Perkins."

Surprised, Cruz let go.

"Perkins? Like the sheriff?"

"Yeah, sure. Who else. Now let me up," scolded Walt. He scrambled to his feet and patted his clothes off.

"And why did you follow me?"

"I wanted to offer my... condolences," Walt replied.

"Offer your condolences?"

"Yes. After all, our elders died together. It seemed appropriate," he said.

"Uh-huh." How on earth did he know the other guy? An image of a man behind the wheel of the vehicle that had run them off the road flashed in his mind's eye. Had that been him? He wasn't sure. "What kind of car do you drive?"

"Car?"

"Yeah. You know, the thing with the four wheels?"

"An old Chevy."

Cruz took a step back. "No offense, Perkins. But next time you want something from me, you better come straight. I don't like people sneaking up."

Walt swallowed. "All right."

"Now get out of here."

With a scowl in Cruz's direction, Walt hurried out of the alley.

"Well, that wasn't very productive." Pat stepped out of the shadows.

"No, it wasn't."

"Do you think he'll leave you alone?"

Cruz shrugged. "I hope so."

Pat patted him on the shoulder. "You know where to find me."

"Thank you."

Pat grinned. "Then I'll say goodbye. I have a lovely wife and a great dog waiting. Definitely better company than you."

Amused, Cruz shook his head and raised his hand in farewell. At the same time, he felt a spark of envy. His friend had already found what he hoped for with Zelda. He sighed. As it was, he had a long way to go before Zelda attached the same importance to their relationship. He was in a competition with a damn treasure of gold. How was he going to win?

A glance at the clock showed him he was already too late for her appointment. Oh, great. He'd hardly win her heart that way. Best he went directly to Zelda. He could take a shower at her place. In a noticeably better mood, he got on his way.

Walt, who had gotten over the initial shock, didn't think about giving up. He just had to pay more attention. Boiling with rage, he brushed the dirt off his jacket. The bastard had almost flattened his windpipe. As soon as he turned the corner, he stopped. There he waited again for Cruz to make his way home.

He couldn't believe his luck when Cruz's friend was the first to leave. To avoid detection, he retreated deeper into the shadows of the front entrance and held his breath until the other had passed. He breathed a sigh of relief. One less problem.

Shortly thereafter, his target reappeared at a greater distance, and Walt resumed his pursuit.

Worried that Zelda would be angry because he was half an hour late, Cruz lengthened his stride. He grimaced. Once again, he'd done a great job. It took him two weeks to convince her to go out with him, and then he didn't even manage to be on time. Really mature.

Suddenly, the tingling sensation in his neck came back. Irritated, he rubbed the spot. What was going on now? Did he have a second pursuer? It was probably just his fear and some after-effects after the confrontation with the stalker. Impatiently, he pushed the thoughts away and concentrated on his way.

Finally, Zelda's little house came into view. Once he was there, he ran his hand through his hair before knocking.

No response.

He knocked again while stepping from one leg to the other and peering through the window. The kitchen was empty. *I wonder if she was still in the shower. Probably not. I'm so late.*

Murphy emerged from the darkness of the garden and stroked his legs, purring. Cruz bent down. "Well, how are you? Where's your mom?" Instead of an answer, the cat pushed his forehead against his fingers. "I see. You'd rather be pet than talk about Zelda," Cruz laughed and squatted down.

Zelda sat, pencil in hand, in front of her maps. The old treasure map seemed to mock her. She almost thought she could hear how countless unsuccessful treasure hunters before her had tapped the walls of the various caves and crevices. Frowning, she followed the marked route again. If only she knew what the various cryptic symbols meant. The tapping repeated. Irritated, she shook her head, but the tapping did not stop. As if emerging from a dream, she blinked twice. The sound was coming from her front door, she realized. Not quite there yet, she glanced at her watch. Was she expecting someone? Cruz! The date! She looked down. She was still wearing the same clothes she'd been wearing all day. She hadn't showered yet either. Where had the time gone?

You forgot, she thought. *Didn't you?*

She glanced at the chaos that reigned over her coffee table. Didn't she intend to let the treasure be, at least for the evening? Looking at the old map, she felt the urge to get behind her quest again. A shudder ran over her, and she deliberately took a step away from the table. The whole thing was scary. But she simply couldn't escape the pull.

Another knock, much more impatient, jolted her.

She hurried toward the front door.

Cruz's guilty conscience evaporated. It was obvious Zelda had forgotten. When she opened the door seconds later, a guilty expression on her face, his suspicions were confirmed. Her cheeks were flushed, her hair disheveled.

"Cruz!"

"Surprised to see me?"

Zelda blushed. "No!" she said. "Of course not."

Cruz raised an eyebrow skeptically.

"Well, that is... not really." She grimaced and ducked her head. "Only halfway. Will you give me ten minutes? I'll get ready really quick. If you want, you can look at my notes."

Cruz waved his hands. "You know what? Forget it."

"No, I..."

"If the treasure is so important to you, then let's just forget it. You concentrate on your treasure hunt, and I'll concentrate on my life."

He turned to leave.

"Wait. I think I figured out why Adela sent your family away."

"Really?"

"I have a strong hunch. Are you coming in?"

"Okay. But only if you promise to forget about gold and treasure maps for the rest of the evening."

"I'll try, I promise."

Cruz smiled. "I'll help you take your mind off it."

"Deal."

Walt couldn't believe his luck. After realizing that Cruz hadn't gone home, he almost stopped tailing him. Only his curiosity caused him to stop behind the cherry tree and listen. When the words treasure and treasure map had come up, he pricked up. It was as he suspected: there was a second map. For some reason it wasn't in Cruz's possession, but in Zelda's. All the better. After the unpleasant encounter with the guy, he dreaded breaking into his house. But Zelda was just a woman. That was not a problem. Soon he'd pay her a visit. His mouth twisted into a smug grin. Soon he'd be rich as Croesus.

When the words *date* and *I'll -get-ready* came up, he listened. Were they going out? This was getting better and better. He wanted to see if they actually left the house.

He inconspicuously moved to the other side of the street and made himself comfortable in the shade of a hedge. Walt was grateful to the bastard. He'd led him straight to his destination.

CHAPTER TWENTY-THREE

Less than an hour later, Zelda and Cruz were sitting together at the Silver Lodge. He could hardly believe he'd succeeded in getting her out of the house. Over the edge of his menu, he studied the woman who fascinated and frustrated him in equal measure. The candlelight made golden points of light glisten in her dark curls.

His girlfriend.

Was she, though? They'd never talked about it or put a name to what they had. Maybe a conversation would be good? His heart wrenched at the idea she might disagree. He wanted to spend endless time with her instead of discussing something that was working. *Nothing more than a meaningless label*, he thought. *Coward*. There was no way he was going to lose Zelda again after they finally got back together. He looked around the restaurant.

The Silver Lodge was a newer establishment that had opened four years earlier. In the financial crisis, the then-owner had lost his log cabin. The current owners, a gay couple named Jeff and Jarvis, had stepped in and made their dream of a Michelin-starred restaurant a reality. Only organic ingredients went into their cooking. Cooking was something where the two of them excelled.

They maintained a good relationship with their service staff and paid reasonable wages, so there was always a pleasant atmosphere in the restaurant. The service was impeccable.

A little more than a year prior, the Silver Lodge had almost burned down. Some members of the mob had engaged in a shootout with Avery, Cole, and the rest of their team in the course of an FBI investigation that had gotten out of hand. Clever as Jeff and Jarvis were, they hadn't completely reno-vated everything, but had left some remnants standing in strategic places that bore witness to the violent incident. This allowed them to make the most of the story for promotional purposes. There were many who got a kick out of dining at the scene of a crime.

All those points, however, led to the Silver Lodge charging rather high prices. Completely justified, Cruz believed. Zelda was worth it. He hadn't picked the restaurant because of its glittering past though, but because of its romantic ambience. If he interpreted the sparkle in her eyes, he had hit the mark with his choice. "Do you know what you want yet?" he asked.

"Difficult, difficult. But I think so."

He smiled. "And that would be?"

"I opt for the salad with braised lamb strips and warm goat cheese."

"Is that all?"

"No, no," she laughed. "If I'm going to get to enjoy Jeff and Jarvis' much-lauded cuisine, I want an appetizer. The crostini with the beet hummus sounds fantastic." She flipped the menu closed and looked at him. "And what about you?"

"I'll join you on the crostini. Hmm. And after that, I'll try the monthly special: pasta with Cajun-style chicken." He shifted in his seat. "Who knows when they'll have New Orleans week again. In my time in California, I was exposed to the cuisines of many different countries and regions, and I developed a soft spot for spicy dishes of all kinds. That variety is one of the few things I miss here in Independence."

"At least there's Café Sweets and the pizza place now, in addition to the diner. It certainly sounds delicious," Zelda said. "Although I'll probably explode just looking at that combination of carbs and cream."

Cruz reached across the table for her hand. "Not true."

Zelda rolled her eyes. "That's very true. I have the metabolism of a Shetland pony. Leslie owns such a pony. According to Paula, all the animal has to do is look at a clump of hay and it gains a pound. I'm the same way. Not with hay, of course. But with pasta."

Cruz smirked at the funny comparison. "But I like you infinitely better than a pony. Plus or minus a pound. I like that you're round and soft where I have rough edges."

He raised his hand to her face and let the tip of his index finger glide from her cheek, down her neck, toward her lusciously rounded breasts.

Zelda's pupils dilated. Her cheeks turned pink. "Cruz!" she scolded but did not push his hand away. She glanced around the Lodge to see if anyone was watching. Phew. Lucky again. Behind her, someone cleared his throat. Her cheeks turned deep red.

"Ahem. We don't offer rooms, I'm afraid," one of the well-trained waiters said with a twinkle in his eye. "But perhaps we can provide a temporary distraction with our food?"

Cruz dropped his hand. Before turning to the waiter, he gave Zelda a smile that promised a sequel.

For the second time that evening, Zelda completely forgot about the treasure map and gold. Instead, all her senses were completely taken up by the man at her side. Her hormones, surfing through her blood, were totally off the hook. Her belly contracted in joyful anticipation. She was looking forward to getting home. But first, there was food. Very tasty food. So, she'd enjoy the evening. Calories or not.

"You meant earlier that you knew why Adela made sure we moved away?" Cruz interrupted her thoughts.

"Oh, yeah right." She gave him a surprised look. "I didn't think you'd bring up the subject again on your own."

Cruz gave her a contrite smile. "I'm sorry. I know I'm not very patient when it comes to this supposed treasure. I admit I've been almost jealous about it. The treasure gets your unrestricted attention at times. A little of that attention—okay, a big portion," he said, "I'd like for me. For us."

"Oh."

Zelda didn't know what to say. A spark of hope stirred in her like a butterfly emerging from its cocoon, slowly unfurling its wings. Maybe they could be more than just a rekindled affair. Should she ask? Better not. She'd rather revel in the feeling of possibility for a while. She cleared her throat. "You remember the summer before you moved?"

"Sure. We spent every spare minute together."

They had. Balmy summer nights under a starry sky, a mountain lake, meadows full of wildflowers, first kisses and endless conversations. The dream of every teenage girl. "We used to go to that spot by the lake. Until one day your great-aunt caught us red-handed."

"True," he said.

That had put an abrupt end to her nightly excursions.

Her parents had been shocked that the otherwise so well-behaved Zelda, who went to church every Sunday and only brought home good grades, actually had the courage to steal away in the night without permission to meet up with a boy. With that one, too. The son of a drunkard and troublemaker. As a result, they'd grounded Zelda for three weeks and never let her out of their sight. Cruz suspected her father kept watch in the backyard, shotgun in hand, the entire three weeks.

His aunt had wasted no time organizing for his family to move to sunny, faraway California. The evening they'd been caught was the last time he'd seen Zelda. So many missed years. Although, he knew the years apart had given them the opportunity to become the people they became. He winced. Zelda had thought he'd died. She could have done without that.

"And you think that had something to do with the treasure?" he asked.

"Think about it, what other reason could there have been to send your family away?" She gestured with her hands. "Adela made me understand that she wanted to preserve the treasure for the next generation. Yours, that is. I guess she didn't want to take the risk of you stumbling on her secret too soon. What do you think your father would have done with the money?"

"Ha. That's a simple question. Booze it up." Cruz laughed.

"See? Adela wanted to avoid that at all costs."

"That still doesn't explain why she went off on you like that."

"No. It doesn't." She shrugged. "Maybe she wanted to avoid me roaming around up by the lake out of sheer nostalgic feelings, meaning lovesickness. Maybe she was sad that she had to send you away, and indirectly blamed me. But really, it doesn't matter, don't you think?"

"That's an extremely generous view."

"Possibly. But it is hard for me to resent her. She has visibly regretted her actions, Cruz. What good will it do me to carry a grudge any longer? I'd rather focus on you."

"And the treasure."

Embarrassed, Zelda averted her eyes. "And the treasure," she admitted. "But let's talk about something else now, as we agreed."

Cruz was only too happy to comply.

When Cruz and Zelda had actually got into the car earlier and left from Zelda's house, Walt felt like jumping for joy. He didn't want to attract any unwanted attention, but his leg had fallen asleep during the wait. The beating Cruz had given him didn't help. He waited a few minutes, ensuring they hadn't forgotten something and would have to turn around.

He decided he'd waited long enough. The longer he put off his house search, the greater the chance they would return home.

The first place he tried his luck was the front door. Unfortunately, Zelda was not one of the careless residents of Independence who left the house without locking up. But he knew what to do. He bent down and picked up one of the large stones and crept around the house to the back door.

He took a swing and struck. There was a clang and a large hole shattered through the pane. He stood there frozen, waiting for someone in the neighborhood to sound the alarm. After five minutes and no reaction from neighbors, did he dare to feel relieved. Walt reached through the opening and turned the doorknob.

In no time he was standing in the house. What now? Of course, he didn't have a flashlight. Nor had he expected to go on a burglary spree. He decided to take the risk and turn on the light. There was nothing else he could do if he wanted to find something.

Systematically, he searched the kitchen before moving on to the living room. Right away, he discovered many books on the subject of treasure hunting. Bingo! The screen of her laptop was dark. Determined, he flipped it shut and tucked it under his arm. Underneath, he found a transparent sleeve, containing a map that looked like his. Too bad he didn't have his own with him. Otherwise, he could have swapped the two.

The inevitable damage to the door and the stolen computer made it clear someone had been in the house. Walt turned the map over in his hands before he pocketed it and carried the laptop into the kitchen. There he deposited the computer along with the map. If he wanted it to be treated as a normal burglary, he had to make it look like one.

Since he was sweating, he took off his jacket and hung it over one of the chairs. Then he set to work. He opened cupboards, dragged out the contents, and threw them to the floor. With a kitchen knife he worked on the sofa and the cushions. What he had first thought of as pure necessity turned out to be very liberating. He imagined Cruz, stuck-up Zelda, his miserable father, and all the other people who didn't see how great he was. He worked himself up into a frenzy.

Breathing heavily, he arrived at the upper floor. The bedroom was waiting. A lecherous grin stretched across his face. The large carving knife in his hand, he walked mind-lessly into the dark room.

As soon as he was inside, something hissed and attacked him. Its claws landed on his face.

A cat, he thought incredulously. A fucking cat had hidden in the room! He tried in vain to get rid of his animal attacker, but the darn critter had clawed its way into his chest.

Finally he got hold of the cat by the tail and flung it away.

With a primal scream, the devilish thing fled.

The left side of his face burned like fire.

Seconds later, he staggered backward out of the room, cursing violently. The knife fell to the floor and landed on the carpet.

He groped his way to the bathroom and took a cautious look in the mirror. Four bloody marks stretched across his face. What a mess. He grabbed a towel and wiped his face. Walt knew he wouldn't be able to go out among people for a few days if he didn't want to cause suspicion.

When he remembered he finally had the real map in his possession, his anger subsided. He had different plans than to be among people anyway. Despite the incessant throbbing in his face, he continued freshly motivated with his destructive action.

Fortunately, the bloodthirsty cat did not show up again.

Not half an hour later, he pulled the door shut behind him and walked out onto the street as if he didn't have a care in the world. He didn't. Not anymore, because the treasure was within reach. It had to be celebrated, he decided.

Slightly buzzed and dizzy from the good California red wine she'd enjoyed with her main course, Zelda leaned toward Cruz.

Cruz, who had to drive, had held back on drinking. Now he smirked, very taken with such a cuddly side of Zelda.

"Are you still coming in?" she said, leaning against his chest.

Cruz stroked the dark curls from her face to look into her eyes. It didn't do much good since her eyes were closed. Through the interior lights of the car, her eyelashes cast long shadows on her cheeks. Fine golden freckles covered her cheekbones and the bridge of her nose. "Should I?" he asked.

Zelda nodded. "Absolutely."

Cruz smiled. "Then I'll be very happy to."

He was sure Zelda would have fallen asleep the second her body touched the mattress. But he didn't care. He was content to finally have her to himself again and not have to vie for her attention with an old piece of parchment. Falling asleep beside her and waking up with her the next morning was enough.

Zelda smiled. "I'm glad." Full of anticipation, she got out of the car. While she was still walking to the door, she fished in her coat pocket for the key.

"You coming?" she called over her shoulder to Cruz.

"Yeah, I'm already there."

Amused and also a little flattered by Zelda's obvious delight he'd stay the night, he followed her.

Barely in the house, she stopped and gasped loudly. Alarmed, he hurried to her side. "What is it?"

Shocked, she pointed to the devastation. "That, that..." Stunned, she looked from one corner to the other.

"Someone broke in," Cruz said, pulling his cell phone from his pocket.

"Who on earth would do such a thing? I have nothing, no money, no jewelry..."

"I don't know either. But I promise you, we'll find out."

CHAPTER TWENTY-FOUR

They sat on the steps in front of the entrance and waited for the police. Jake promised to be there in ten minutes; he couldn't get there fast enough. Even though Cruz had his arm around her, she was cold. The little house had been her sanctuary. Her home. And someone had broken in, a stranger, and destroyed that magic. How was she ever going to feel at home again? Let alone spend the night? What was she supposed to do? Where was she going to go?

Zelda's upper body swayed. Cruz felt her shoulders rise and fall with each shaky breath. He knew such a way of breathing happened when you were trying not to repress your emotions.

He had a memory of how, fourteen years ago, he'd arrived home one evening to find his mother and sister packing, tears in their eyes. While the panic in his chest had grown at the thought of never seeing Zelda again, he'd demanded an explanation. His mother only shook her head while his father bragged that luck had finally come. Nothing made sense then. He remembered that all too well. His youthful instinct for self-preservation ensured he'd suppressed the memory. Secretly, he was relieved it came back. He had been wondering why it had been so easy for him to forget Zelda back then. The closer they got over the past weeks, the more incomprehensible it seemed.

Zelda sniffled and pulled up her nose. Cruz searched in his jacket for a handkerchief. When he found it, he held it under her nose. His gesture elicited a snort from Zelda, despite her tears. It didn't quite pass for laughter, perhaps, but still, it was something nice. Glad to have cheered her up a little, he pulled her closer.

Cruz imagined how the burglar had invaded her very private space. Knowing Zelda needed his support kept him from going in search of the culprit. He had a pretty good idea of who the burglar was, too. It was certainly no coincidence Zelda's house had been broken into on the same day he was being followed. God knows Independence was not an ideal world, but the two events were not coincidental.

Murphy came strutting around the corner and let out a questioning meow. "Oh dear, poor you. Your home has been turned upside down, too."

Zelda stretched out her arms to the cat. To her surprise, he marched straight to her and hopped onto her lap. "The poor thing is obviously in shock," Zelda said.

"Obviously," Cruz said.

"What am I going to do?" Zelda's voice sounded quite lost and as if she knew there was no answer.

"Well, that's obvious. You're coming with me." He gestured toward the house behind them. "I guess you can't stay here tonight."

Surprised, Zelda and the cat looked up at him. "To your place? Including the cat?"

"Sure." He pointed his chin at Murphy. "He certainly

doesn't look like he'll be letting you out of his sight anytime soon."

Zelda used the handkerchief to dry her damp cheeks before trying to free Murphy's claws, which were caught in the fine knitted fabric of her top. "Letting go of his claws is more like it," she said, nuzzling her face into the warm, contented purring of the otherwise aloof animal. It looked as if the cat had settled down on her for the time being. "He doesn't do things by halves either. Either all the way or not at all. I'm just wondering why he's sitting on me now instead of you. You're his favorite."

Cruz didn't have an answer. He shrugged.

At that moment, the police car drove up.

Jake and two of his deputies jumped out and approached.

Murphy stood up, humped, and hissed as the sheriff stopped beside them. He did not leave his place on Zelda's legs. "Would have been smarter if you'd waited in the car," Jake said. "Who knows if he's still in there."

"I don't think so. I haven't looked, though."

"Very good. That would have been extremely reckless, too. We're going in. In the meantime, please sit in your vehicle or go to the neighbors," Jake instructed.

Cruz gave Zelda a look. "Do you know your neighbors?"

Zelda shook her head.

"Well, come on, back in the car."

"We would have been better off staying in the car from the beginning," she said. Zelda tried to put the cat on the ground, but he clung to her with every claw at his disposal. "I'll just have to take him with me," she said apologetically to Cruz.

"No problem. We already decided he was coming along anyway."

Spontaneously, she wrapped her cat-free arm around his

waist and pulled him close to kiss him on the mouth. Surprisingly, Murphy abstained from any protest, even though he was squeezed between Cruz and Zelda during the kiss. Had he approved of the connection?

"What was that for?"

"For being who you are," she said and got into the car, the cat still in her arms.

A smile on his lips, he slipped into the car behind her.

A few minutes later, Jake knocked on the car window. Zelda lowered the window.

"There's no one in the house. The intruder got away."

Relieved, Zelda let herself fall back into the seat. She hadn't even been aware that she had been worried that the burglar might still be there. "That's good, isn't it?"

Jake grinned. "Any way you look at it. It would have been easier for me if he'd been stuck in the bathroom window. Would have made it easier to arrest him."

"Did he come through the bathroom?" Zelda asked with wide eyes.

Jake shook his head in denial. "No. He broke a window on the back door."

Zelda groaned. Not only was her little house completely devastated, but now she had to find a glazier. She really didn't have time for that. With work and the treasure hunt, she was completely occupied. *The map! Her documents!* They had probably also fallen victim to the burglar's destructive frenzy.

"Zelda?" asked Cruz, shaking her shoulder.

"What is it?" she asked as she became aware of the concerned looks on the faces of the two men.

"Jake asked if you felt well enough to go through the

house. It would be good if you could make a list of the things that are missing."

She felt really sick at the thought of walking through her home.

"But we can put it off until tomorrow if you'd rather not go in there today," Cruz assured her caringly.

She shook her head. "It's no use, after all. At some point I'll have to face the extent of the destruction. I'd better get it over with now." She straightened her shoulders. "Is right now okay?" she asked the sheriff.

"Sure," Jake replied, opening the door for her.

"Okay, wait."

She reached for the bundle of fur on her lap and wanted to hand it to Cruz. But Murphy would have none of it. He hissed like a world champion and once again clung to her knitted top. The garment would not survive the night, though for a different reason than the rest of her wardrobe. Finally, she gave it up. He'd come with her, then. She placed him in the crook of her right arm and got out.

Cruz did the same. He wanted nothing more than to undo the incident. Once again, anger gripped him, mixed with a feeling of helplessness. For, of course, he could not simply conjure away the burglary. Instead, he placed his hand lightly on Zelda's back as a silent support.

Amazed, Zelda turned to him and gave him a grateful smile.

He admired her for her calmness in this crisis situation. Apart from the tears after the initial shock, nothing was noticeable. He didn't know if he himself would have remained so calm during such an invasion of his privacy.

"If it gets too much for you, let me know."

She gave him a strange look. "Of course, it's too much for

me. I'd rather be anywhere else than right here. But as I said earlier, wishing doesn't help."

Her voice sounded impatient and a little stubborn, so it was instantly clear to Cruz that she was going to go through with this inspection, no matter how much strength it would cost her. Admiration for her courage rose in him.

"This way," Deputy Toby said. "Don't touch anything, please."

Zelda blinked. "Because of my fingerprints?"

"Not directly because of yours. Yours are all over the place anyway. But forensics are just on their way. If the burglar left any behind, it would be beneficial if you didn't accidentally obliterate them."

"Oh, I see. All right." She shifted Murphy on her arm. "There's no such danger with me. I've got my hands full, so to speak," she said, gesturing with her free hand at the cat. He still made no effort to move from his place on high.

What new things you learned every day, Zelda thought to herself as she followed the deputy through the house. She resolutely suppressed the hysterical giggle that forced itself up her throat.

Arriving in the living room, she was again overwhelmed by the destruction. Countless broken pillows, the sofa with stuffing coming out of slits, the scattered books and DVDs. Under the window lay a broken pot. The scattered potting soil and the tulips that had just poked their heads through the surface lay careless and trampled on the floor. She had to really get over herself to put one step in front of the other.

Jake, knowing all too well how overwhelming the marks of a violent intruder could be, touched her lightly on the hand.

"Do you notice anything missing right off the bat?"

Helplessly, Zelda pointed to the devastated room. "How

am I supposed to answer that? There's not a stone left standing here."

"I know it's difficult. But just try to ignore the chaos and look beneath the surface. The TV is still there, after all. He obviously didn't take that with him."

"I wouldn't have either. From the looks of it, I doubt it still works," she muttered, hoping her insurance would cover the damage.

"True. Still, it tells us something about the perpetrator," the sheriff patiently explained to her.

"And that would be?"

"This wasn't some random burglar looking for loot he could easily peddle. Clearly, he was looking for something specific. What else did you have in this room that might be of interest to someone?"

Zelda took a deep breath and let her eyes wander around the room again, while Jake's question echoed in her head. What did she have that could be of interest to anyone? Nothing. Nothing at all. Her life was boring and her bank account empty.

"Do you have a computer?"

Abruptly, she turned to face him. She almost would have lost her balance if Cruz hadn't had the presence of mind to grab her by the elbow. As if she had seen a ghost, she stared at Jake before lowering her gaze to the coffee table. Like everything else, it had fallen victim to the burglar. It had tipped to one side. A few sheets of paper and books lay scattered beside it.

"Why, sure," she said in horror. "My laptop. And..." Out of the corner of her eye, she squinted at Cruz.

His expression remained inscrutable. Presumably it was a stroke of luck in his eyes if all the clues to the treasure had disappeared, she thought angrily.

"Your laptop and?" Jake prompted her to continue speaking.

"The map," she whispered. At least the unfortunate incident was now beginning to make sense. The treasure map and the prospect of the fabled treasure were, of course, excellent motives. At the realization that someone else was in possession of the old map, her pulse began to race. Involuntarily, she pressed Murphy tighter against her chest until the cat complained with a pitiful meow. On the spot, she loosened her grip.

"Sorry, little guy," she murmured between his ears, rubbing the tip of her nose over his fur.

As if in a trance, she walked over to the table and pushed the various documents aside with the tip of her foot. No sign of her laptop. Or the map.

Jake cleared his throat. "What map are you talking about?"

Zelda could read into Cruz's face the conflicting emotions raging inside him. On the one hand, he must have been very relieved that the treasure map was finally gone. At the same time, she sensed he knew and sympathized how devastating the loss was her.

"It was a map that supposedly showed the way to the treasure from Treasure Mountain," Cruz said. "Adela left it for me." The words came out harsh. She knew that to him, this bullshit hunt for a treasure that most likely didn't exist was like a red rag.

Zelda flinched imperceptibly when she heard his harsh tone. What else had she expected? Sure, they had been reasonably civil about their research. But that had been in the restaurant. Very different from reality. Cruz had never made any secret of the fact that he found her efforts to get to the bottom of the matter pointless.

When she thought of the treasure, she felt the hunting fever take hold of her, as it had so many times before. Determinedly, she straightened her shoulders. He didn't have to approve of her search. She would find it on her own.

"I'll check over here," she informed Jake and wandered into the next room.

"Wait, I'll go with you."

Cruz hurried to her side. Zelda gave him a critical look. Involuntarily, he pulled his head in a little. It looked like he at least had a guilty conscience because of his harsh tone earlier, she thought, a little mollified, and concentrated again on the task ahead.

As she had already suspected, nothing else was missing. Relatively composed, she took in the chaos in the kitchen. Flour covered the kitchen counter and floor. The cutlery drawer had been ripped out. Knives and forks lay scattered everywhere. Eager to get the ordeal over with as quickly as possible, she courageously continued on her way.

From his vantage point on her arm, Murphy watched the events around him with wide eyes. It wasn't until they arrived on the second floor and headed for her bedroom that life came to him. In one leap, he jumped off her arm, bristled his fur, and ran, snarling, into the bedroom.

Zelda and Cruz exchanged puzzled looks.

Jake, who had followed them and seen the cat's action, laughed softly. "Now I realize a few things."

"You realize some things?" repeated Zelda uncomprehendingly.

"Yes. In this room we found traces of blood. And a few tufts of cat hair. If I'm not mistaken, your cat was playing watchdog and attacked the burglar. Now we can only hope we'll get lucky, and someone will notice the bloody welts left by his claws."

Speechless, Zelda looked after her cat. Murphy? A guard dog? Or more precisely, a guard cat? Did that word even exist? Filled with new appreciation for Murphy, she followed him into the room. She should have left that alone. When she discovered her tattered clothes carelessly strewn about the room, bile rose in her throat. Suddenly she could no longer breathe. Panic-stricken, she turned and rushed out of the room, straight into Cruz's arms.

"Calm down," he whispered in her ear. Gently, he stroked her back.

Satisfied with the results of his inspection, Murphy stepped out of the room with his tail raised. He walked straight up to the closely entwined couple and stroked their legs.

This behavior, so unusual for her cat, was enough to push back Zelda's panic. She leaned back a little and looked at Cruz.

"Thank you. The sight of my clothes... he... my underwear."

"Shh." Cruz put an index finger to her lips. "I understand you all too well. When I get my hands on that bastard..."

The irony of this did not escape him. Only a few hours ago, he had had the culprit in his power and had let him go. But that wasn't all, he had obviously led him directly to Zelda. These thoughts just wouldn't let him go.

Zelda twisted her mouth into a wry smile.

"Then I hope you never meet him. I have no interest whatsoever in mourning you again before the next fifty years have passed."

Cruz stared at her in amazement as he heard the fierce determination in her voice. It almost sounded as if she planned to spend the next fifty years at his side.

"Nothing else is missing," Zelda informed the sheriff. "Can I go now?"

"Of course. Why don't you come by the station tomorrow sometime so we can get the paperwork done? You'll need that for the insurance too. Do you have a place to go tonight? Otherwise, you're welcome to stay at my house."

Zelda's heart warmed. Independence may be full of curious, gossipy residents. But when it came down to it, everyone stuck together and were there for each other.

"She's coming with me," Cruz said.

To her amazement, she felt the corners of her mouth twitch again at Cruz's statement, which brooked no contradiction. A great quality about this man who actually felt more like her boyfriend. Perhaps clarifying talks of their relationship status would simply become superfluous in the face of burglaries and other disasters.

Murphy meowed loudly. He stood on his hind legs and fished for Zelda's fingertips with his paw.

She looked down at the cat. "Do you want to go back up?" Testily, she squatted down. Without hesitation, Murphy jumped up onto her knees. Dumbfounded, she stroked his back.

"But then you have to go with me to Cruz," she informed him.

Murphy blinked.

CHAPTER TWENTY-FIVE

Zelda looked around as Cruz led her inside his apartment. She'd never been there before since he'd always gone to her place. It made sense, too, now that she had a four-legged roommate to be responsible for. She looked at the bundle of fur in her arm. Still, he made no move to leave his safe place. Poor thing. Surely, he had suffered a shock when he had encountered the burglar. She couldn't explain his sudden change of heart any other way.

She turned her attention back to the new surroundings. Cruz had placed his bag on a small shelf under the coat rack. The lower half of the walls were painted gray blue, the upper half a pleasant, muted white. It gave the apartment a masculine touch without seeming harsh or cold. A leather armchair in an alcove invited people to read. Otherwise, the hallway was empty.

"I'll get Murphy's toilet and his basket out of the car in a minute. Let's go to the kitchen first," he said.

Zelda nodded and followed him down the long hallway. Several doors opened on the left. He opened each one a crack.

VIRGINIA FOX

"Bedroom. Office. Bathroom. Do you want me to leave your stuff in the bathroom right now?"

"Sure." She thought of the contents of the small white bag in Cruz's hand. After she hadn't been able to bring herself to take any of her own things—things that some stranger had touched—they had stopped at the convenience store. Of course, she found only the absolute basics there. A toothbrush. Toothpaste. A moisturizer for her face. Fortunately, her pharmacy carried her favorite skincare line. So, at least she could replace those things the next day.

Zelda just wanted to go to bed and pull the covers over her head. Forget what had happened. She was aware her problems would not go away by doing so but surely she was entitled to a few hours of self-pity, pretending her life was in perfect order.

She sighed and put the cat on the ground. Murphy lifted his nose and sniffed. He explored the apartment, checking every corner of his new, temporary home. When he finished the first round, he continued his tour one floor higher, on the wooden chairs, and the comfortable leather sofa.

"Is that all right?" asked Zelda. After all, he didn't have a cat. Probably for a good reason. What if he hated cat hair? Bengal cats didn't shed excessively. But like most fur-bearing animals, Murphy shed hair from time to time.

"Yeah, sure. I want him to feel at home."

"I'm really grateful to you."

"If you thank me again," he said, "I'm afraid I'll have to put you over my knee."

It wasn't just her nerves that were on edge when he resorted to such threats, Zelda thought, even though she had to admit a part of her noted the threat with great interest. She smiled. They could skip the part about bending over his knee, after all. But losing herself in Cruz, spending a few hours just feeling and not thinking, sounded... perfect.

"With that, you have successfully taken my mind off things."

"Really?" asked Cruz. He ran a hand through his black hair and grinned, giving him a boyish look. "I mean, you're welcome."

Zelda walked up to him until their bodies touched and put her arms around his neck. "Where were we before reality set in?" she whispered against his lips.

"Right here, I'd say," he said. He grasped her hips and pulled her closer.

With a soft, longing sigh, Zelda let herself fall against him and kissed him.

After a few seconds, he reluctantly pushed her a little away from him. "Let me jump down for a minute, get Murphy's stuff. I wouldn't want to put him through having to abuse my only potted plant as a litter box."

"I'm sure he wouldn't mind," she said, taking a step back.

Cruz smirked. "But my plant probably would."

While Cruz took care of Murphy's belongings, Zelda walked around the apartment. When she spotted the computer in the office, her heart leapt. The treasure hunt! Wisely, she had scanned the map and saved it to online storage. She looked at the dark screen. *I wonder if she should ask Cruz for help.* At that moment, Murphy appeared and began using her pant leg as a scratching post.

"Hey!" she scolded him and lifted him up. Purring, the cat dropped into the crook of her arm. *Strange animal,* she thought, and scratched his belly.

"You found my office." It was Cruz. Zelda turned and looked at him. Her breath caught in her throat when she met his intense gaze. All thoughts of the treasure vanished. Without her noticing, Murphy jumped off her arm. Cruz approached. What was he up to? A tingling sensation spread down her stomach and southward. All the way to the tips of her toes, that is. And all the regions in between. She swallowed.

Lithe as a panther, Cruz walked toward Zelda. With one fluid movement, he lifted her into his arms.

"What... This is becoming a bad habit," she said.

"What is?"

"Well, that you carry me from A to B. You're about to get a herniated disc, and then what? Sue me for a million dollars?"

Ashamed, she realized she was babbling irrelevant stuff.

"Are you nervous?" asked Cruz.

Zelda hid her hot face against his chest. "Of course not!"

Cruz smiled. "All right, then."

Without breaking a sweat, he carried her into his bedroom and laid her gently on the bed. His eyes sparkled in the light of the streetlamp that fell through the window. Her chest rose and fell with each breath, betraying her tension. With a finger, he stroked her cheek, down her throat, to the top of her collar.

If Cruz didn't make a move soon, she would burst into flames, Zelda thought. The beautiful evening and the adrenaline rush had shaken her hormonal balance. Or maybe it was just his proximity?

Cruz lowered his head and kissed her. Slowly. Lovingly. As if he wanted to make sure she was actually there. Amazed, Zelda realized that this kiss was exactly what she needed. It was strange. Earlier, she hoped for a wild attack that would make her forget everything but the two of them. But Cruz's disarming tenderness was just as efficient. With a content sigh, she snuggled against him and surrendered.

When Cruz woke the next morning, he met Zelda's chipper gaze.

"Morning," he growled, kissing the tip of her nose. "What are you doing up so early?"

"It's a beautiful day and you're lying next to me. Isn't that enough of a reason?"

Cruz rubbed his eyes and stretched. "Hm. Yes, that's true. On the other hand, I was hoping you like to sleep, too." He squinted. "For a long time. Snuggled up to me. So what is it that keeps those busy brain cells of yours going?"

"How is it that you know me so well after only a few weeks?"

Cruz grinned. "That will probably be because that's how everything I used to know gradually returns to mind."

Zelda dropped onto her back, half amused, half annoyed. For her part, she knew Cruz well enough to know he wouldn't let up until she gave him a satisfactory answer. Only it would very likely not please him.

With an expectant "And?" he confirmed her assumption right after.

"I was just wondering where I could get a computer today." She glanced at him from under her lashes. To give her hands something to do, she cuddled the cat who had snuck into bed with them sometime during the night.

"A computer? What for?"

"I have a copy of the treasure map stored in my cloud." Although she knew he wouldn't be very enthusiastic about the subject, she couldn't help a certain pride. For once, her foresight and meticulous notetaking had paid off.

"A copy of the treasure map?"

Zelda nodded.

As if she could see in Cruz's brain, the gears that were still asleep came to life. Everything came crashing down. The near crash after the visit to Perkins. The mysterious death of his great-aunt. The damn map. And yesterday: the break-in.

"You're obsessed!" he yelled.

Murphy put his ears flat against his head, hissed in his direction, and jumped off the bed with a mighty leap. He didn't like loud noises.

Zelda pulled her head in involuntarily. *Obsession?* She wasn't obsessed with the gold. Or was she?

"Can we talk about this in peace?" she asked.

His eyes widened. "Calmly?"

"Uh, yeah?" she replied. "Did you really think I was going to give up now?"

Upset, Cruz looked to the side and swallowed. "Honestly, yes." His voice grew louder. "What else has to happen to convince you that there's a curse?"

Zelda couldn't help but laugh. "The curse? That's your argument to convince me to stop researching?"

Cruz scowled. "How else do you explain all the incidents? The break-in?"

"A criminal who broke into my house wasn't caused by a curse. I'm not going to let some run-of-the-mill thief stop me from my goals, damn it."

"Do you care so much about the gold?"

"It's not about the gold," Zelda said. "It probably belongs to the state anyway. And if it doesn't, I can always put it in the contest fund so it benefits the community."

"But if it's not about the gold, what is it about?"

Zelda raised her shoulders. She couldn't explain the mysterious pull the treasure had on her either. "I want answers." She averted her eyes. "Somehow I feel that if I end up finding the treasure, it will have been worth it. The years without you. The move. My grief. For you. My life. My innocence."

Cruz ran his hand over his face and got out of bed. "I love you, Zelda. But this obsession with the treasure scares me. I'm sorry. I can't and won't help you in your quest."

Zelda looked after him. His words echoed.

I love you.

I can't and won't help you with your search.

As she realized, she had been longing to hear those words for quite a while. The first ones, of course. Because, if she was honest, she loved him, too. Very much. But there had been the other sentence. Her heart hurt. He did love her. But apparently not enough to support her in what mattered most.

The front door slammed.

She blinked back the tears and pushed the bedspread away. If that was the case, he might as well keep his words! Regardless, she wouldn't let him stop her from pursuing her goals. She got up and went in search of Murphy. In the meantime, the poor cat must have been half-starved.

Cruz sat brooding in front of his coffee at the Sweets café. Zelda's astonished look when he had confessed his love to her earlier played in his mind. The joy in her eyes and the disappointment that had followed after. What had he expected? That she would fall around his neck and return the words? Hardly, when in the same breath he trampled her dreams.

Annoyed with himself, the impossible situation, and relationships, he pressed two fingers against his eyes.

"Problems? Or just too little coffee?" Aileen inquired amiably as she approached his table with a full coffee pot.

With a wave of his hand, he pointed to his empty cup. "Both," he admitted. "Any advice?"

Aileen laughed. "If it's not about making delicious eclairs..."

Cruz shook his head.

"Then no, I'm afraid. What's it about?"

"It's Zelda. I love her. I really do. But I just can't deal with what she's up to. But I do want to be there for her." He looked up at Aileen. "I guess I don't make much sense, do I?"

"I don't know," Aileen said. "You don't have to agree with everything Zelda does. After all, that doesn't stop you from being there for her in other ways."

Surprised, Cruz stared. "How did you get so wise? Is it the coffee? If so, I'd like a pot."

"I'd attribute that more to chocolate." Aileen winked at him and disappeared to the next table.

Chocolate. Zelda loved chocolate. He would bring her some, he decided. What else did she need? The state of her little house came to his mind. *I wonder if I should help her clean it up.* He certainly wasn't her favorite person right now, though.

His spotted Charlie, who was standing at the counter placing her order. She'd dyed her hair orange with purple tips. Despite his bad mood, he had to smile. Zelda would definitely like the new color, too. But would she make it to the bookstore? An idea came, and hastily, he stood.

"Charlie? Do you have a moment?"

When he left the store ten minutes later, his heart was lighter. Charlie and Aileen had promised to activate their circle of friends. After the store closed, Zelda would have a whole cleaning crew at her disposal. Aileen had promised to bring chocolate and Paula was going to take care of drinks. Probably high-proof drinks if he had interpreted Aileen's look correctly. The thought of half a dozen friends singing loudly while cleaning up made him smile. Hopefully Zelda would be pleased.

The best part was he himself didn't have to face the chaos and danger Zelda had been exposed to again. Perhaps that allowed him to gain a little distance from the whole situation. Not having to clean and tidy up himself was an added bonus.

He glanced at the clock. Almost nine. Perfect. He'd have time to talk to Brenda before the first meeting. Maybe he could persuade her to contribute something edible for the evening. Elated, he continued on his way toward the office.

CHAPTER TWENTY-SIX

Completely exhausted, Zelda closed her pharmacy for the evening. Since she'd left her car in front of her house the previous night, she had to walk. But maybe a little fresh air would do her good, she thought, and headed for the shortcut through the park.

She wondered how Murphy was doing in his new temporary home. That morning she practically had to throw him back into the apartment and pull the door shut behind him, so eager had he been to accompany her going out. She would've loved to go straight to Cruz's apartment and curl up on the sofa with the cat, a good book, and a cup of tea. But alas, she had things to do. At least that way she could avoid meeting Cruz for a short while longer. She grimaced.

His words had been haunting her all day.

I love you.

Her pulse quickened every time she thought about it. Knowing her love was reciprocated was great. *I wonder if he really meant it.* And what did it mean exactly? Didn't love also mean supporting the other person achieving their goals? Or was that too much to ask? She wished Cruz had left it at that. His subsequent, "I can't and won't help you in your quest" had cast a dark shadow over what should have been her happiest moment. Depressed, she kicked a stone that lay on the path. It rolled a long way until it stopped at the edge of the grass.

"You're such a drama queen," she said. "Just find the treasure and everything will be fine."

She was itching to delve into the maps again, both the old and new. But first, she hadn't made it to the library because Astrid had called in sick. For a computer, she would have to go to Breckenridge, if she found anything there at all. After that, probably a trip to Denver was in order. Or maybe she'd ask Charlie for help? She would print out her notes and copy of the map.

In a much better mood, she quickened her steps until she remembered where she was headed. To the chaos that had once been her home. The surge of energy she'd felt dissolved. Her shoulders slumped. If she had a choice, she'd rather volunteer for a tooth extraction than rather face her small house and memory of the burglar. Unfortunately, she had no more wisdom teeth to offer, so she had to tackle the cleanup.

As her small house came into view, she sighed. Somehow she was just overwhelmed by the idea of the task ahead. Anxiously, she pushed open the garden gate. She didn't know where to begin.

"Pull yourself together," she said. "After all, the burglar isn't going to jump out from behind the one rather pathetic-looking bush growing next to the house." No sooner had she spoken than she bristled. A light was burning on the lower floor. She blinked. In her shock the day before, she hadn't thought to ask the sheriff to turn out the lights after the forensics team finished their work. She thought that was a given.

She continued on her way with a queasy feeling in her

stomach. At the front door, she heard music. Music? Since when did burglars listen to rock music? She was irritated. It was her home, damn it!

Angrily, she put the key in the lock. Nothing moved. She tried again. Had the intruders come with their own locksmith this time? Zelda pushed the door handle. The door swung open.

Without thinking about the danger she might be putting herself in, she stormed into the house in a rage. As soon as she was inside, she stood rooted.

Countless women, many of them friends, scurried through her house like elves on steroids. They swept away broken glass, sorted cutlery into drawers, and stacked books and magazines into neat piles. Zelda almost felt dizzy watching them. The kitchen gave off a promising aroma of food. Her stomach growled.

"Hey, there you are. Long day at the pharmacy?" Jaz was carrying a garbage bag over her shoulder toward the back door.

"Could someone pinch me? I think I'm dreaming," Zelda said.

Paula, who was passing by with a bucket of water in one hand and a mop in the other, stopped. She put down the bucket, stretched out her arm, and complied with her request.

"Ouch!" Zelda gave the helpful culprit a nasty look.

Paula shrugged and lifted her bucket again. "You wanted to get pinched!"

Zelda rolled her eyes. "Yeah, yeah." She gestured toward the women. "What's happening here?"

Paula smiled. "That, my dear, is Independence in action."

Zelda's friends and acquaintances had created a true miracle. From where she stood, there was hardly anything left of yesterday's mess.

"No slackers here," Charlie teased, kissing her on the cheek. "Chop, chop, we still need to paint."

"Paint?"

"Well, sure. Your walls have to match your new pillows, after all."

"New pillows?"

"Did you swallow a parrot or is there something wrong with your ears?" Charlie grabbed her by the sleeve and pulled her along. "Come on. Let me show you what we've done so far."

"Is the kitchen on the way? Because something smells heavenly here."

"Your house isn't that big, so I'm sure we can make that work," Charlie said, brushing an orange-purple strand from her face.

She followed Charlie. It was incredible how different everything looked.

"I'm afraid your sofa wasn't salvageable. But Rose still had an old one that Jaz used to use when she came for sleepovers."

"And what did you do with the other one?"

"Right now it's sitting outside, along with the other things that couldn't be salvaged. Donovan from the auto shop is coming by later with his little truck. Then he'll drive it all to the junkyard."

Zelda stroked the faded pink fabric. Tears came to her eyes. Hastily, she blinked them away.

Paige emerged from the kitchen and thrust a glass each into Zelda and Charlie's hands.

Charlie groaned. "I don't think that's a good thing."

Zelda eyed the brown liquid suspiciously. "What is this?" she asked and took a cautious sip.

"This is my cure-all," Paula said, patting her on the back.

The combination of the strong alcohol and Paula's chummy greeting triggered a coughing fit in Zelda.

"Don't spill all over the floor again," Paula chided.

Zelda gave her an evil look and gasped. "What kind of devil stuff is this?"

"Well, good old Jack, of course. And a sip of Coke," she added after a little pause for thought.

"But really, just a little sip," Zelda said. "If I drink this before my stomach gets any food, I'll be singing the Rolling Stones in no time."

"Can you sing?" asked Paige.

Quinn joined the ever-growing group. "Zelda can only whisper. With moose, specifically." She winked.

Zelda snapped out of her trance-like state. "Hey! I've been good about staying away from moose."

"It's probably for the best," Paige said. "Come on. Let's get something to eat. The others just finished up on the second floor. Then we can start painting later."

"Good idea," Quinn said.

Food was good, Zelda thought. The kitchen was really shining. The oven was half open, revealing grilled chicken, lemon slices, and onions. A basket of pita bread and what looked like yogurt sauce were on the table.

Overwhelmed, she dropped into a vacant chair that hadn't been there yesterday. "I have to say, when you guys tackle something, you tackle it right. A cleanup crew, delicatessen catering, and home improvement," Zelda said.

"Well, most of it was easy," Aileen said, shrugging apologetically as Lily gave her a venomous look. "It was."

Laughing, Zelda held up her hands. "Stop, stop, stop! You really don't have to fight on my account. Remember, I was here yesterday. I know very well the level of destruction here." She looked around. "Or rather, what prevailed." Her voice trailed off. "I still can't quite believe what you've already accomplished."

"Here," Quinn said, shoving a piece of pita bread filled with grilled chicken breast and yogurt sauce into her hand. "You better eat something before you get stir-crazy."

"Where did my vegetarian version go?" asked Jaz after checking the oven.

"Here," Brenda said, unwrapping a filled pita roll from aluminum foil.

"You are the best mother-in-law in the world."

"I've got to make sure my second grandchild doesn't starve to death."

"Where is Lara, anyway?" asked Becca, who had come from upstairs.

Becca was, if Zelda remembered correctly, Hank's sister. Hank, a real cowboy, and a gifted horse trainer if she believed the rumor mill, was married to Lara, a Swiss woman. The two lived together on the Lone Wolf Ranch, which also housed the wildlife sanctuary where Quinn worked in her capacity as game warden. Sometime in the spring, the two were expecting their first child.

"She sends her apologies. Seems she's welcoming a visitor from Switzerland in the next few days and has some preparations to make," Quinn said.

Paula lowered her pita roll. "That's right. I forgot about that. No wonder Leslie and Shauna were so excited. They both can't wait to welcome an exotic exchange student."

Zelda frowned. "What's exotic about her?"

"Having never been to the other side of the Atlantic, that's already enough for them to dub her exotic," said Paul. "Plus, she's a few years older than Shauna. Fifteen, if I remember correctly."

"This is bound to be an adventure for everyone involved,"

Brenda said with the knowing smile of a mother who'd raised five children of her own.

"Especially when the new baby comes around. My brother as a dad..." Becca shook her head as if she couldn't quite believe it herself.

"And you became a mother by surprise," Jaz said with a wink.

That's right, Zelda thought. Becca had also reconnected with her childhood sweetheart sometime last fall. Not entirely unlike her and Cruz, actually. The only difference was that Adrian brought his son Jonas with him. That hadn't stopped them from starting a family, though, although it certainly hadn't been easy. Zelda sighed. Here she was, willing to give up over a difference of opinion with Cruz. Maybe she should just grow up?

"So," said Aileen, still leaning against the kitchen counter. "You and Cruz."

The women in the kitchen focused on Zelda. Of course she blushed, even though she couldn't have said why. She lifted her chin and returned Aileen's gaze defiantly. "What are you saying?"

In her typical, very French manner—at least Zelda imagined French women had similar body language, although she didn't know anyone else who could lift and drop a shoulder so elegantly—Aileen said, "He was very upset when he stopped by the café today."

Zelda's guilty conscience reared its ugly head. "Oh. Really?"

"Really. The incident has taken a lot out of him. I think he's pretty worried about you."

"You think so?"

Paula laughed. "You kidding?" She gestured around the

room with a sweeping motion of her hand. "Who do you think organized all this?"

"That… you... It was Cruz who organized you to help?"

"He gave the idea for it. Paula and I were responsible for organizing people and materials. But once the first five people knew about it, most of everything else took care of itself."

Speechless, Zelda stared around until Charlie broke the silence. Her friend propped herself up on her thighs and grinned.

"We want to hear details. How are things going with you and your lover boy?"

Zelda avoided their gaze and studied the floor. With all the mess the burglar had made, it would have been nice if he'd also left a hole in the floor. She could really use one.

Unfortunately he hadn't, and one didn't suddenly open up that moment. She sighed.

"That good?" asked Quinn, raising an eyebrow.

"Or that bad?" asked Charlie with concern.

"Both," Zelda said, slapping her hands in front of her face.

"Oh no," Charlie said. "Don't tell me the problems started with your treasure hunt."

Zelda gave her an evil look. Did she have to blurt it out? After all, this was her private project.

Charlie rolled her eyes in annoyance. "Oh, come on. You didn't really think you could keep this a secret?"

"Why not?"

"Because you talk about practically nothing else!" said Charlie.

"That may be so. But that's only until I find the treasure," she insisted.

Brenda clapped. "You're welcome to continue your

discussion at work. We have walls to paint. And to you, my lady," she pointed at Zelda, "falls the important task of choosing the colors."

Relieved to have escaped the spotlight, Zelda stood. A woman who had remained in the background joined her and grabbed her hand before anyone could ask another question. Zelda let herself be pulled along. Out of the corner of her eye, she regarded her. The olive skin tone and black hair showed her Hispanic heritage.

"I'll show you where the paint pots are. The selection isn't that big," she said apologetically when they stood in front of it. "I'm Valentina, by the way. One of the employees at Avery and Cole's security company."

"That's right. I've heard of you."

Avery had described her team in conversation with Zelda.

"I hope only good things," the other woman replied.

Zelda laughed. "Of course."

"Then I'm relieved."

"Thanks for getting me out of there." Zelda pointed toward the kitchen.

Valentina grimaced. "You're welcome."

Curious, Zelda eyed the woman. "I suppose you don't like to talk about your private life either?"

Valentina shrugged. "It depends. Sometimes I do. But then when I don't want to, is when a few well-meaning friends get together and start an inquisition." She thought briefly. "But enough about me. What do you think of this dark raspberry color? Too dark? Or just right for the living room?"

Zelda accepted that Valentina did not want to talk about herself any longer and focused on the available colors.

Three hours, two more whiskey-cokes, and many brush strokes later, Zelda was lying on the floor next to Charlie in the living room.

"But aside from your fixation on the gold—how are you doing otherwise?"

Zelda turned her head and grinned wordlessly.

Charlie started laughing. "*Oh, la la!* That good?"

Zelda nodded and joined the laughter. Why not? She had a raspberry-colored wall in the living room, a lavender-colored wall in the bedroom, new pillows Rose had sewn on her sewing machine over the course of an afternoon, a secondhand sofa, and a new mattress from the outlet in Breckenridge. There was even a new lamp for the coffee table next to the sofa.

"She's old, after all," Zelda had said.

Paula only laughed. "I doubt that was the reason. She probably just didn't want to ruin her manicure."

"Like you?" Tyler teased her sister.

"Yeah, sure," Paula replied, waving her short-trimmed fingernails.

"Are you sleeping here tonight?" asked Charlie.

Although her house was now practically like new, the idea of staying there all alone caused her a queasy feeling. "No, I don't think so. It stinks of paint. Besides, the poor cat is still with Cruz. I hope Cruz fed him."

"I'm certain Murphy made sure," Charlie assured her. After a moment of silence, she asked, "Are you scared?"

"Yes," Zelda admitted.

"Shall we get on our way then? We still have a nice walk ahead of us."

After the amount of alcohol she'd had, there was no way she could drive Charlie home.

"Where is Ethan, anyway?"

"At Jake and Cammie's house."

"Oh my. Didn't he think that sucked being there?"

"Not after Jake promised to drive him through town running the blue lights and sirens." She grinned. "Guys."

"You can say that again," Zelda said. Even Cruz would be happy doing that. Speaking of Cruz? Was she seeing ghosts again? Or was there really a double of him standing in the doorway? She blinked, expecting her daydream to disappear. It would be too embarrassing if he were actually there and discovered her lying on her back, drunk, and probably more colorful than a bird of paradise.

Cruz laughed. "Looks like the action was a complete success."

At the sound of his voice, Zelda straightened up in horror. "You're not a ghost at all," she said.

"I thought we had already worked that out?"

"No! Yes. Oh. Can you just pretend you didn't see us?"

Shaking his head in amusement, he knelt down next to Zelda. "Unfortunately, no. Your cat was very clear. He's been prancing around the apartment all evening, meowing indignantly for you."

"Tell him I'll be there soon." She closed her eyes. "Even without an escort."

"Not so fast," Charlie said. "I suppose your sweetheart has a ride?"

My treasure, Zelda repeated in her mind and giggled softly. She already had a treasure. What did she need the French gold for? Before the thought could take root, she realized what else Charlie had said.

"You're here with the car?" she asked, turning to Cruz.

He nodded.

"All right. Take us with you, then. But I don't want to hear any complaints about purple paint on your seats later."

Cruz laughed. "Well then... your carriage awaits." Gallantly he gave a bow and pointed to the door.

Charlie and Zelda glanced at each other and burst out laughing.

Cruz looked at the ceiling. It was going to take a little longer until they'd finally get home.

CHAPTER TWENTY-SEVEN

The next morning, Zelda woke up with a terrible headache. It felt like a herd of buffalo was rushing through her skull. And her mouth felt... furry. Furry? She opened an eye. It was already light outside. *I wonder what time it is.* Crap, she had to go to work. She groaned at the thought of spending a day encouraging people and selling medicines. Promptly, something furry tickled her mouth. She opened the other eye and pulled her chin a little to look down at herself. Indeed. The cat slept relaxed in the hollow of her neck. And purred. She wiped her lips to get rid of the cat hair.

"You even purr," she said, half asleep. "Did the burglar give you a personality transplant?"

Murphy lolled and turned onto his back. Zelda pulled a hand from under the covers and stroked his silvery fur with the leopard pattern peculiar to Bengal cats. "You're a beauty,"

It was incomprehensible how someone could simply leave a pet behind; whether that had been the case for Murphy, she'd probably never know.

She blinked and knew that she had to get going.

"If you can party, you can work," her grandfather had

been fond of saying. One of those uncomfortable truths you only really understood as an adult.

With difficulty, she straightened up and grabbed her throbbing head. She desperately needed an aspirin. Or two. The light falling through the window hurt; she reached for her cell phone on the nightstand. As she did, her fingers brushed a piece of paper. She opened her eyes a crack. A note. Next to it, two tablets. Cruz must have placed them there before he left.

She smiled. When it wasn't about the treasure, the man was perfect. With a big gulp of water, she washed down the medication. "Ah! Much better." It was amazing what a glass of water could do. She reached for the paper.

Astrid called. She is healthy again and said I should let you sleep in. She can open the pharmacy on her own. Details of yesterday's clean-up party have come to her attention. (Anything else I should know? ;-)) Enjoy the day. I'll see you in the evening. —Cruz

Next to his name, he'd scrawled a crooked heart. Zelda sighed. Being in love had its nice sides. And Astrid deserved a medal. She decided to make time to sit down with her co-worker and discuss the future. The pharmacy was doing well. Not long, and Astrid would have her degree in pharmacy. Many would consider it overkill to have two trained pharmacists in a small town like Independence. But Zelda found that carrying the responsibility alone and being available all the time stressed her out. So why not take the opportunity to try to make a half-time position palatable to Astrid?

But first she had treasure to find. She was tired of this issue standing between her and Cruz. From her point of view, the only solution was to find the gold as soon as possible.

Vaguely, somewhere in the back of her mind, she realized the urge to go treasure hunting wasn't as overwhelming as usual. Strange. It had to be the hangover.

She glanced at her phone. It was already nine o'clock, she realized, and she dropped the device on the bed. No time to lose. Ignoring the pounding in her head, she jumped out of bed. Murphy sat up in bed and yawned heartily.

"You've probably already been fed by Cruz."

The cat indignantly closed his eyes and began to preen himself.

Zelda made her way to a pile of clothes. She winced at the sight. Unless she was planning to stop by the kindergarten to provide some amusement, she couldn't possibly be walking around in any of it. But what was she going to wear instead? Most of her clothes had fallen victim to the burglar's destruction. As much as her friends had helped her yesterday, there hadn't been a complete new wardrobe among the souvenirs. She squinted at Cruz's closet. Surely, he had a sweatshirt and a pair of jeans he could spare. She and him were almost the same size, after all.

Five minutes later, she found some, although Cruz's toned rear end was different from her well-rounded one. With a frustrated growl, she pulled a pair of sweatpants out of the closet. Cotton and spandex. This fabric combo was supposed to be able to handle her curves, after all.

It did, she was relieved to find. A glance in the mirror showed she was quite presentable. At least for a quick breakfast at Aileen's. She bribed Murphy with a piece of cheese and slipped out of the apartment.

It was cold outside. Did she have a jacket at the pharmacy? Did she really want to go by there when she was off work? With a deep sigh, she turned back to the apartment, grabbed a windbreaker from Cruz's dressing room, and offered another piece of cheese to calm the cat, who was plagued by a sudden abandonment anxiety. Secretly, she suspected he planned it that way. But cats were like that. Definitely smarter than their humans.

Walt cursed as he eyed the rough terrain around Adela's cabin. After the successful break-in at Zelda's house, he'd retreated to his father's cabin to lick his wounds. That damn cat had done a first-class job with its claws. Fortunately, he found some antibiotic wound ointment in his old man's supplies. Still, the welts burned like hell and remained bright red. That hadn't stopped him from going on a treasure hunt though. Ever since he had the map, he couldn't wait to get his hands on the gold. He felt it in his heart, just waiting to be discovered.

Although pretty sure no one would follow him to the cabin, Walt had left his car a little distance away. No one was with him except the two goats standing in their enclosure eating hay. Despite the cool wind blowing over the mountains, he was sweating like a pig from the exertion. Frowning, he looked over at the two mountain lakes. From the looks, he still had quite a way to go. The prospect of the gold waiting for him gave him the energy he needed to continue his search. He kept moving.

Zelda needn't have worried. As soon as she held the map in her hands again—okay, only a cheap copy of it, but still—the now familiar hunting fever returned. She felt a tingle in her fingertips, and her breathing quickened. She folded the paper and stowed it in her jacket pocket.

"Thank you," she said to Charlie, who was sitting in her recliner with a coffee-to-go mug in her hand.

Zelda had brought it as a bribe. That'd worked brilliantly. A single glance at the Sweets logo, printed on the side of the cup, had been enough. Already in caffeine-induced seventh heaven, she nodded at Zelda's question about whether she could use her computer and printer. "What do you need?"

"Oh, just a few things from my cloud. My laptop was stolen," Zelda explained.

"You mean the treasure map," Charlie stated, yawning. "Heavens, I'm tired. I've never been so glad that my customers usually don't drop in until the evening."

"We really need to change that," Zelda reminded her, glad to have something else to talk about. She didn't want to discuss the treasure. She would find it, she was sure. After that, the subject would be settled.

"Yes, yes, I know. You had all kinds of ideas to liven up the store. I have to admit that by now I'm ready to listen. I just don't seem to have the entrepreneurial spirit to do it. And the sales numbers... The numbers are so low, they're underground. People just don't read enough anymore. Or only electronically."

"That bad?"

"No, no," said Charlie, who was not used to so much caring. "Don't listen to me, it's probably just the not-yet-evaporated caffeine talking. Go find your treasure." She made a shooing hand gesture toward the store door.

"Are you sure?" Zelda didn't like leaving her alone when she was in such a melancholy mood.

"I'm sure. Now go on. My problems will still be here tomorrow."

It was the last remark that convinced Zelda to finally set out. After all, she was no longer the only one who had the treasure map. The thought of accidentally running into the criminal responsible for breaking into her house sent chills down her spine. Fortunately, she was miles ahead of him in terms of research. It would give her a much-needed head start. She wasn't about to share her treasure with a runaway thief.

Walt wiped the sweat from his brow and consulted the map. *Here. Right here should be the damn entrance.* He followed the rock wall on the west side of the lake, and his frustration grew. He was close, he was sure. He rounded a boulder that lay in the way. Abruptly, he came to a stop. A crevice, not much wider than a person, opened the way into the mountain. There were no signs anyone had set foot in the natural tunnel recently.

He squeezed himself and his fat belly into the tunnel. Fortunately, the opening was enough. Once he was inside, the rock tunnel opened up into a larger chamber. Cautiously, he followed the path. After just a few steps, the passageway curved around, effectively shutting out daylight. Darkness surrounded him. He turned back and took a few steps along the same path he had come. In the pale light that fell through the gap, he fumbled with the headlamp he had brought with him. Not for the first time, he was glad his paranoid father had taken precautions. It would have been unthinkable if he'd had to do all the research himself. If his father had ever confided in him, they might have shared the treasure together. He let out a laugh. It echoed off the walls. Who would have thought he would one day outdo his father?

In the cone of light from his headlamp, a side tunnel appeared. The worm-eaten support beams proved the presence of other people, even if it'd been a long time ago. He looked at the second tunnel entrance. Should he try his luck? He consulted the map. There was no turnoff to be seen. Satisfied, he stuffed the map back into his shirt pocket. He ignored the side tunnel and continued on his way.

Shortly before noon, Cruz paused in the middle of work. Forgetting the business plan in his hand, he gazed out the window. Something had jolted him. *Only what?* He listened to the sounds. Except for the voice of the secretary and two other businessmen in the building, and the moderate traffic outside, there was nothing. Nothing out of the ordinary, that was. He frowned and tried to focus again on the contents of the papers. It was in vain. He couldn't shake off the unmistakable feeling of having overlooked something important. *I wonder if it had something to do with the burglary...*

He thought of Zelda and smiled. He would have liked to have woken up next to her. It'd been far too long since he'd felt her velvety skin under his fingers, smelled her scent, and listened to the beating of her heart. Briefly, he allowed himself to be distracted by the tantalizing daydream. He sighed. *I wonder what she was doing with her day off.*

As if struck by lightning, he sat up. Zelda's day off. Of course! No question what she was doing, he thought. She would be looking for the damned treasure. The treasure the unscrupulous criminal who'd broken into her house also had a map to. He suspected it was Perkin's son, Walt. This meant he was in possession of all the research his father and Cruz's aunt had compiled over the past fourteen years.

A queasy feeling in his stomach grew stronger.

Cruz took out his phone.

At Cruz's house, Zelda's phone rang. Murphy jumped on the bed and looked at the frantic blinking. He tentatively reached for it with his paw. When it stopped shortly after, he lost interest and went back to sleep.

Walt stumbled in the semi-darkness. The batteries of his headlamp had worn out. Afraid of sitting in the dark, he quickened his steps. The passage became narrower and lower. Loose stones and broken logs hindered his progress. After negotiating a pile of boulders that had collapsed, the path descended steeply. Huffing and cursing, he slid down. For the first time, he began to worry about how the hell he was going to salvage the vast amounts of gold. He'd be lucky to make it back himself. How he was going to do that with additional weight, he wasn't sure. *Didn't think that one through, did you?*

When he reached the bottom, he spotted a shapeless lump in the middle of the room. Was that a chest? An object shone golden in the sparse glow of his lamp. Excited, he stepped closer and almost tripped over something. At the last moment, he was able to brace himself against the wall with one hand. What the hell had it been? He lowered his head to scan the ground in front of his feet. A branch? He bent down and picked up the culprit. No sooner had he realized what it was, then he flung it away. A bone, he realized in disgust. Many bones. Was there a whole skeleton? Cautiously he walked around it. After he had overcome the first shock, he didn't care. He would rather meet a dead man. At least someone dead would not dispute the treasure.

Beyond the bones, there was a large chest with a burnt candle stub stuck on the lid. Dried herbs tied in a bundle lay next to it. He wiped them away. He shook the lid. It opened quite easily. When he discovered the contents, he recoiled. The eerie grimace of a skull stared back. With a shaky hand, he reached for the paper lying next to it. Was this a bad joke?

After dialing Zelda's number for the third time and only getting her voicemail, Cruz admitted defeat. Either she didn't want to talk to him and ignored his calls, or she had forgotten the phone somewhere. The latter seemed more likely. She was probably sitting in the diner. Or at yoga. Or at the bookstore with Charlie. An image of Zelda's punctured mattress and the blood in the bathroom flashed before him. He was worried she might be in danger if she was off on the hunt without her phone. What if Walt was there before her?

He dialed the sheriff. "Hi, Jake."

"Hi, Cruz. How can I help you?"

"I suspect Walt Perkins is behind the break-in at Zelda's house as well as the attack on us, running us off the road on the pass," he stated.

"Now slow down. Are you sure?"

"Pretty sure. But that doesn't matter. Zelda has gone on a treasure hunt."

"This isn't the first time, is it?"

"No. But this time she doesn't have her cell phone with her. And the burglar also has a treasure map. I just have a bad feeling about this."

Jake sounded interested. "You mean there might be a danger of the two of them meeting?"

"It's a very real possibility. Listen, I'll try to catch up with Zelda. At least then there will be two of us."

"Where does she think she'll find the treasure?"

"Near Adela's cabin. Charlie has a map. If you don't hear from me in two hours, send a search party."

CHAPTER TWENTY-EIGHT

Outraged, Walt crumpled up the letter and dropped it back into the box. That was what he had gone through all the trouble for? Suffered his father's wrath? Committed a burglary? Desperately, he felt around inside the box. His fingers bumped against something hard. There! He held it up to the light. A jam jar? With salt and a few herbs? That couldn't be true. Some hocus-pocus from the old witch. The jar slipped from his fingers. He burst out laughing, bordering on hysteria. Even from the grave, Adela had everyone in her grasp. Adela had been no more successful with her treasure hunt than his old man.

He would succeed where neither had. He just had to study the map again.

The light from his headlamp danced across the skull. The empty sockets that once housed eyes seemed to mock him. Hastily, he took a step back, and then another. Something poked him in the ribs. With a yelp, he jumped away and turned. A second skeleton leaned against the wall. A silent guardian of time. Walt turned and ran.

Halfway out, he had to stop briefly to gasp for air. So much exercise was certainly not good for his heart. A noise. Had he heard voices? But that was impossible.

"You're chasing a phantom. Let's turn back," he heard a man's voice.

"You promised not to try to change my mind," a woman's voice replied.

Of course. That damn Cruz and annoying Zelda. The two were arguing. Angrily, he pushed himself toward the wall. This was all their fault. Zelda's. Cruz's. Adela's. If it weren't for these people and their machinations, his father would have found the treasure long ago and would still be alive. And he would have had time to make his father understand.

They had spoiled all that for him.

Quick as a flash, Walt disappeared into a side tunnel. If he didn't find any gold, he would at least teach them a lesson.

"Did you hear something?" Cruz asked.

Zelda rolled her eyes. Ever since he'd found her up here, Cruz acted like he'd seen a bad guy around every corner. His "intuition," as he had called it.

As if anyone but them could have found the cave. And even if someone else had figured out the map, they were alone, she was sure. Although she had to admit she was glad not to be by herself. Not because she feared an attack. But the flashlight feature on his phone was extremely helpful. She couldn't believe she'd been so stupid as to go treasure hunting without a reliable light source. How amateurish. How embarrassing.

"It was probably a rat."

"A rat," Cruz repeated.

"Yeah, you know. Those furry, cute animals with the naked tail. Very cute."

"You think moose are cute, too," he said.

Zelda didn't say anything back. In fact, she'd just discovered a fork in the road. She took a step toward it.

"Where are you going?"

"Well, there's a left turn, deeper into the mountain." She eyed the dilapidated beams. "Maybe that's where we should...?"

"Come back," Cruz's voice rang. "The map is clearly pointing west, not south."

"Okay," she answered. The urge to explore this corridor was almost overpowering. The darkness seemed to beckon and call her. But Cruz was right. There was no turnoff marked.

After a last curious look into the dark hole, she turned back. How exciting it all was!

Only when their voices faded in the distance did Walt dare to breathe again. Now he just had to be patient. Then his chance would come. He laughed softly to himself as he thought of the slow and violent death that awaited them. He who laughed last laughed best.

Zelda approached the box in awe.

"What do you think is in there?" Cruz asked.

"Well, the treasure, hopefully."

Cruz doubted that. He could not imagine they'd actually

find any. Especially not the legendary gold of the French. But he kept his doubts to himself. They would find out soon enough. With the beam of the cell phone flashlight, he searched the area. He didn't see any nasty surprises.

When he spotted the skeleton in the corner, he whistled through his teeth.

"Say hello," he prompted Zelda. "We have company."

She whirled around and couldn't suppress a small holler when she caught sight of the bone man.

"That was mean," she said, embarrassed she'd let herself get so scared. After all, she was the one who claimed the treasure hunt was harmless.

Cruz laughed. "I'm sorry. But that was just too tempting."

"I can imagine," she said. The corners of her mouth twitched. After the initial shock, she recognized the humor. "Will you shine a light over to the box or whatever this thing is?"

"Sure."

Zelda got down on her knees next to the hulking box and peered over the edge. "It is indeed a box. It's open, though," she noted.

Were they actually too late? She refused to believe so.

The first thing her eyes met was a skull.

"Ew! More bones." Zelda shuddered.

"Not your thing?" asked Cruz.

"Only if they're plastic."

She gathered her courage and felt around in the box.

"No gold," she moaned with disappointment. She lifted the two things she found to the light.

"What is it?"

"I'm not sure. It seems to be an old jam jar with different things inside. I think it's part of Adela's magic para-phernalia."

"Do you believe that nonsense about witches and stuff?"

"It's not about what I believe or don't believe, it's about what this could be. And it looks like all the elements are combined. The white substance is probably salt. Salt represents the element of earth." Carefully, she unscrewed the rusty lid and held her nose over the rim. A faint scent of sage rose. "Sage represents air. The chili pepper is probably fire, and the blue stone represents water."

"Why a stone and not real water?"

"That would have evaporated by now," Zelda said.

"I see," Cruz said. "What's the other one?"

Zelda put the chili pepper back in the jar and screwed it shut before reaching for the crumpled ball of paper and unfolding it. She tried to decipher the contents. "It's a letter. From Adela."

"From Adela?" Cruz asked. "What's it say?"

Zelda read.

"My dearest family. For many years I believed in the existence of a treasure, even sacrificing my happiness, and especially your happiness, to this mystery. I always wanted to be able to leave an inheritance to you, my nephews and nieces. What is better suited for this than a historically documented gold treasure? But that was a mistake. The true treasure in life is a loving family. Exactly what I destroyed with my secrecy and machinations. Please forgive me. Only when you were gone, and my life was suddenly incredibly empty and lonely, did I realize it. Do it differently than I did. Live your life. Be brave. Take risks. Laugh with each other.

Love, Adela."

Zelda looked up at Cruz. For a moment, time stood still.

An unspoken message vibrated between them. Cruz was the first to break the connection and cleared his throat. "I have to admit I'm a little disappointed."

"I'm a little disappointed we didn't find gold too, but the message is priceless. This was the best answer we could have received."

A rumble filled the room. The floor shook. Dust and lime trickled from the ceiling. Instinctively, Cruz pulled Zelda close and cradled her head against his chest. He pushed her against the wall, away from the threatening sound. Wood burst, and gravel splattered on all sides. Boulders rumbled down the steep section of the tunnel. Larger chunks came loose from the ceiling.

Zelda pressed closer to Cruz. Surely, they would be killed any moment.

After what felt like an eternity, Cruz raised his head. "I think it stopped."

"You think?" She kept her eyes closed. Maybe it was all just a bad dream.

Cruz let go and crossed the chamber to inspect the extent of the destruction.

She coughed. The air was filled with dust. Her eyes, nose, and mouth felt as if she'd been caught in a sandstorm.

"At least none of those rocks fell on our heads. We probably wouldn't have survived." The light from Cruz's cell phone flashlight flitted across the ground, revealing a view of huge debris.

"The only question is how long we'll be alive," Cruz said.

"What do you mean?"

"The rockfall has buried the only path out," he said.

Zelda stared at him with wide eyes. "No," she said. "It can't be." She ran to the other side of the cave. She fell and scraped her shin. "Ouch, fucking hell!" she cursed, and scrambled back up.

"What are you doing?"

"Well, what do you think? Getting us out of the mess I got us into."

Like a savage, she began blindly shoveling dirt and sand aside with her bare hands, pulling at the larger stones. Immediately, more debris rolled down.

Desperate, she redoubled her efforts.

Strong arms embraced her waist with a firm grip and pulled her away.

"Shh," Cruz whispered. "You're only putting us in danger. You'll hurt your hands. Let me see."

He reached for her hands and inspected them under the flashlight. Several nail tips had broken off. A bloody scrape stretched across the back of her left hand.

This was not how she had imagined her great adventure to end. She had only just gotten used to the idea of Cruz back in her life and now would be responsible for his death.

"You must hate me."

"Why should I?" he asked.

"Because I lured you here. To your grave."

Cruz laughed. "How dramatic."

"But it's true," she said.

"Is that it? As far as I remember, you didn't force me at gunpoint into the tunnel."

"Maybe not," she said, "but you tried to explain to me that it could be dangerous. And I didn't listen."

He shrugged. "To be honest, I was more worried about getting robbed."

"A robbery?"

"First we almost get run off the road, then my great-aunt falls to her death. I pick up a tail, and your house gets broken into." He paused, staring into the darkness. "I wouldn't be surprised that this rockslide was intentional."

"Oh, come on. We were the only ones here," she replied.

"That's what we thought. But who knows. Anyway, I'm just hoping the cavalry will come to our aid."

Zelda frowned. "The cavalry?"

"Didn't I tell you? Before I went looking for you, I let Jake know."

No, he had definitely forgotten to mention this detail.

"That's great news," Zelda said. "But half the mountain between us and the exit has collapsed. I'm afraid it won't do us much good. Unless they've switched from horses to moles."

On the other side, Walt rubbed his hands together in satisfaction. Nothing more would be heard from those two. It was fun to hurt them. And so surprisingly easy. After he'd pulled the first big stone out of the wall and brought down a beam, everything collapsed. He was lucky the damage had been limited to the last part of the tunnel. With a final glance at the ceiling, he hurried toward the exit.

The fact he hadn't found the treasure puzzled him. Clearly, he'd have to go in search again. Adela had gotten in his way for the last time. He simply had to study the maps again. Eventually, he'd find the treasure. He didn't consider that her letter could actually be true, and the treasure didn't exist.

Farther ahead, he caught sight of the first streak of light. At last. He'd had enough of the miserable darkness. Walt hurried toward the crevice.

After Cruz called to tell him he had found Zelda and was going to explore a crevice with her near the larger Yule Lake, Jake could no longer concentrate on his paperwork. Realizing that he had just read the same section for the third time, he put his papers aside in disgust. Had he still not learned that he couldn't fight his intuition? His intuition was telling him loud and clear that the two of them were in danger.

So, he left everything on his table and reached for his gun. He would at least take a quick look. He let Polly know and drove off.

Half an hour later, he stopped in front of Adela's cabin. Zelda's and Cruz's vehicles were both parked in the driveway. They were still nearby. On an impulse, he opened the glove compartment and took out his binoculars. Then he got out of his old police car and set off on foot toward the lake. Everything looked peaceful. The two goats had sunk their heads into the hay. The first wildflowers were poking their heads up from the meager grass. The two lakes shimmered deep blue in the sunlight. Individual clouds passing high in the sky were reflected on the surface of the water. But he knew extremely well how deceptive the outer impression could be. Something was wrong. Only what? Considering the vehicles present, they were the only ones here. With the help of the binoculars, he gazed over the idyllic surroundings. There was no sign of any imminent danger.

A dull rumble that seemed to come from within the earth spurred him on. What had it been? A rockfall? An avalanche? He didn't know, but the uneasy feeling in the pit of his stomach grew stronger. Moving at a run toward the larger of the two lakes, he pulled a copy of a crudely drawn map from his pants pocket. As suspected, it had been easy for Charlie to print out again the last document Zelda had looked at.

"The printer has its own memory," she had told him. "Zelda didn't admit it, but I was pretty sure she was going to print it out. After all, she'd had nothing else on her mind for days. Do you think something happened to them?" she had asked, concerned.

"I'm sure they're both fine," Jake had tried to reassure her. "I'll just take a quick look up there. Maybe they need some help with all that gold."

In his pathetic attempt at a joke, Charlie had only smiled wryly and wished him good luck.

None of it helped. He had to stop briefly to make sense of the map. Squinting his eyes against the blinding sunlight, he tried to make sense of the cryptic drawing. There was the lake. And here was the rock wall jutting up into the air. That much was clear. But where did it go from there?

His searching gaze found the narrow path that ran between the shore and the mountain. So that's where he had to go. Suddenly, something red flashed by. What was that? Alarmed, he raised his binoculars.

Who was that? Cruz? As soon as the thought occurred, he dismissed it again. Cruz was smaller than the man in the red shirt. And not as fat. He registered every detail about the stranger. Having appeared out of nowhere, he was leaning against the wall and seemed to be supporting himself with his hands on his knees, as if he needed to catch his breath.

The sheriff squinted at the map. If he wasn't mistaken, the man was at the exact spot where the entrance to the hideout was marked. It had been some time since Jake had encountered Walt Perkins. But he was pretty sure it was him he was looking at. Coincidence? Jake didn't believe in coincidences. A smile stole onto his lips. It was always nice when suspects took the trouble out of looking for them. He had no intention of confronting the stranger on the narrow riverside path, though. Not when he might as well wait for him at the end of the path. Unconcerned that the other man would spot him, since his brown uniform shirt blended in well with the landscape, Jake assumed a position behind a tree and waited.

CHAPTER TWENTY-NINE

Finally, enough air seemed to flow into Walt's lungs again. Groaning, he straightened up. He would have liked to keep searching for the treasure but had to make sure he got out of here. He had no idea how long it would take before someone would miss the two idiots in the mountain. Besides, he desperately needed a drink. And his cheek was still burning like hell. Damn cat! With shaky knees from the exertion and the waning adrenaline rush, he stumbled along the narrow riverside path. He cursed as he remembered he had taken the precaution of leaving his car far from Adela's cabin in the woods. As if anyone would find him.

Zelda and Cruz must have driven all the way to the cabin. Perhaps they had carelessly left the key for him? In any case, they didn't need the car anymore. The thought cheered him up so much that he began to whistle.

The whistle, however, gave away his spot. Someone approached him at the end of the riverside path. The sheriff. He began to sweat. What was he doing here?

"Walt Perkins?" asked Jake.

"That's me," Walt answered. He couldn't let on that

anything was amiss. After all, there was no evidence he had anything to do with the disappearance of the other two. "Is there a problem?"

Before he finished the sentence, Jake twisted his arm behind his back.

"You're under temporary arrest." Without taking a breath, he quoted him his rights.

"Arrested?" asked Walt, trying to free himself.

"You're suspected of burglary and attempted murder."

"Murder?" said Perkins. "But there's no evidence at all. You don't have any dead people."

Jake pulled the handcuffs closed. "Dead people? Plural? Now it's getting interesting. You can tell me all about it on the way to the car."

He pushed and dragged the protesting prisoner to his car. There he pushed him roughly onto the back seat. "Where are Zelda and Cruz?" he demanded to know.

Perkins didn't answer.

Frustrated, Jake slammed the car door. He didn't have time to wait for Walt Perkins to grow a conscience. Every minute counted. He pulled his cell phone from his pocket and dialed the number for his deputy, Toby Winters.

After informing Toby of the situation, Jake set off for the lake. He was dreading what he might encounter. Hopefully, he wouldn't be too late.

Somewhere water dripped from the wall. Time seemed to stand still strangely. Zelda was freezing, and Cruz tried his best to keep her warm. But it didn't do much good. It wasn't just the actual cold that was getting to her; her insides felt frozen, too. Even though Cruz tried to make her feel hopeful, she knew better. Their situation was hopeless. Even if Jake set out to find them, he never would. How could he? They were literally buried under tons of rock.

"Don't give up," Cruz said.

"There's no point," Zelda said.

"They'll find us. I'm sure help is on the way."

"You can't know that. We'll die here. Slowly and painfully. And I'm to blame after I've just found out you're still alive after all these years." She added, " And I love you."

"Zelda..."

"No, wait. When you told me that yesterday morning, I was angry."

"Angry?"

"Yes. Because you vehemently opposed this treasure hunt right after you said it. I thought if you really loved me, you'd support me in everything."

"You're right," Cruz replied.

"No," she contradicted him. "I'm not. Loving someone doesn't mean giving up the right to your own opinion."

"I guess not. But if we had gone looking together, we might have come another day."

"Maybe so," she said. "But mostly, I regret I didn't just pull you back into bed with me and tell you I felt the same way. That I love you. And how happy it makes me that you return my feelings." She laughed. "Until then, I wasn't even sure we were officially a couple. Crazy, huh?"

As much as she longed for the daylight, she was glad for the darkness at that moment. It was much easier to be honest when you didn't see the other person.

Cruz laughed. "That makes two of us. I didn't know if

you just wanted to have a casual fling while I fell in love with you all over again."

"Honestly?"

"Honestly," he replied, kissing her.

Jake spotted the crevice when he arrived at the spot where he had seen Walt. He took a picture from his phone and sent it on to Toby. Inside, he would have no reception. Having no need for binoculars in the crevice, he pulled the strap over his head and placed it in the grass beside the rock opening. Fortunately, he'd brought a powerful flashlight and shone it into the mountain, peering into the narrow passage. Finally, he sighed and squeezed through the entrance.

To his relief, the passage became wider the deeper he got into the mountain. In the light of the flashlight, clear tracks were visible. Filled with new hope, he rushed.

He came to a fork in the road where the prints separated. He hesitated. Which trail should he follow? Torn, he consulted the map. There was definitely no turnoff marked.

Hoping Cruz and Zelda had kept to the original path on the treasure map, he continued, ignoring the turn. Fifty yards later, he stood at a collapsed wall. The sight sent a shiver down his spine. The dark marks in the sand on the ground and the musty support beam lying farther away told a clear story.

"That fucking bastard!"

He tried to think of another, less horrible explanation. But found none. The passageway had collapsed, probably with Walt's help, and now Zelda and Cruz were stuck. If they were still alive.

Jake turned. He couldn't do anything on his own. He had to get help. He could only hope there was still time.

The call reached Ace while he was having coffee in the diner. His laika dog, Lilo, sat attentively beside him, observing the comings and goings in the restaurant. In a moment, Paige would come and pick her up while he would spend the night at the fire station. Although he was the chief of the fire department, he made a point of taking a certain number of night shifts like everyone else. His men and women—after all, he had Sunny, an extremely capable firefighter, on his team—appreciated that and repaid him with excellent work.

"What are you saying? A rockslide?" Ace asked. "What were they doing in there? Don't they know these old mines and smugglers' hideouts aren't safe?"

He frowned as he listened to what Jake was saying on the other end of the line.

"A treasure hunt," he repeated incredulously. "Where did they get that crazy idea?"

"Adela must have left Cruz some kind of treasure map."

"Okay. I'll alert the others right away. We'll be with you as soon as we can. But Jake..." He didn't finish the sentence. But the likelihood of finding them alive was vanishingly small.

Eve Lartimer, sitting next to him at the counter and elegantly sipping her martini, stopped him with the outstretched index finger of her perfectly manicured hand.

"Did I hear that right? Zelda wanted to find Adela's treasure?"

Ace ran his hand through his military short-cropped hair. Actually, he had no time for long explanations. Every minute counted. But the intelligence that flashed in her gray eyes kept him from simply fobbing her off with a sentence.

"I'm afraid so. And now the tunnel has collapsed."

The old lady listened attentively as he mentioned all the details the sheriff had just shared with him. Finally, she nodded.

"Just as I thought. You won't get them out through the main course. It'll take you days, if not weeks. Before you get to the treasure cave, the tunnel goes steeply down."

Dismayed, Ace listened to her. This was the worst news ever. Unless they blasted their way through the rock, they had no chance of reaching them.

"But..." she continued, sipping her drink again. "There is a second entrance. Just follow the turnoff to the left. It leads in an arc to the chamber. The entrance is blocked with boards and stones, so it looks like there's no way through. But it can all be cleared fairly easily."

She gazed fully over Ace's whole body. "With your muscles, that shouldn't be a problem."

Uncomfortable, Ace shifted his weight first to one foot, then to the other. Eve had always been a little scary to him. That she now came up with ancient gold-digger knowledge while devouring him with her eyes as if he were her favorite dessert didn't necessarily make things better.

"Ma'am?"

"Yes, what are you waiting for? Go and save them."

Ace didn't need to be told twice.

Half an hour later, he and Jake tackled the man-made and cleverly camouflaged second entrance. The rest of the fire crew was on its way. He had gone straight to Adela's cabin with his good news. There wasn't enough room here in the narrow passage for more people anyway; already it was pretty cramped just for the two of them. They worked tirelessly in the glow of the spotlight Ace had brought.

"If only we knew what was waiting for us on the other side," Jake said, pulling a beam out of the pile of boulders. Their progress was slower than expected. Presumably the shock of the rockslide had shaken things.

Ace nodded. "No idea how big this chamber is. It's quite possible they're buried under the rocks."

Clear words, but he knew Jake had the same thought.

Doggedly, they continued their task.

"Do you hear that?" asked Cruz.

"What do you mean?" Zelda would have preferred to curl up and sleep. But Cruz decided sleeping was a very bad idea. So, he disturbed her whenever she was about to doze off. Terrible. If she would have been able to see anything, she would have punched him. But in the dark, she was more likely to run into the wall. Not necessarily the point.

"That scratching. And before that, I could have sworn I heard voices."

"Voices?"

At that moment, they heard a colorful curse that included the rear end of a donkey, the intelligence of a sea cucumber, and other unfriendly things. At the same time, a slim beam of light crossed the small chamber.

Zelda ran over. "Hello? Can you hear us?"

"Zelda! Are you okay? Is Cruz with you?" Another stone was removed. Jake's relieved face came to light.

"We're fine," Zelda said. "Especially now since you got here." Ace came behind the sheriff.

Less than five minutes later, the opening was large enough for the two to slip into the other passage.

Zelda went first, then Jake, and finally Cruz and Ace.

"Thank you, thank you, thank you! You saved our lives."

"Don't mention it," the sheriff said. "Let's put off the thank-yous until later. I'd rather we get out of this death trap as soon as possible. Who knows how things have changed with the rock fall."

"Good idea," Cruz agreed and grabbed Zelda's hand.

Ace pressed a flashlight into Zelda's hand. "Here. You might be glad to have your own light source."

Zelda nodded and gratefully accepted the offer. Exhausted, she followed the two through the narrow tunnel. Suddenly, her light revealed something shiny. Her pulse quickened and she let go of Cruz's hand to get to the bottom of it.

"What is it?" asked Cruz.

Zelda gave no answer. As if spellbound, she sat in front of a hole in the wall. The vibration in the mountain had opened up a crack. Behind it was a hollow space. Scattered all over the floor were numerous gold bars.

"I don't believe it," Cruz said, dumbfounded, crouching beside her. "You found it."

Zelda reached out and stroked the uneven surface of one of the gold bars.

Cruz picked one up. "I can't believe how heavy these are," he remarked.

"How sad Adela missed the treasure by just a few feet," she said. "So close, yet so far. Do you think she would have been happier if she had found it?"

"I think," Cruz said, "she would be very pleased with how today turned out. You are the best treasure of my life."

Zelda hugged him. "You, too."

"You guys coming?" Jake called from farther ahead.

"You want to take the gold?" asked Cruz, bending down to pocket one of the gold bars.

She shook her head.

"Let others get it with proper equipment. Let's get out of these tunnels. It's not safe."

Cruz laughed. "Agreed." In Jake's direction, he called out, "We're coming!"

Zelda took one last look at the gold. Briefly, the desire to pocket as much as possible flickered inside her. Her fingertips tingled. But it was easy for her to suppress the impulse. Her future life was waiting for her outside. She wasn't going to risk her second chance.

EPILOGUE

The next few days passed in a flurry of activity. Walt Perkins had been transferred to another, larger jail farther away and was awaiting his court sentence. Considering that he was charged with attempted murder, the judge had set bail very high. But as it was, there was no one interested in his fate.

Zelda might have felt sorry for him if he hadn't tried to kill her and Cruz twice. She was just glad that he was far away and, above all, locked up.

After she and Cruz presented the gold bar to the mayor under the seal of secrecy, the big question was what to do with the treasure. These discussions would probably occupy the community for some time. Zelda had suggested a scholarship fund be set up; Adela had intended something similar with it if she had ever found it. A secure future for her children's children. What better way to achieve that than by making a good education possible? Mr. Wilkinson had not been averse to her proposal but could not promise anything. The legal situation was too unclear. To whom did the treasure belong? To the finder? Zelda, that is. Or to the municipality?

The state? All these were things to which an answer had to be found first.

However, everyone agreed that the gold had to be recovered as soon as possible. Already loose tongues rumored that Zelda had found the treasure and hidden it again.

When she had glanced in the mirror in the diner's restroom after being rescued by the sheriff and fire chief, she had recoiled in horror. Her hair had been a disaster. More gray-brown than black, it had stuck up from her head in all directions. Traces of dirt stretched across her face. Fine dust covered her from head to toe. Her clothes were best to be thrown away, as she didn't think they were salvageable. The pants had a tear at the knee. The jacket didn't look much better. When it occurred to her that these weren't her own clothes at all, but Cruz's, she laughed until tears ran down and left bright marks on her cheeks. Briefly, she had been tempted to ask Cruz to keep the gold bar, so that she would at least have a decent budget to start a new wardrobe.

Of course, she had not done so. Unfortunately. But it wasn't so bad. Heavily pregnant, Jaz had talked Tyler into taking Zelda on an extensive shopping spree in Denver. Thanks to her insurance company's promises to pay, she dared to use her credit card. Tyler had been an extremely pleasant companion. They had laughed a lot together while she provided her with a sharp eye, advice, and assistance. Now she had a whole new wardrobe of cool clothes. She was still mourning one or two former favorites she had lost during the burglary, but overall she couldn't complain.

In general, she felt lighter and happier since she had narrowly escaped death. The experience had sharpened her focus on the essentials. Murphy seemed to approve of her change, too. At least he was still very affectionate. Even the fact that they were still living with Cruz, and he wasn't allowed out, he took in stride. Soon, she would return to spend the night in her own little house again, but hopefully Cruz would come, too. She didn't know if she could make it on her own. Her cat certainly kept her excellent company, but human company in the form of her battle-hardened boyfriend was more preferable. Maybe that made her a coward, but she didn't care.

"Bye," she said to Astrid, who could close the pharmacy for her later. She had an appointment with Cruz. He had asked her to come along when he packed up Adela's belongings at the cabin. Of course, she said yes.

Cruz was waiting for her when she arrived at his apartment, and he greeted her with a kiss. Zelda let herself sink into the embrace, enjoying the feeling of coming home. Murphy, not wanting to stand back, stroked around her legs and meowed.

"Oh my," Zelda said, breaking away from Cruz to pet the cat. "Now you're so happy that I'm home already, and then I'm about to leave."

"Why don't you take him with us," Cruz suggested.

Surprised, she looked at him. "Take him with us?"

Cruz shrugged his shoulders. "Why not? He can roam around up there in peace while we sort Adela's things."

Zelda looked at the cat, who had dropped and now presented his belly to her. The message was clear. The belly should be scratched. She complied with his request while thinking about Cruz's suggestion. In fact, why not? The way he had behaved in the last few days, he would not leave her side.

"Adela had a cat, too," she suddenly remembered.

Cruz raised his eyebrows. "Really?"

Zelda nodded.

"Well, all the better. Then we'll see if they get along."

"You want to take the cat?"

Cruz grinned. "Not me. You. *You* want to take the cat. You're the cat-suited homeowner with a garden and everything." He didn't mention he was hoping she would also take him to her home for the long haul. That was a topic for another day.

When Zelda stared at him with wide eyes, he said, "What is it? The Diner Sisters were happy to step in and take turns looking after the animals with their friends. But I'm sure they won't do that forever. Were you going to leave the cat up there by herself?"

"Of course not," she replied. "I just hadn't thought about it until now." Was she really supposed to do that? Get a second cat? After all, she had just barely managed to call a truce with Murphy. Suddenly, something occurred to her. "And what about the goats? Should I put them in my garden?"

Laughing, Cruz waved it off. "I've already promised those to Paula. Shauna is apparently already beside herself at the prospect of now having goats to teach tricks to."

"Typical Shauna. I can vividly imagine that. Alright, you've convinced me. Let's take this gentleman here."

She lifted the cat and placed him in her elbow. He looked around with interest but made no effort to flee as she carried him down to the car.

Arriving at Adela's cabin, she put him on the ground. Like a watchdog, he stood at the edge of the cliff and lifted his nose into the wind to sniff all the foreign smells.

Cruz closed his eyes and took a deep breath. "Every time I'm here, the beauty of this place overwhelms me. And it's not even particularly good weather today."

That was true. Dark clouds hung over the mountain tops and covered the sun. A cold wind blew and pressed the young grass to the ground. Zelda brushed a strand of hair from her face. It would probably snow again in the next few days, although she'd hoped the snow would be over for the year. But that happened frequently in the Rocky Mountains. Still, she didn't want to live anywhere else in the world.

"I was thinking we could fix up the cabin and keep it as a weekend cottage. What do you think?" Uncertainly, Cruz looked at her. When she didn't say anything, he said, "You could also continue Adela's tradition and dry herbs here. Then it would be more like a workshop. Or is there a special name for that?" Embarrassed at his torrent of words, he looked to the side. "Sorry. Actually, I didn't want to blurt it out in the first five minutes. My plan was to clean out the cabin and then talk to you about the potential. But whatever," he added self-deprecatingly.

Zelda grabbed his hand, strangely touched by the signs of his uncertainty. Most of the time, he seemed so sure of himself. It was reassuring to realize he was no different from her.

"I think your idea is fantastic. I can't think of anything better than spending weekends here with you. After some much-needed improvements to the cabin though. Shall we go in?"

"Gladly. Looks like we won't be needed out here anyway." He pointed to the black cat, which approached Murphy cautiously. Murphy pricked up his ears, but didn't move from the spot, waiting until the other cat almost touched him with the tip of his nose. Only then did he stand up and greet her.

As Zelda and Cruz walked to the cabin, however, Murphy left his new acquaintance and followed them inside the small, warped house.

"I thought we could replace the front wall with glass." He

gestured to the wall, which now had only a single, tiny window. "That way we'd have more natural light, and we'd have an unobstructed view of the whole valley from the bed."

Zelda studied the wall in detail and tried to picture his proposed change. The resulting view would be breathtaking. The idea of converting this into a retreat just for the two of them was extremely tempting. Feelings of happiness spread around her heart. Had they actually already reached this point where they were making future plans as a couple? It sure looked like it.

"It sounds like you've already given this a lot of thought," she said. She was grinning from ear to ear. No matter; it was impossible to keep so much joy inside.

"Of course. In fact, I've already scheduled our next few weekends that we'll spend here together."

Amused, Zelda gave him a look from under her long lashes. "You mean after the remodel?"

"Of course."

"And what would those plans be?"

Cruz cleared his throat. "Well, let's just say we don't have to leave our bed much to do it." He winked at her.

Zelda laughed and felt the blush rise to her face. This playfulness in connection with sex was still foreign to her, but she was getting more used to it every day.

A short time later, they were sitting in the middle of a hodgepodge of things. Zelda tried to identify the herbs from the old notebooks, while Cruz sorted Adela's other belongings.

"Adela's knowledge of herbal medicine was enormous," Zelda marveled. "It's really too bad I didn't have more time to learn from her." Her voice sounded wistful.

Cruz put the pile of old clothes he had taken out of the

box on the bed and went to Zelda. He put a hand on her shoulder and gave it a gentle squeeze.

"After all, you still got to know her a little. And who knows what you'll find in her notebooks that you might be able to use. From the looks of it, she wrote everything down meticulously."

Zelda nodded and wiped a single tear from her face.

Murphy crawled out from under the bed and purposefully crossed the room. Adela's black cat sat in the open doorway and watched the unusual goings-on in the cabin with an unmoving expression, as if none of this really interested her.

Murphy stopped and began scratching at the wall.

"What's wrong with him?" asked Zelda.

Cruz turned to the cat. "I don't know. Maybe a mouse hid between the beams?"

"Possibly," Zelda said. "But then wouldn't the other cat react, too?" She still didn't know her name. She hoped one of the Diner Sisters could answer that for her. After all, she couldn't just call her Cat. But just giving her a new name didn't seem fair.

"Right." Cruz walked over to the cat and took a closer look at the spot Murphy was still incessantly working on with his claws.

"Do you see anything?" asked Zelda. She joined the two and crouched down next to them.

"No." He ran his index finger over the rough layers of wood. "Wait! Is there a rift here?"

Zelda leaned forward a bit to be able to look over his shoulder. Cruz took the second hand to help. After some shaking, pulling, and scolding, he succeeded in detaching a piece of wood from the wall paneling. Behind it, they found a small compartment.

"Looks like a secret lair," Cruz noted.

"Is there anything in it?"

"I don't know. I can't see anything. Your cat is in my way," he replied.

Murphy had his nose in front once again. Much like when he was in hunting mode, he emitted a bleating meow. Then, in a flash, he reached out with his paw. "Maybe there is a mouse," Zelda guessed.

When he pulled back his paw, however, it wasn't gray fur that had gotten caught in his claws, but a piece of black velvet.

Cruz grabbed Murphy's paw and freed the caught fabric. The cat sniffed at it once more, then lost interest. With his usual nonchalance, he turned away and began to preen himself.

"Not after all this," Zelda said, shaking her head. "Don't keep me in suspense. What has Murphy dragged into the light of day?"

Carefully, Cruz knocked the heavy, black fabric aside.

For a few seconds, they both stared at the contents. Their eyes met. Together, they burst into raucous laughter. Murphy and Adela's cat fled outside.

"I don't believe it," Zelda said. "She knew where the treasure was all along. But how come she never got it out of the mountain?"

Cruz shrugged.

"I suppose she didn't think it was necessary. After all, she obviously had everything she needed to live." He looked around the barren cabin. "Although we may find this hard to believe, I think she lived her life the way she wanted to."

"I have that impression, too."

"And after the only nephew who was in the region did not even bother to visit..." Cruz said.

"Don't be so hard on yourself. She could have sought you

out, after all. I think she simply concluded that you have no need for gold. You were, and are, successful on your own merits. The gold was there. In the mountain. She probably thought you would find it if you needed it. Or maybe she intended to leave a will with specific instructions. I'm pretty sure she knew how sick she was."

Cruz weighed the gold bar in his hands. "If it's all right with you, I'd like to keep the existence of that one gold bar to myself."

"Sure. Whatever you want." Adela had been his great-aunt, after all. Thus, that was his gold bar, too. But she was still curious. "And why is that?"

A sly smile played around Cruz's lips as he rewrapped the bar and slid it back into its hiding place. Once he had it safely stowed away, he straightened up and turned back to Zelda. "This is a wonderful story to tell our grandchildren and great-grandchildren in front of the fireplace while one passes the gold bar to the other."

Zelda smiled and returned his gaze. Was he really serious about what he was saying? Grandkids? She hoped so. "You mean when we're old?"

"Exactly. At least ninety or maybe even a hundred."

"Why not a hundred and ten," Zelda said, amused.

"No time to start better than right now," he replied, kissing her.

The End.

AUTHOR'S NOTE

Dear Reader,

If you liked the book, I would be very happy if you took the time to write a short review on Amazon and tell all your friends about it. This way you help me and this book to become a little more visible.

Many, many thanks for your support!

Love and greetings,
Virginia

FREE NOVELLA

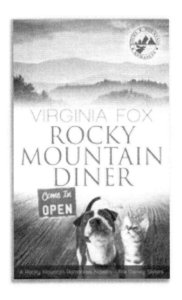

Sign up for my newsletter to get insider information, more recipes, give aways and receive the FREE ebook of the Rocky Mountain Romances prequel, *Rocky Mountain Diner*.

https://books.virginiafox.com/rmdiner_novella

ABOUT THE AUTHOR

Author, mother, horse whisperer, and part-time healthy food cook, Virginia Fox is a woman who cares deeply about family, animals, the environment, and friendships.

Creative from a young age, she turned her love of books into a prolific career as a writer.

Virginia Fox lives on a small ranch with her family, her Australian cattle dog, and two moody tomcats. When she isn't writing, she delights in caring for her horses and cooking for her family. Discover more on her website:

www.virginiafox.com

BOOKS BY VIRGINIA FOX

The Dragon Sisters Trilogy (British English)

The Dragon Sisters, Volume 1

The Rocky Mountain Romances Series

Rocky Mountain Yoga, Volume 1

Rocky Mountain Star, Volume 2

Rocky Mountain Dogs, Volume 3

Rocky Mountain Kid, Volume 4

Rocky Mountain Secrets, Volume 5

Rocky Mountain Fire, Volume 6

Rocky Mountain Life, Volume 7

Rocky Mountain Race, Volume 8

Rocky Mountain Lion, Volume 9

Rocky Mountain Gold, Volume 10

Printed in Great Britain
by Amazon

56118864R00167